Praise for the novels of Phaedra Patrick

"Sweet and resonant." —*People,* **"Best New Books" Pick**

"Phaedra Patrick understands the soul. Eccentric, charming, and wise… This book will illuminate your heart."
—**Nina George,** *New York Times* **bestselling author of** *The Little Paris Bookshop*

"One of those lovely, heartwarming stories that restores your faith in human nature."
—**B. A. Paris,** *New York Times* **bestselling author**

"A heartwarming and tender tale of growth and redemption…. Curl up by the fire with a cup of tea and a biscuit and be entranced by this delightful story." —*Library Journal,* **starred review**

"[A] charming, unforgettable story." —*Harper's Bazaar*

"A laugh-out-loud, globe-trotting adventure… A witty, joyful read."
—*Bustle*

"An endearing celebration of life." —*RealSimple*

"As cozy and fortifying as a hot cup of tea on a cold afternoon."
—*Kirkus Reviews*

"It's a sweet quest and a thoughtful reminder that sometimes the person who loves us most knows us better than we know ourselves."
—*MarthaStewartWeddings.com*

Also by Phaedra Patrick

The Curious Charms of Arthur Pepper
Rise and Shine, Benedict Stone
The Library of Lost and Found

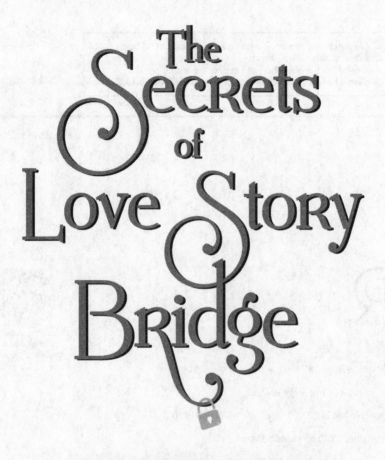

The Secrets of Love Story Bridge

PHAEDRA PATRICK

PARK
ROW
BOOKS

PARK
ROW
BOOKS™

Recycling programs
for this product may
not exist in your area.

ISBN-13: 978-0-7783-8943-9

The Secrets of Love Story Bridge

First published in 2020. This edition published in 2021.

Copyright © 2020 by Phaedra Patrick

This edition published by arrangement with Harlequin Books S.A.

Park Row Books
22 Adelaide St. West, 40th Floor
Toronto, Ontario M5H 4E3, Canada
ParkRowBooks.com
BookClubbish.com

Printed in U.S.A.

To my family and friends

The Secrets of Love Story Bridge

THE LILAC ENVELOPE

The night before

As he did often over the past three years, Mitchell Fisher wrote a letter he would never send.

He sat up in bed at midnight and kicked off his sheets. Even though all the internal doors in his apartment were open, the sticky July heat still felt like a shroud clinging to his body. His nine-year-old daughter, Poppy, thrashed restlessly in her sleep in the bedroom opposite.

Mitchell turned on his bedside lamp, squinting against the yellow light, and took out a pad of Basildon Bond notepaper from underneath his bed. He always used a fountain pen to write—old-fashioned he supposed, but he was a man who valued things that were well constructed and long lasting.

Mitchell tapped the pen against his bottom lip. He knew what he wanted to say, but by the time his words of sorrow and regret traveled from his brain to his fingertips, they were only fragments of what he longed to express.

As he started to write, the sound of the metal nib scratching against paper helped him block out the city street noise that hummed below his apartment.

Dearest Anita,
Another letter from me. Everything here is fine, ticking along. Poppy is doing well. The school holidays start soon and I thought she'd be more excited. It's probably because you're not here to enjoy them with us.

I've taken two weeks off work to spend with her, and have a full itinerary planned for us—badminton, tennis, library visits, cooking, walking, the park, swimming, museums, a tour of the city bridges and more. It will keep us busy. Keep our minds off you.

You'll be amazed how much she's grown, must be almost your height by now. I tell her how proud I am of her, but it always meant more coming from you.

Mitchell paused, resting his hand against the pad of paper. He *had* to tell her how he felt.

Every time I look at our daughter, I think of you. I wish I could hold you again, and tell you I'm truly sorry.

Yours, always,
Mitchell x

He read his words, always dissatisfied with them, never able to convey the magnitude of guilt he felt. After folding the piece of paper once, he sealed it into a crisp, cream envelope, then squeezed it into the almost-full drawer of his nightstand among all the other letters he'd written. His eyes fell upon the slim lilac envelope he kept on top, the one addressed to him from Anita that he'd not yet been able to bring himself to open.

Taking it out, he held it under his nose and inhaled. There was still a slight scent of her violet soap on the paper. His finger followed the angle of the gummed flap and then stopped. He closed his eyes and willed himself to open the letter, but his hands began to shake.

Once more, he placed it back into his drawer.

Mitchell lay down and hugged himself, imagining Anita's arms were wrapped around him. When he closed his eyes, the words from all the letters weighed down upon him like a bulldozer. As he turned and tried to sleep, he pulled the pillow over his head to force them away.

1

A LOCKED HEART

The lovers who attached their padlocks to the bridges of Upchester might see it as a fun or romantic gesture, but to Mitchell, it was an act of vandalism.

It was the hottest year on record in the city and the morning sun was already beating down on the back of his neck. His biceps flexed as he methodically opened and squeezed his bolt cutters shut, shearing the padlocks off the cast-iron filigree panels of the old Victorian bridge, one by one.

Since local boy band Word Up filmed the video for their international smash hit "Lock Me Up with Your Love" on this bridge, thousands of people were flocking to the small city in the North West of England. To demonstrate their love for the band and each other, they brought locks engraved with initials, names or messages and attached them to the city's five bridges.

Large red-and-white signs that read No Padlocks studded the pavement. But as far as Mitchell could see, the locks still hung on the railings like bees swarming across frames of honeycomb. The constant reminder of other people's love made him feel like he was fighting for breath. As he cut off the locks, he wanted to yell, "Why can't you just keep your feelings to yourselves?"

After several hours of hard work, Mitchell's trail of broken locks glinted on the pavement like a metal snake. He stopped for a moment and narrowed his eyes as a young couple strolled toward him. The woman glided in a floaty white dress and tan cowboy boots. The man wore shorts and had the physique of an American football player. With his experience of carrying out maintenance across the city's public areas, Mitchell instinctively knew they were up to something.

After breaking away from his girlfriend, the man walked to the side of the bridge while nonchalantly pulling out a large silver padlock from his pocket.

Mitchell tightened his grip on his cutters. He was once so easy and in love with Anita, but rules were rules. "Excuse me," he called out. "You can't hang that lock."

The man frowned and crossed his bulging arms. "Oh, yeah? And who's going to stop me?"

Mitchell had the sinewy physique of a sprinter. He was angular all over with dark hair and eyes and a handsome dorsal hump on his nose. "I am," he said and put his cutters down on the pavement. He held out his hand for the lock. "It's my job to clear the bridges. You could get a fine."

Anger flashed across the blond man's face and he batted Mitchell's hand away, swiping off his work glove. Mitchell watched as it tumbled down into the river below. Sometimes the water flowed prettily, but today it gushed and gurgled, a bruise-gray hue. A young man had drowned here in a strong current last summer.

The man's girlfriend wrapped her arms around her boyfriend's waist and tugged him away. "Come on. Leave him alone." She cast Mitchell an apologetic smile. "Sorry, but we're *so* in love. It took us two hours and three buses to get here. We'll be working miles away from each other soon. *Please* let us do this."

The man looked into her eyes and softened. "Yeah, um, sorry, mate," he said sheepishly. "The heat got the better of me. All we want to do is fasten our lock."

Mitchell gestured at the sign again. "Just think about what you're doing, guys," he said with a weary sigh. "Padlocks are cheap chunks of metal and they're weighing down the bridges. Can't you get a nice ring or tattoo instead? Or write letters to each other? There are better ways to say I lov—well, you know."

The man and the woman shared an incredulous look.

"Whatever." The man glowered and shoved his padlock back into his pocket. "We'll go to another bridge instead."

"I work on those, too…"

The couple laughed at him and sauntered away.

Mitchell rubbed his nose. He knew his job wasn't a glamorous one. It wasn't the one in architecture he'd studied hard and trained for. However, it meant he could pay the rent on his apartment and buy Poppy hot lunch at school each day. Whatever daily hassle he put up with, he needed the work.

His workmate Barry had watched the incident from the other side of the road. Sweat circled under his arms and his forehead shone like a mirror as he crossed over. "The padlocks keep multiplying," he groaned.

"We need to keep on going."

"But it's too damn hot." Barry undid a button on his polo shirt, showing off unruly chest curls that matched the ones on his head. "It's a violation of our human rights, and no one can tell if we cut off twenty or two hundred."

Mitchell held his hand up against the glare of the sun. "We can tell, and Russ wants the bridges cleared in time for the city centenary celebrations."

Barry rolled his eyes. "There's only three weeks to go until then. Our boss should come down here and get his hands dirty, too. At least join me for a pint after work."

Mitchell's mouth felt parched, and he suddenly longed for an ice-cold beer. A vision of peeling off his polo shirt and socks and relaxing in a beer garden appeared like a dreamy mirage in his head.

But he had to pick Poppy up from the after-school club to take her for a guitar lesson, an additional one to her music class in school. Her head teacher, Miss Heathcliff, was a stickler for the school closing promptly at 5:30 p.m., and it was a rush to get there on time. He lowered his eyes and said, "I'd love to, but I have to dash off later."

Then he selected his next padlock to attack.

Toward the end of their working day, Barry sidled up to Mitchell and wiped his brow. He crouched and packed up his toolbox before staring at his mobile phone. "Brilliant, a lady I've been messaging can meet me for a drink."

Since Barry had lost three stone at Weight Whittlers, he'd discovered the enticing world of dating apps and was now like a dog let off its leash. Mitchell had long since given up advising him quality was better than quantity when it came to women.

"You have *another* date?" he asked. "And we're not supposed to finish work for another five minutes."

Barry smiled proudly. "Five minutes doesn't matter, and going out beats sitting on my own all night. Tonight's lucky lady is Mandy." He side-glanced at his friend. "Maybe you should get back out into the wild, too. Start to live a little."

Mitchell shuddered. "I'm fine as I am, thanks, just me and Poppy."

If he ever thought about going out with someone new, his head spun: getting dressed up, meeting someone in a bar, making light conversation, laughing politely at their jokes, debating who was going to pay for the drinks, going through that excruciating moment when you might offer to see them again, moving in for a kiss or not. And that was on top of the babysitting logistics, because his few family members lived miles away. Before he even went on a first date, he could already picture first arguments, awkward silences and accusations at him for being emotionally frozen. And the line "I'm a single dad to a nine-year-old girl" wasn't an ideal conversation starter. He looked at his watch. "You go enjoy yourself," he said. "Have a pint for me."

"Will do," Barry shouted over his shoulder as he walked away.

Mitchell stared at his own trail of padlocks and at Barry's petite pile on the other side of the bridge. A couple of lads from the Maintenance Team pulled up and began to shovel up the scrap metal. Mitchell gave them a wave and rushed off along the street that followed the edge of the river.

As he hurried, he didn't notice the clustered rows of black-and-white Tudor shops, or the intricate carvings on the twin towers of Upchester cathedral, the tallest building that loomed over the medieval walled city. He didn't stop to admire the glistening River Twine that gushed fiercely a few meters lower besides him, or the architecture of the five bridges that spanned it. He had given his own nickname to each of them.

The Slab was a drab concrete construction on the far side of the city. Built in the 1970s to ease traffic flow, it was more useful than attractive and, in Mitchell's opinion, spoiled the aesthetics of its surroundings.

Vicky was the next one along, the Victorian bridge he and Barry had been working on that day. It had handsome stone arches and ornate panels depicting flowers and leaves. It connected the cathedral on one side of the river to the library on the other.

When he reached the third bridge along, his palms itched as he spotted dozens of fresh padlocks hanging there. This was the oldest bridge in the city, with parts of it dating back to the fourteenth century. Mitchell christened it Archie, because it had three pale stone arches.

The newest bridge had been commissioned to celebrate the centenary of Upchester's city status. Due to open soon, Mitchell named it the Yacht. It was supermodern, all sleek white railings and thin white struts that looked like the laces of a lady's corset, securing two tall white masts to the road.

He called his favorite bridge Redford, because of its red bricks. It was a sturdy construction, erected one hundred and fifty years ago. It might look dull and traditional, but it did its job.

As he crossed over Redford, the people he passed came at him in twos, like animals boarding Noah's Ark. They laughed and kissed with abandon, and Mitchell picked up his pace, finding it painful to witness.

He still saw Anita sometimes, catching glimpses from the corner of his eye of her copper-brown curls in a crowd or a flash of her favorite tomato-red coat. Every time he felt as if someone had stabbed his heart. His breath would catch, and he'd crane his neck to look for her, desperate to see her one more time.

As he strode on, Mitchell noticed a woman standing in the middle of the bridge's pavement. Her dress was vibrant, a daffodil yellow. Everyone else was heading across the bridge, but she was stationary, absolutely still, so people had to part and move around her. As Mitchell drew closer, he noticed her nose had a bump on the bridge that made him feel an immediate kinship with her. Her walnut curls reminded him of Anita's hairstyle.

Her warm, familiar smile seemed to say, *Oh, fancy seeing you here.* But he was certain he'd never seen her before. He couldn't help staring at her, as if catching sight of his own reflection in a shop mirror and doing a double take.

As they caught each other's eyes, a wash of color circled his neck, but he found it difficult to look away.

You're still in love with Anita, remember?

Mitchell's eyes fell upon the sweep of her collarbone and her shoulders, before stopping on the shiny thing in her hand. It was large, heart-shaped and glinted intermittently gold and then white in the late afternoon sunlight.

A padlock.

He gritted his teeth as the woman stepped toward the railing and stooped to secure her lock. After straightening back up, she tossed its key into the river and peered down at the water. She brushed her hair back with her hand then patted her ear. Her forehead furrowed and she spun around on the spot, searching on the pavement. She then looked over the railing at the narrow ledge on the other side.

Mitchell wondered what she'd lost, but told himself he didn't have time to help her to find it anyway.

His view of her was obstructed by a young man carrying a large shiny shovel on his shoulder and a few other passersby. When he saw the woman again she was leaning over the railing on her tiptoes, reaching for something on the other side. Her fingers padded around and she raised a leg off the ground, pointing her foot to balance herself as if performing a ballet move.

A feeling of worry reared up inside him at her precarious position. "Hey, be careful," he called out.

His view was interrupted again by a large group of students traipsing along. When they had passed, Mitchell stared at the spot where the woman had stood. Except she was no longer there.

He saw a flash of her yellow dress through the railings, vivid in the rushing river below.

"Damn," he said out loud.

And in that split second, all thoughts of Poppy flew from his mind. He dropped his toolbox to the ground, ran and swung his legs over the railing with ease.

When the base of his back caught against the ledge on the other side, he knew a jolt of pain should accompany it, but Mitchell didn't feel anything as he crashed down into the violent water.

2

PIZZA BOXES

Mitchell had never been a strong swimmer. He hadn't been that great at any sports or classes in school, except for physics, where he loved learning about fulcrums, loads and motion. He and Poppy used to enjoy swimming sessions together until recently, when she got out of the pool after a couple of lengths, arms folded. "I like swimming with Mum better," she said. "This isn't as fun. You always set targets for me." And she hadn't wanted to go to the pool with him since.

As Mitchell plunged into the river, icy cold water gushed over his head and plugged his ears. When he stopped sinking, he pushed upward and broke to the surface with a gasp. He squinted and saw the woman in the yellow dress was twenty meters or so in front of him, being sucked along by a strong torrent. She flailed her arms, clutching at the air, before her head disappeared underwater.

People along the street at the side of the river slowed down to stop and watch, gaping down at the crisis occurring in front of them. Mitchell was only vaguely aware of them as he kicked off his shoes and began to swim.

He arched one arm and then the other, kicking his legs as quickly as he could. After every few strokes, he fixed his eyes on the woman as she was swept along. "Hold on," he called out, spitting out the bitter water that filled his mouth. "I'm coming for you."

He urged himself onward, but although he was using all his strength, it felt like he wasn't moving anywhere. He clenched his jaw as the river tugged him backward, like it had strong arms wrapped around his thighs. The young man who drowned last summer had lost his battle against the currents that swirled forcefully beneath the surface.

Mitchell pushed himself to swim harder, trying to find a rhythm with his limbs. *One-two, one-two, one-two.* He lost all sense of the geography of the city. All he could see was grayness sloshing around him, and a circle of yellow fabric in front of him like a beacon.

Fear made him focus. The dread of not reaching her, not managing to save her, pushed him onward.

Pain seared across his shoulders and his throat tightened so much his breath was shallow through his nose. He told himself he was getting closer to her, mind over matter, but he wasn't really sure.

After what seemed like forever, he spotted a fallen tree, split by lightning in a storm, that hung over the river at a right angle. The flow of water suddenly pulled the woman toward it, and spindly branches stuck out like daggers to greet her. Mitchell watched as she became entangled in them, and then she was gone from his sight.

He thrust his face into the water, swimming harder than ever before. All he could see was blackness until he felt something sharp scrape his arm, and he was there alongside the tree. Next to her.

A section of her dress had snagged on a branch and the rest of it billowed around her.

He fought against the branches to reach her and took her into his arms. While treading water, he gently lifted her chin with his fingers. "Are you okay?" he spluttered. "Can you talk?"

Her lips moved, but she didn't reply. Her face was ashen and strands of her wet hair hung down over her eyes.

"Try to hold on to me, if you can. I'm going to swim and get us both to safety."

Mitchell unhooked her dress from the tree and managed to recall snippets of the few lifesaving sessions he'd watched Poppy have at the pool. He helped the woman to lie on her back and, after cupping his hand under her chin, he swam backward, pulling her along with him.

Fortunately, he found a calmer current that assisted their movements.

The riverbank was lower on one side than the other, with a long grass verge in front of a series of waterfront bars. Mitchell headed toward them, his eyes intermittently flicking between the woman's face and his destination.

"We're nearly there," he said. "Only a bit farther. You're doing so well."

A few people stood, clutching pints of beer and staring at him as if he was competing in a swimming race. The edge of the river shallowed and Mitchell pushed himself forward onto the grass and pulled the woman out of the water. She lay in his arms with the back of her head pressed against his chest. "You're okay. You're safe," he blurted with relief.

They stayed there together, his arms wrapped around her as the blazing sun warmed their cold bodies.

The woman's eyes were shut, but her eyelashes danced against her cheeks and she smiled serenely.

This moment, being here with her, reminded Mitchell of the contradictory mixture of stillness and exhilaration he felt when Poppy was born, when he first held her in his arms. Anita had smiled at him weakly and he had wanted to burst into tears and laugh at the same time, as exhaustion, joy and responsibility sent his feelings into a tailspin. When he looked down at the woman, he pictured Anita with her damp curls pressed against her forehead. The closeness to this stranger, her body in his arms, was both tender and unnerving and his hand shook when he brushed her hair away from her eyes.

She squinted against the daylight. "What happened?" she rasped. "Where am I?"

"My name is Mitchell Fisher. You were standing on a bridge in Upchester, attaching a padlock. I think you dropped something and were looking for it. You leaned right over the railing and fell." He held his breath for a while. "You could have gotten yourself killed."

She smiled weakly and reached up to take his hand. Their wet fingers entwined tightly. "I'm so clumsy recently. I don't make a habit of this, honestly. I usually just knock glasses of wine over or forget my door keys."

Mitchell liked how she managed to find humor in her situation. "So long as you're safe. Do you think you're ready to try to stand up?"

She crooked one knee, then frowned in pain. Her head slumped back against his chest. "Not yet." She looked upward at him, and again he felt a tug of *something* for her. It caused more memories of Anita to trickle back and he didn't want to think of her, not here and now. The shame he often felt could bury him like an avalanche.

"I do *know* you, don't I?" she said.

Mitchell looked away. "I don't think we've met before." He wondered if her fall was causing her confusion, but as he opened his mouth to reply, a hand clamped down on his shoulder. A man with a thin mustache and horn-rimmed glasses stood above him.

"I'm a doctor. Can I help?" the man said.

Mitchell nodded gratefully, and he slipped his fingers away from the woman's hand. He cradled her head and helped her to lie down flat on the grass, then he shuffled backward out of the way.

The doctor crouched down. "What happened?"

The woman swallowed but didn't reply.

"She fell into the river, and I jumped in to help her," Mitchell said.

"How long was she in for?"

"Ten or fifteen minutes, I think. I don't really know." His sense of time had flown and his stomach plunged when his watch showed 5:40 p.m.

His attention snapped back to Poppy. She was at school and he was very late. He'd also left his toolbox on the bridge. "Sorry, I have to go," he said to the doctor and the woman.

Mitchell stood up and took a few unsteady steps along the grass verge in his soggy socked feet. He hunched away from the well-meaning pats that rained down on his back. When a couple of mobile phones appeared, he resisted the impulse to bat them away.

He told himself the woman would be fine. She was with a doctor.

Heart thumping, Mitchell thrust a hand into his trouser pocket and tugged out his own phone to call the school. But the screen was blank and tiny bubbles emerged from the camera hole.

He limped to where the grass verge ended, made his way

back up onto the street and headed toward Redford to quickly look for his toolbox. When he reached midway along the bridge, he stood in the rough spot the woman in the yellow dress had fallen.

He searched frantically around for his tools and his shoulders sagged when he realized they'd gone, perhaps stolen.

When he looked back over the railing, he saw the woman and doctor were heading in his direction. The sun made her wet dress shine like gold, and a thought struck Mitchell like a lightning bolt.

I don't even know her name.

He looked at her again and his pull toward her was magnetic. But she was over thirty meters away from him, and he had to get to the school.

He would rush past and ask what her name was.

He *had* to know.

He turned and saw a cyclist whizzing along the pavement toward him at great speed. Pizza boxes were piled high on the handlebars. Mitchell tried to jump out of the way, but the bicycle smashed into him, knocking him to the ground.

As boxes went flying in the air, Mitchell heard the thwack of his own head on the pavement. Pain bloomed and his vision blurred. Someone shouted for an ambulance, and legs surrounded him like trees in a forest.

When he strained to raise his head, a hand pressed his shoulders back down.

Mitchell wasn't sure how long he lay there for, but through a set of fleshy knees in long khaki shorts, he thought he saw the swish of a yellow dress.

Then he closed his eyes and everything went blank.

SMALL SHOES

While he was out cold, Mitchell dreamed.

It was another kiln-hot summer day where the air shimmered and people gathered in the pub for shelter from the sun. A woman with copper curls pushed in next to him at the bar.

"A pint of cider, please," she said, even though it was Mitchell's turn to be served. She glanced at him and pressed a hand to her mouth. "Oh, sorry, you were next?"

He shrugged, a little irritated. "It's fine."

"No, it's not. Really. The barman was cutting into a lime and the smell always reminds me of this holiday I went on to Ibiza in my early twenties. It was supposedly cool to drink beer from a bottle with a slice of lime sticking out of the neck. Even though I didn't like the taste, I drank it for a whole week and..."

Mitchell laughed despite himself. "I once forced myself to drink the same thing at a barbecue because my friends liked it."

She returned his smile. "Anyway, what I'm trying to say is *sorry*, and can I get you a drink?" When he started to protest against her offer, she jokingly placed her elbow in front of him. "I'll get this," she said to the barman.

She wasn't his usual type, with a round face and messy red hair when he was usually attracted to brunettes. But when she grinned at him, he liked how her eyes crinkled at the corners in a fan shape.

Mitchell asked for a cider, too, and they carried their drinks outside together, grumbling about the hot weather, and sat down at the only free table. She told him her name was Anita and she was waiting for a friend who was always late.

She raised her glass at him. "Cheers."

"Cheers." He clinked his in return.

When Anita pressed her lips against the glass, she savored every sip of the fizzy amber liquid as if it was the finest champagne, and Mitchell realized he actually fancied her. She was the kind of person who could find adventure in the simplest of things.

A delicious sensation tingled in his chest as he thought about where their conversation might take them both.

Mitchell closed his eyes as he drank his cider. However, when he opened them again, his glass had vanished from his hand. The table and the pub were no longer there. Anita had gone, too.

He woke up and found himself woozy and sore, lying down on a hospital bed. There was an electronic beeping sound to his right, and a cannula tube taped to the back of his hand. He wore a starchy, patterned gown and a wristband with his name on it.

He forgot about his dream and tried to sit up. *"Poppy,"* he cried out.

A bag with an Upchester Hospital logo sat on a chair beside his bed and he could see his clothes were folded inside it. On top of the small table next to him, his keys, wallet and mobile phone were sealed inside a plastic bag that was foggy with condensation. He stretched to reach for it, but realized a nurse was pointing a finger at him from the end of the bed.

"Leave that alone," she ordered.

Mitchell tried to sit up again. "You don't understand—yow!" A pain shot down his spine and he screwed his eyes shut.

"What do you think you're doing, sweetheart?"

Mitchell opened one eye and took in the nurse's blue uniform, tight black curls and steely brown eyes. "Sorry, but I need to get out of here," he said. "I'm late to get my daughter from school. She'll be worried..."

"Even if you have a dinner date with the queen, I'm not letting you go anywhere." Her name badge said Hello My Name is Samantha and it made her sound friendlier than she looked.

He clawed at the neck of his gown. "I'm absolutely fine, honestly."

"That's for me to say, not you. As it stands, your oxygen levels, temperature and blood pressure are okay. You've had a CT scan, and the good news is you'll be fine." She tapped the side of her own head. "You've had a couple of stitches."

Mitchell felt like he'd been battered with a meat tenderizing hammer. He reached up to feel the spongy softness of gauze taped above his right ear. "Poppy's only nine, and she has a guitar lesson. What time is it?" When he saw a wall clock displayed 7:25 p.m., his insides cramped. "I have got to *go*."

He imagined Poppy staring expectantly at her watch as the other kids were picked up from the club and she was left behind. She'd be twitchy, frightened even. Exactly the same as the fateful day Anita didn't arrive to collect her.

"You need to calm down," Samantha ordered. "Won't her mum have things covered?"

Mitchell wondered why she'd assume this. He tried to reply, but the words stuck in his mouth. "No. She's…"

Samantha crossed her arms expectantly.

"There's only me." Mitchell looked down at his hands. "Poppy's mother…well, she died."

Samantha unfolded her arms and fiddled with her name badge. "I'm very sorry," she said softly. "I'll find out what I can."

Mitchell nodded. "Please."

He'd never fully settled on how to describe Anita. She wasn't his wife because they weren't married, and they'd never got engaged. The word *partner* sounded like a business arrangement, and *soul mate* was too soppy. *Girlfriend* was too young, and *the mother of my child* suggested Poppy was the result of a one-night stand. He usually called her *Poppy's mum.*

If he ever had to explain his circumstances, he often found himself consoling people, rather than the other way around.

"You weren't to know…"

"I'm sorry to tell you…"

"It's one of those things…"

What he really wanted to say was, "Imagine being told you'll never feel sunshine on your skin ever again. That's what life is like without her. And every minute and hour of each day, I feel like it's my fault she's no longer here."

But he kept this to himself.

He tried to picture himself as an armadillo, curled up against the world and displaying an armored shell. Even though three years had passed, he still needed this protection.

Samantha returned a few minutes later. "Your friend Barry

Waters is listed as an emergency contact at the school. I understand he picked up your daughter and took her to her music lesson."

"But that will have finished…"

"That's all I can tell you, I'm afraid." Samantha passed him a small paper cup that contained two round white tablets. "Are you allergic to paracetamol? Do you feel sick at all, or dizzy? Any memory loss? Do you know where you are?"

"In prison?" He eyed the pills with suspicion. "I'm totally fine, genuinely. Do I really need to take these? Don't I have to sign something to agree to it? What are the rules about these things? I just want to leave."

She looked at him disparagingly. "Just take the tablets, please, Mr. Fisher. You're not going anywhere until I say so. Those are *my* rules."

Half an hour later, Barry arrived. He wore faded double denim and his chest hair spewed out from the open neck of his shirt. "I've seen you looking better, mate. You feeling all right?"

"I'm fine." Mitchell strained forward. "But how's Poppy? Is she okay? Was she upset?"

Barry moved the bag off the chair and sat down. "No need to worry. The school called me when you didn't show up and they couldn't reach you. The hospital found some council ID in your pocket and rang me, too, to say you'd been brought in. I collected Poppy from school and told her you'd been in an accident but were fine. She was a bit shaken, though still wanted to go to her music lesson rather than for a burger with me. She had an appointment card with the teacher's address on it." He reached in his pocket and handed it to Mitchell before looking around him. "God, I hate these places."

Mitchell did, too. He refused to think about the last time he was here in the hospital with Anita. The memories were beginning to seep back and he tried to banish them by talking quickly. "Thanks. I've not met Miss Bradfield properly yet, just spoken to her on the phone."

"She's really nice and said it's no problem if you're late to pick Poppy up. She'll feed her, too." Barry leaned down and deposited a pair of shoes on top of Mitchell's bedsheets. "I've brought you some dry ones."

Mitchell turned one over. "Thanks. Um, they're two sizes too small."

"They're good shoes, though, got nice laces. I'll leave them anyway. Do you know you've been on the local news?"

Mitchell gaped at him. "On TV?"

"Online." Barry located a photo on his phone of Mitchell sitting on the riverbank dripping wet, his head bowed. "The reporter called you the Hero on the Bridge."

"That's rubbish, anyone would have done the same." Mitchell pictured the woman in the yellow dress standing on the bridge, wearing her enigmatic smile. He wondered again why she thought she knew him. "What did they say about the woman? Is she okay? What's her name?"

"It only really mentions you. This stuff gets updated all the time, though." He put his phone away. "You really don't need this drama in your life, do you?"

"I've spoiled your evening and lost my toolbox," Mitchell said glumly. "You had a date lined up."

"Nah, it's fine. I had a quick beer with Mandy before I got the call about you. She was nice, but…" He squirmed. "I'm seeing Megan later. I've met her before, but it was messy. We had a great time, until her husband rocked up and wanted to take the party back to his place. Totally awkward."

Mitchell stared at him in disbelief.

Barry held a palm up. "I didn't go," he said defensively. "Anyway, I'm meeting Tina tomorrow. She's an artist."

The number of women's names spilling from Barry's lips made Mitchell's temples throb. "Good luck, Casanova," he said.

Barry stayed with Mitchell a while longer before excusing himself to meet Megan. "I'll ask around about your toolbox," he said. "Make inquiries."

"Thanks, the tools cost me a packet."

After Barry left, Mitchell lay in bed, stewing and urging Samantha to reappear. When she eventually returned with a clip file and paperwork, she removed the tube from the back of his hand and stuck a plaster on it. "Yes, you do have to legally sign these papers to discharge yourself," she said and handed him a pen. "You have an appointment at the clinic here next week to have your stitches removed. I'll give you a leaflet about concussions to read. Your back is bruised and might be sore for a while."

Mitchell closed the curtains around his bed and sat down heavily on the mattress. His polo shirt still had patches of dampness and felt strangely stiff. After pulling on his trousers, he stuffed his keys, wallet and phone into his back pockets.

The realization of what he'd done was beginning to dawn on him.

He wasn't a hero at all. He was a stupid person for putting himself in danger, when the outcome could have been a lot worse.

If he hadn't felt a flicker of interest for the woman in the yellow dress, he would have walked on by and not seen her fall. He wouldn't have spotted the padlock in her hands. Helping her had triggered a chain of events he wished hadn't been set in motion.

A sob suddenly reared inside him, threatening to break out like a lion's roar, and he gulped it away. He dropped Barry's shoes to the floor and tried to stuff his foot inside one of them, even though he knew it wouldn't fit. When he bent down to pick them back up, tears blurred his eyes and he clutched the shoes to his chest like a child with a teddy bear.

It was his job to put Poppy first and he'd let her down.

As he pulled back the curtain from around the bed and stepped beyond it, he took a pained breath.

When he shuffled off the ward, guilt clenched his gut that he'd been able to help a stranger, but not Anita.

4

PINK FRIDGE

Mitchell eased himself into a taxi outside the hospital and asked the driver to take him across the city to Miss Bradfield's house. Anita had always spoken of arranging for Poppy to take extra music lessons and the teacher came highly recommended by another parent. She gave independent lessons in the evening, as well as her daytime job teaching in several local schools, including Poppy's school, Hinchward primary.

As his damp trousers squeaked against the leather car seat, Mitchell watched the red illuminated digits of the taxi fare rolling higher and higher. The cost distressed him almost as much as his aching body.

Budgeting for him and Poppy was always tight. Things like family days at theme parks, lunch without thinking about the bill and popcorn buckets at the cinema were resigned to the past. Now he scoured the internet for cheap things for them to do together. He had discovered that strolls in the countryside, making cheese sandwiches and attending free events in libraries were just as much fun, and provided the opportunity to chat with Poppy more. Or it meant he could try.

Sometimes Poppy still swung his hand in hers, chitchatting away about school and new songs her friends had downloaded. Other times she wore a cloak of sadness that he couldn't break through.

"I want people to like *me*," she said when she moved to Hinchward after Anita died. "Not just be nice to me because Mum's gone."

And her words had seared into him, making his guilt bloom like dye in water.

When Mitchell slid out of the taxi, he clamped Barry's shoes under one arm and looked up and down the road. There was a curve of pretty small white houses, many with hanging baskets bursting with colorful flowers. He felt a pang of envy that they had small front gardens, when his own apartment didn't have any outside space.

When Mitchell rang Miss Bradfield's doorbell, he placed one foot on top of the other in an attempt to disguise the fact that he wasn't wearing shoes.

The woman who answered the door wore large red-and-white spotty earrings that reminded him of toadstools, and had rows of black dogs on her white shirt. Her brown hair had streaks that shone purple like a beetle shell when she moved her head.

"Hey," she said. "Poppy's dad? I'm Liza Bradfield."

"Yes, I'm Mitchell Fisher. I'm so sorry I'm late."

"It happens, though maybe not *this* late." She raised an eyebrow. "Come inside."

He followed her into a glossy powder-pink kitchen that looked like something a child would design. Poppy sat at the dining table.

"Are you okay?" He rushed toward her.

"You're *really* late, Dad," she said, her bottom lip trembling. Her straw-blond hair snaked into a waist-length plait, with wispy curls along her hairline. She was going through a blue clothes phase, not wanting to wear her more girlish pink things any longer. When she stood up, she launched into a ferocious hug, her fingers clutching his back. "Don't *ever* do that again."

They held each other until she dipped her head and pulled away.

Miss Bradfield smiled at them, as if watching a play.

There were chunky fish fingers piled on Poppy's plate like Jenga blocks with no vegetables to be seen, and her drink was a shade of chemically enhanced orange. A ginger wiry-haired terrier sat on the floor, wagging its tail at him.

Mitchell was too tired to make small talk and wanted to go home. If he hadn't had an accident, Poppy wouldn't be eating and drinking this stuff.

Poppy guzzled the orange liquid. "Hmm," she sighed, as if it was the best thing she'd ever tasted.

Miss Bradfield picked up her dog and held it, legs dangling, under one arm. "You finished it all, yay."

"It was *so* good. Thanks."

Miss Bradfield turned to Mitchell. "Poppy's done great. She was a bit upset at first, but I played her some classical music. A sonata can soothe the soul." Her voice had a lyrical quality, as if she sang some of her words.

"I can't thank you enough," Mitchell said.

"We learned how to hold the guitar and practiced a few notes. She's a natural, I can tell."

He wondered if she said this to all her pupils. "We should go and leave you in peace."

The dog leaned forward and licked the back of his hand, its wide pink tongue leaving a shiny trail on his skin.

"Ah, Sasha likes you," Miss Bradfield said in surprise. "That's rare, you know, her taking to a man like that. She's choosy—used to bite one of my exes. Drew blood sometimes, ha. A better judge of character than me."

When she lowered the dog to the floor, Mitchell wiped his hand on his trousers.

He glanced at her fridge, covered in a scrapbook of photos. He spotted Miss Bradfield posing in front of the Golden Gate Bridge, the Eiffel Tower and a purple VW campervan. She was accompanied by two other women, one who looked startlingly similar to the woman he helped from the water. He rubbed the space between his eyebrows and wondered if a bump to the head could bring on hallucinations.

"So, you had an accident?" Miss Bradfield said. "Are you okay?"

"I'm in one piece."

"Didn't you jump into the river to save someone?"

"It was nothing," he said, wondering how much Barry had told her. "We mustn't keep you any longer…"

She picked up an apple and bit into it leisurely. "You're an architect, right? Clever?" she asked between crunches. "Poppy told me you designed the new white bridge, the one that looks like a yacht?"

Poppy slid her eyes guiltily to the ceiling, and Mitchell felt his cheeks burn. He'd left his job in architecture when Anita died, and he hated to think about his involvement with the new bridge for many reasons.

"I no longer practice," he said. "I changed jobs and work for the council now instead. No out-of-office meetings or travel."

Miss Bradfield's eyes swept to the Maintenance Team logo on his chest. "Ah, okay," she said lightly.

Poppy carried her plate and glass over to the sink.

Miss Bradfield sped over to her. "Now, you leave those for

me to wash. Have you got room for ice cream? I have vanilla, strawberry or both."

"I *love* strawberry!"

"Great choice."

"We have bananas and apples at home," Mitchell said. He picked up Poppy's blue Word Up schoolbag.

"I have sugar sprinkles," Miss Bradfield said. "And caramel sauce."

Poppy shot him a pleading look.

Mitchell shook his head and zipped up her bag. "It's past nine o'clock. Let's do that some other time."

"When?" Poppy said immediately. "Next week?"

"We'll sort something out, okay?" Miss Bradfield said. She placed her hand behind her head and fanned out her fingers to form a crown. "Remember what we learned, Poppy? Always be a pineapple."

"Stand tall, wear a crown, but be sweet on the inside," Poppy added to her quote with a smile. She moved away from the sink and took her bag from Mitchell. "Thanks for looking after me, Miss Bradfield."

"Oh, call me Liza outside school. And just look at Sasha's sparkly eyes. She's missing your dad already."

Mitchell headed for the front door, desperate to sink into his own sofa. "Thanks again," he said.

"No problem, Mr. Hero. Shall I call you a taxi?"

"It's fine, we'll walk."

"Um, you're not wearing shoes, Dad," Poppy said.

Mitchell curled his toes. Their apartment was around two miles away, but he didn't carry credit cards and there was only a five-pound note left in his wallet. "I fancy some fresh air," he said.

Poppy wilted against the doorframe. "Pleeease. I'm so tired, and I've got my bag to carry."

Miss Bradfield pursed her lips. "If you need a little money?" she said quietly. "You can pay me back, along with the lesson money. It's eighteen pounds for a half hour lesson. Not as cheap as other teachers, but I'm good."

Damn, Mitchell had forgotten about that, and he would have to pay her more for looking after Poppy. If he'd been alone, he'd be stubborn and limp home in his socked feet.

However, he reluctantly agreed to Miss Bradfield's offer and she phoned and ordered a taxi, before covertly slipping him a ten-pound note. "Call me tomorrow, let me know you're okay," she said.

He reached for the latch on the door. "I'll be fine."

"Just to check. Or for a chat. Poppy said you're on your own…"

His cheeks flushed with embarrassment. "I'm really okay," he said. "I'll be back in work tomorrow, as usual."

Mitchell saw Poppy's and Miss Bradfield's eyes meet, unconvinced.

"I think the cab is here." He raised his chin and pulled the door open, glad when a breeze outside cooled his fiery face. "Thanks again, for everything."

5

ANGEL HOUSE

The shadows cast by the setting sun made the crumbling white bricks of Angel House look almost pretty. The 1920s building had originally been built as commercial offices for a detergents company and was named after its most popular cleaning fluid, Angel Liquid. It had been converted into apartments in the 1990s and retained its name.

Mitchell and Poppy lived at the top of the building in the eaves, where the ceilings sloped at acute angles. The roof slates soaked up the heat in summer, turning the place into a sauna, and in winter it was as cold as an igloo. The landlord described it as a penthouse, but it was more like an attic.

Mitchell started to rent the apartment four years ago as a weekday base away from home to be closer to his job at Foster and Hardman Architects. Work had been difficult to come by in the rural area he, Anita and Poppy lived in, and Anita wanted to remain close to her job teaching art at a local school, and her friends. They'd both lost their parents before Poppy was born, so these connections were important to her.

Mitchell was initially reluctant to stay in the city, but Anita assured him it was a more sensible option than commuting four hours a day. His work contract was for only eighteen months, and he'd be home three nights out of seven.

He initially liked that the apartment was uncluttered by family life. There were no piles of books and clothes on the stairs, or lipstick marks on towels or toys littering the floor. He could go to bed when he wanted, at 8:00 p.m. with a book or after a late-night movie. He discovered Minecraft on his iPad and sat up for hours crafting virtual bridges and buildings.

He often had to work over the weekends, too. At these times, when he and Anita didn't see each other for up to a fortnight, they wrote letters to each other.

He wished he had shared her same eloquence for words. Her joie de vivre shone through in each letter she sent him, and his heart leaped when he found them waiting for him in the lobby or in his mailbox. Poppy sent him crayon drawings and small notes, and her handwriting flourished from the extra practice.

In return, Mitchell's letters were practical and concise to prevent the stresses of work showing through. As his workload increased, the passion for his job faded, and so did his words home. But the money was good, and he was doing it for his family to have a better life. The foundations he laid now would strengthen their future.

Mitchell prayed to himself that the Angel House lift was going to be working, or else there were five flights of stairs to climb to the apartment. He just wanted to clamber into bed and go to sleep so he could be productive at work the following day. He could ask around to try to find out what happened to the woman in the yellow dress and put his mind at rest.

A fresh wave of exhaustion hit him when he saw Carl, the live-in concierge, mopping the checkered floor of the lobby. Carl was occupying the role to cover for his uncle, who was looking after a poorly relative overseas. In Mitchell's opinion, Carl was overly keen on his new job. He greeted the residents too eagerly, with a big smile and many questions. In his mid-twenties, Carl's hair was butter yellow and he wore a white shirt and tie underneath his khaki overalls. He could often be found folding origami shapes out of colored paper.

"Evening," Carl said, looking grateful to have someone to talk to. He rested his arm on top of his mop. "You two are out late. Do you have school in the morning, young lady?"

Poppy gave him a tired smile. "Yep."

Carl reached into the breast pocket of his overalls and passed a tiny green paper crane to her. She cupped it gently in her hands. His eyes then swept down to Mitchell's socked feet. "Why are you carrying your shoes, Mr. Fisher?"

Mitchell flexed his toes, too fatigued to reply properly. He groaned inwardly as he saw the Out of Order sign on the lift.

"I have a letter for you." Carl darted eagerly across the lobby toward his tatty oak desk. He moved a few origami frogs to one side and picked up a pink envelope. "A lady on the third floor asked me to give you this. Is it your birthday?"

"No." Mitchell reached out to take it, but Carl kept it pincered to his chest.

"I can see hearts through the paper," he said. "Very romantic."

Mitchell whipped the envelope from Carl's grip. He placed a hand on Poppy's back and urged her toward the door to the stairway. "Thank you."

Carl called after him, "I have another letter here, too, Mr. Fisher. This one's for me. I wonder if you could just—?"

However, Mitchell had already opened and closed the door behind him. He looked up the stairs spiraling above them.

Poppy glanced back toward the lobby. "I think Carl wanted you to look at his letter, Dad."

"Why would he want me to do that?"

She shrugged a shoulder. "Don't know."

"Well, I'm sure he'll find someone else to do it," Mitchell said as he mounted the first step.

After reaching the apartment, Mitchell panted as he unlocked the door. Even though the sun was almost down, the apartment was still baking hot. The small rooms were sparsely furnished, with stripped wooden floors. He'd bought the bare minimum of sleek Scandinavian-style furniture to kit the place out. In his sitting room, there was a three-seater sofa with a textile print featuring block-printed stags, and a coffee table that looked like a tree stump with rings in the wood. In Poppy's bedroom, there was a shiny white bed, desk and wardrobe that he'd hastily bought and assembled from Ikea.

When Poppy dropped her schoolbag onto the floor of the hallway, pieces of paper pinned to corkboards on the walls fluttered like butterfly wings—recipes, an exercise itinerary, Poppy's school timetable and the diary of their activities he'd planned for the school holidays. Whenever Mitchell thought of new plans of action, he wrote them out neatly and pinned them here. After Anita died, he'd become obsessed with planning his and Poppy's lives. There was a beauty to structure, like mortar between bricks, holding things together.

"That's not the right home for your bag, is it?" he said.

Poppy picked it back up, huffing as if it was really heavy. She pushed it onto its allocated labeled shelf in the storage cupboard. "Okay?" she asked blearily.

"Good. A tidy house is a tidy mind, even though it's technically an apartment."

"*Yes*, Dad."

The handwriting on the pink envelope was indigo, with large looping letters. Mitchell opened it up and winced when he saw the hearts on the card that Carl mentioned.

Dear Mitchell,
My name is Vanessa and I live on the third floor. I hope you don't mind me writing to you, but I saw you online, on the local news, and recognized you from our apartment block. What you did is totally admirable. Bravo, you!

If you'd like to pop over for a bottle of vino or coffee some-time, feel free to knock on number 25.

Love,
Vanessa xx

Poppy peered at it excitedly over his shoulder. "That's nice of her."

"It's kind of weird," he said. "How does she even know my name?"

"Maybe from Carl?"

Mitchell felt prickly at Vanessa's attention. She'd put two kisses and used the word *love*.

He often thought he'd been born in the wrong era and belonged to a more old-fashioned time instead. He couldn't understand why hooking up with someone you'd only just met was called *getting lucky*. What was lucky about having a stranger in your home and being intimate before you even knew their surname?

He'd been on only a few dates since Anita died and through-out them he felt as if he sweated guilt through his every pore.

He knew Isobel through work, and she was obsessed with Spain. They'd met for tapas and, although the dishes of food were tiny, Mitchell couldn't eat a thing. Isobel didn't notice and devoured his portions anyway.

Beatrice was an intellectual. She wore black-framed glasses that made her look like a 1950s scientist. Her favorite word was *existentially* and she had learned her periodic tables at the age of seven. She said Anita's death was *lamentable* and, at the end of the night, invited him back to her place.

Mitchell still felt ashamed that he'd succumbed to her offer. After eighteen months without Anita, his body had ached to be close to someone else. He wanted the comfort of listening to another person's breathing as they slept beside him, even if it was for only a few hours.

Afterward, in bed, he and Beatrice talked sleepily about their favorite seasons and things they liked to do on Sundays. But a voice in his head told him he shouldn't be here, that it was far too soon.

After napping for a while, Mitchell had sat up in bed and pulled on his shirt. "Sorry," he said into the darkness of the early morning. "I have to dash. I had a lovely time."

"Me, too," Beatrice murmured with a smile in her voice.

Mitchell paused, wondering what the etiquette was here, if he should ask to see her again. But Beatrice spoke first. "Please make sure the front door is closed properly when you leave."

"Yes, of course."

"It sticks sometimes."

"Sorry," Mitchell whispered, stubbing his toe against her bed as he slipped out of her room. And when he hurried away from Beatrice's apartment, he said, "Sorry," once more, this time to Anita.

Now he gripped Vanessa's card in his hand. "I won't go around for coffee. She might be a serial killer," he joked at Poppy, trying to get her to agree. But she shook her head at him very slowly.

"She might just be lonely, Dad," she said. "Like you."

Mitchell stared at her for the longest time. "How can I be lonely when I have you?" he said and kissed the top of her head.

Later that night, Mitchell moved stiffly around Poppy's bedroom, putting her books away, reminding her to put her worn clothes in the laundry basket and to choose her clothes for the next day. As she changed into her pajamas in the bathroom, he picked up his favorite family photo of him, Anita and Poppy at the top of Conwy Castle. Poppy had insisted they climb each of its towers, and afterward they'd rewarded themselves with huge ice creams.

After Poppy finished cleaning her teeth in the bathroom, she jumped up onto her bed. "Hop on, Dad," she said, and Mitchell placed the photo back down.

Poppy's bedroom had ceilings that met in a point, so it resembled the shape of a tent. A large window built into the slope of the roof opened outward, so she could stand on her bed and poke her head and shoulders through it.

They stood on the bed next to each other and looked out of the window at the night sky and the twinkling lights of the city. Laughter rang from the late-night cafés below, and at the edge of the silvery rooftops a pigeon lay huddled in the nearby gutter.

After they'd breathed in the night air for a while, Mitchell said, "Come on, Pops, it's bedtime."

She walked her fingers along the warm roof slates. "I miss our garden."

"This is kind of outside space," Mitchell said, his eyelids growing heavier.

"I could make daisy chains, and friends came over to play."

"I loved it, too, but we go to the park. You see your friends at school."

"It's not the same." She dropped down to her knees on her bed and sat with her head bowed. She picked up her floppy black cat, the last toy her mum had bought for her. "Can we go *home* one day, Dad?"

Mitchell shut his eyes and felt the same way. He missed their house and how Anita's bras tangled up with his socks in the laundry basket. She sang when she smoothed new sheets onto the bed. He wished he could lounge outside on warm evenings and drink cider with her again.

He shut Poppy's window, leaving a small gap, and sat down on the bed beside her. He took her hand in his, knowing the city apartment wasn't ideal for a young girl. "I couldn't afford to pay the rent on the house with only my wage coming in, especially after I switched jobs. Plus, living here I get to spend more time with you."

She cocked her head and played with the bow around the cat's neck. "One day, I'll get a job. Then *I'll* buy our old house," she said with a wobble in her voice.

It was his impossible dream to buy one, too, and he turned off her main bedroom light. "Come on, Pops, it's been a long day. You get some beauty sleep."

"I'm beautiful enough. Mum says so."

"And I agree, but you still need to sleep."

Poppy turned and lay on her side. When she pulled her sheet up over her nose, her eyes shone with tears.

"Hey, what's wrong?" He dipped his head closer to her.

She gave a small sniff. "Will the woman you helped be okay?"

"Yes, she'll be as right as rain," Mitchell said, trying to convince himself as well as Poppy. He picked up her plait and gently brushed the end of her nose with it. "I left her with a doctor."

She peered up at him. "What's her name?"

"I don't know. I wished I'd asked her. But look, get some sleep and we'll chat in the morning."

She was quiet for just a second. "Was she pretty?"

Mitchell cleared his throat. "I didn't notice." But in his head, the woman smiled at him on the bridge and he saw the sunlight kissing the tip of her nose. He thought of Barry's words, not to invite drama into his life, and knew it was good advice. He tugged Poppy's sheet down to expose her face and her words tumbled out.

"I thought you weren't coming to get me from school. You said you'd never be late, but you were, and Mum did the same thing…"

Her words made him sway. "The woman was in danger, and I was there."

"I know, but…" She swallowed a sob.

Mitchell gathered her into his arms and they sat together in the dark. He held her until she grew drowsier and heavier in his arms. When her breathing slowed, he kissed her forehead and helped her settle under the covers before he stood back up.

As he moved away Poppy said quietly, "No one saved Mum."

Her words felt like a thump to his gut, and he gripped the door frame. "People tried to…"

He waited for her reply, but it didn't come as she drifted off to sleep. His footsteps were leaden as he walked back to his own bedroom and fell onto his bed, fully clothed. He took Anita's sealed lilac envelope out of his bedside drawer and held it to his chest, still unable to open it.

After pulling out his notepad from under the bed, he clumsily took the top off his pen. He propped his head up with his hand and began to write.

Dearest Anita,
Something happened today and I wish you were here, so I could talk to you about it. I helped a lady who fell, but I wasn't there for you...

His words stopped as a fog descended on his brain. Mitchell pushed himself to write more, but could only manage two additional words.

Love always

Then the pen slipped from his fingers, and his eyes fell shut as he slipped into a deep slumber.

EARRING

The next morning, Mitchell woke with alarm. His bedroom was brighter than usual, and his eyes shot open when he saw the time on his watch. He was already two hours late for work. He was still wearing his clothes and, when he kicked off the bedsheets, his writing pad skidded to the floor.

Across the corridor, Poppy snored lightly as he hobbled into her room.

"Pops," he hissed. *"Poppy."*

When she didn't stir, he reached out to touch her shoulder. He calculated he could make her a late breakfast, rush her to school and make it there before lunchtime. Then he could go into work.

But tomorrow was the last day of the school year and the lessons would be winding down. He knew deep down that, last night, Poppy wasn't okay.

And he wasn't okay, either.

He had leaped from a bridge, saved someone, been knocked unconscious and woken in hospital. He tried to survey it all technically and without emotion, but he couldn't deny his body felt like it was filled with wet sand.

Even though his brain urged him to wake her, Mitchell brushed a lock of hair off Poppy's cheek and he decided to leave her in bed. He made himself a bowl of muesli and sat alone at the dining table to eat it. He noticed the light bulb that hung down above his head was dusty and didn't have a shade.

Whenever Anita used to visit, she would say the place looked like a bachelor pad. At the time he thought it was amusing, but now it felt rather tragic.

Instead of browsing the national news on his iPad as usual, Mitchell opened the Upchester News website. If Barry had seen a photo of him online, there might be an image of the woman in the yellow dress, too. He felt a desperate need to find out if she was okay.

On the main page, there was a photo of the bridge and he read the large sub headline: Man Saves Woman from Raging River.

He shook his head at it in dismay. *I didn't save the woman, I helped her. The water wasn't raging.*

The piece was written by someone called Susan Smythe and was full of theatrical words such as *selfless* and *courageous* and *dashing*—words he didn't associate with himself. Thankfully the article didn't mention his name, but it didn't give the name of the woman in the yellow dress, either.

He read through it twice and his concern increased. Perhaps she'd ended up in hospital, too. He felt annoyed with himself for not making inquiries while he was in there.

When he scanned the last sentence of the article, he sucked in a breath.

Have you attached your own padlock and why? What would you say to the Hero on the Bridge? Write in and you could win £200.

There was another square image below this, featuring a large red triangle. When Mitchell clicked it, a video played. The air around him chilled as he watched himself sitting by the river edge. His polo shirt clung wet to his body and he hadn't realized how slim he'd become.

The woman in yellow sat in front of him and bent her head, so he couldn't see her face. The film ended with a zoomed-in frozen image of her eye and ear on the screen. Her earring was the shape of a large gold cactus that he hadn't noticed when he'd helped her.

Somehow, she seemed to look straight at him and Mitchell rubbed his fingers together, wanting to reach into the screen. "I hope you're okay," he said quietly. "Who and where are you?"

His thoughts were broken by footsteps thudding along the hallway. "Aargh, *Dad*," Poppy yelped, her dressing gown hanging off one shoulder. "I'm late for school."

He waved a hand to calm her down. "It's okay."

"But I've missed my bus."

"It's not the end of the world."

"Tell Miss Heathcliff that."

He gently took hold of her shoulders. "I don't feel well enough to go into work today," he said, the words sounding alien to him. "I'm taking the day off, and so are you."

Poppy gaped at him. *"What?"*

"I was going to wake you, but you needed to rest after last night."

She chewed the side of her cheek. "Sorry, Dad."

"You don't need to apologize. How do *you* feel today?"

"Starving."

"Well, why don't you have some cereal while I call the

school? I'll tell Miss Heathcliff you'll be back in tomorrow. I'm sure she'll understand."

"*Will* she?"

"Leave it to me. You could take a nice bath after breakfast."

Her words were cautious. "But don't we have a plan?"

Mitchell glanced across at his schedules in the hallway. "Not even one action point," he said, ignoring his uneasiness.

"Great." Poppy grinned as she picked up the muesli box.

Mitchell's mobile phone screen was still blank, so he used his landline to call his boss. He explained he'd been in an accident and needed to rest up.

Russ already knew about Mitchell's hospitalization from Barry and agreed with his time off. He was committed to the city council's mantra of providing *a supportive working environment for all*, and he loved to win trophies and awards to prove it.

"Has the woman I helped come forward?" Mitchell asked.

"No, and let's hope she doesn't," Russ said. "We don't want any negative stories kicking around before the centenary celebrations. Someone falling from a bridge is not good for the city's image, might raise health and safety concerns. So do not, I repeat, *do not* say anything to the press, or put stuff on Twitter or Facebook. We need it to settle down, nice and quiet. You got that?"

Mitchell decided not to mention the online news article. "Loud and clear," he grumbled, shifting on the sofa. "I never use social media anyway."

After her bath, he let Poppy eat a bowl of Coco Pops for her lunch, just this once. He insisted she drink a glass of milk.

He sat next to her at the table and jiggled his leg, unused to convalescing.

Poppy pushed her empty bowl away. "I got some homework yesterday and it's deadly boring." She began to recite the assignment in a singsong manner. "Produce a piece of work during the school holidays to celebrate Upchester's centenary of city status. It has to include photos and more than one quote."

Mitchell liked projects, especially the planning stages. He secretly relished helping Poppy with her schoolwork, and his juddering leg stilled. "You could write a story about the architecture of the city bridges," he said. "Did you know the concrete one is called a beam bridge? It's the simplest kind, like a tree chopped down and placed across a river."

"You've told me before." She rolled her eyes teasingly. "It's *my* homework. Did you look for the lady on the internet?"

He nodded. "I found a short video." Mitchell played the clip and showed Poppy the text about the competition.

"That's rubbish," she said. "You can't see her properly."

"I know."

"And *no one* will write in."

The landline phone rang, and Poppy stared at it suspiciously. Mitchell once overheard her talking about it to her school friend Rachel, as if it was invented in the Dark Ages.

"I'll get it," he said and picked up the receiver. "Hello."

"Mr. Fisher?" The lady's voice was breathless and he wondered if Vanessa had got hold of his phone number.

"Um, yes?"

"It's Miss Bradfield."

"Oh, hi," he replied. "If you're calling to see how I am, I'm absolutely fine."

"But you're off work?"

"Well, yes."

There was a moment's silence. "Look, I know this is a big ask," she said. "But can you come over to my place? Like ASAP."

He frowned. "What, *now*?"

"Yes. I'd like to talk to you. I have ninety minutes free before my next lesson."

Mitchell didn't feel like traipsing across the city today, even though she'd been so helpful. He wondered if Poppy had left something behind at her house. "We kind of have plans."

"Oh," she said dejectedly. "Only I've just watched a small film of you online, and I need to ask you something. It really *can't* wait."

"About the film?"

"About the lady in the film." She paused, as if carefully considering her next words. "I think the woman you rescued might be my sister."

"Don't use your posh voice, Dad," Poppy whispered as they stood waiting for Miss Bradfield to answer her door. They'd taken a bus across the city and got here within forty-five minutes of Miss Bradfield's call. "It's embarrassing."

"What posh voice?"

"The one you use on the phone and in expensive shops."

"I never go into expensive shops."

"Just speak normally, okay."

Mitchell had started to recite words in his head to see if he did pronounce them in a grander manner, when Miss Bradfield opened the door. She was wearing red shorts with a frayed hem, and a blue-and-white striped shirt. Her feet were bare. "Glad you could come over," she said.

"Hi." Poppy fanned her hand behind her head. "Pineapple."

Miss Bradfield returned Poppy's gesture. "Come in and get comfy."

Poppy jumped inside with both feet. "I wasn't in school today," she said.

"She stayed at home with me for a bit of recovery time," Mitchell explained. He covertly gave some money to Miss Bradfield to cover the taxi fare and music lesson.

"We talked about my homework, though," Poppy said. "The history of Upchester. Yawn."

"Well, history can be can be anything, even something that happened five minutes ago. Only boring people get bored." Miss Bradfield led the way through the pink glossy kitchen and out into a small yard. A book lay flat on her striped deck chair and a small guitar was propped against the wall. Poppy picked it up, strummed it then held it up in one hand like a rock star.

Sasha trotted over and flopped onto her side with her head on Mitchell's shoe.

"She lubs you." Miss Bradfield smiled, but it didn't quite reach her eyes. In fact, Mitchell thought she looked a lot paler than she did yesterday. "Can I get you guys a drink?"

Poppy smacked her lips. "I loved that orangey stuff."

"We'd both like a glass a milk," Mitchell said.

Miss Bradfield reappeared a few minutes later with three glasses of frothy yellow liquid. Poppy's glass sported a pink paper umbrella and Mitchell's a green one. "I made banana milkshakes, so everyone is happy," she said.

After sucking nervously on her straw, she reached behind her cushion and passed a couple of photographs to Mitchell. "These are of me with my two sisters."

The first shot showed three brunette women, laughing and raising cocktail glasses to the camera. Miss Bradfield stood in the middle wearing her aviator sunglasses. The woman on the left sported a black top and a striking gold pineapple pendant. "This one is Naomi, my younger sister. And I think you helped my older sister, Yvette." Miss Bradfield tapped the pretty lady to the right of the shot.

Mitchell's mind raced at the potential coincidence of it being her. He couldn't be certain, because the woman's face was partially hidden by a cocktail glass. But her chestnut curly hair was similar. He looked at the next photo and this time he could see her more clearly. Her dark eyes, her smile. He could picture her in his arms again.

It was *her*.

Relief tidal waved over him that he'd found her. "*Yes*. Yvette." He found he liked saying her name.

Miss Bradfield stared at him and stood up abruptly. She glanced at the photo again before rushing back toward the house with a stumble.

Poppy stared after her. "What's the matter, Dad?"

"Hmm, I'm not sure. Will you keep an eye on the dog while I go and see?"

Poppy scooped Sasha into her arms. "Come on," she said. "I'll look after you."

He found Miss Bradfield standing in the kitchen, staring at the photos on her fridge.

"Sorry." She shook her head. "This is all super weird. I recognized Yvette's earring first, in the clip. I bought them in Mexico for her birthday. They're golden cacti and she wears them a lot. I bought Naomi a gold pineapple necklace, too. It's great when you buy something and the person likes it, isn't it? Makes you feel good inside."

Mitchell could recall the woman's yellow dress, her eyes and her smile. However, he felt a sliding sensation inside him that something wasn't right. "Have you heard from Yvette since she fell?"

Miss Bradfield looked down at the floor. "The thing is—" She jumped as the doorbell chimed and she glanced at her watch. "Oh, what? It's too early for my next pupil."

She made her way to the door and stopped dead when she saw two people behind the frosted glass. "It's Mum and Naomi," she hissed. "What are they doing here? Mum's supposed to be staying at Naomi's place tonight."

"It's okay," Mitchell said. "Maybe we can catch you next week—"

Miss Bradfield shot out a hand and gripped his arm. "No." Her eyes flashed. "You stay."

Mitchell stared down at her fingers.

She let them slowly fall away. "Sorry, it's just that—"

The doorbell sounded again, twice.

"Look, let me just get that. Patience isn't one of Mum's virtues. You and Poppy can wait in the lounge. It's nice in there, quite glam."

"Um, okay."

Mitchell opened the door to a small, cozy room with a striped carpet. There were gold-framed paintings of cherubs on the walls and various instruments sat under the window. He called Poppy back inside and she skipped along the hallway to join him.

"What?" she asked.

He ushered her into the room. "We're waiting in here for Miss Bradfield."

"We can call her Liza. She said so." She plopped down on the sofa.

Mitchell heard the front door open and the sound of kisses planted loudly onto cheeks. After a few moments, a large lady bustled into the room. She had dyed raven-black hair set in coarse waves, and she wore an overlong purple shirt over white linen trousers. Her gnarled fingers were like roots of ginger and adorned with chunky gold rings. Mitchell saw she shared the same dark eyes as her daughters. "I insist on meeting your friends, Liza," she said.

Miss Bradfield followed her in and mouthed *Sorry* to Mitchell in an exaggerated manner. Another woman, whom he recognized as Naomi, entered as well, and gave him a warm smile.

"And who do we have here?" Miss Bradfield's mother asked Poppy as if she were a toddler. "How old are you, honey? What instrument do you play and what grade are you on?"

Miss Bradfield stepped forward. "Mr. Fisher and Poppy popped by to talk about some, um, school stuff," she said. "Guitars, sheet music, that kind of thing. They aren't stopping."

Miss Bradfield's mother held out her hand toward Mitchell. "I'm Sheila," she said. "Seeing as Liza hasn't introduced us properly." After Mitchell shook it, she refocused on her daughter. "Do you know your shorts have threads hanging from them, Liza? They're a disgrace."

"Yes, Mum. It's kind of fashionable, you know."

Naomi took hold of her mum's arm. "Let's go to the garden, and we'll get you a nice glass of water." She led her out of the room.

"I'm almost ten," Poppy shouted after them. "I'm learning the guitar. No grades, yet."

There was a bustling noise in the kitchen and the sound of a tap running. When Miss Bradfield returned, she semi-closed the door behind her. "Sorry about that. Naomi's had a burst water pipe at home, so Mum can't stop there. The spare bed is all wet. She's insisting on staying with me instead, which is not what I need. A sure way to bring on a headache." She looked at her watch. "Now, tell me how you came to save my sister, Mr. Fisher."

Mitchell explained how he saw Yvette fasten a padlock then lean over the railing, looking for something. He mimed swimming motions and explained how he'd also ended up in hospital, omitting the detail about being hit by a pizza delivery bike so he didn't sound like an idiot. "I don't know what happened to her after that. I didn't even know her name until you told me."

Miss Bradfield sat down, massaging her temples in a circular motion. "What on earth was Yvette doing on the bridge? Why didn't she call me? This is so strange."

Mitchell didn't say anything, assuming her questions weren't meant for him.

She raised her head. "Aren't those padlocks on the bridges supposed to be love tokens or something?"

"People call them love locks. They leave names or messages on them."

"Hmm, I'd never think to do that." She twirled a thread on her shorts around on her finger until it snapped.

"Is there something wrong, Miss Bradfield?" Mitchell asked her cautiously.

"Oh, just call me Liza."

"*Told* you," Poppy chirruped.

Mitchell shook his head to show her this wasn't the right time. "Okay, Liza. And please call me Mitchell."

"Well, Mitchell." She found a small smile. "The thing is, Yvette went missing almost twelve months ago. Vanished."

His forehead wrinkled. "Um, missing?"

"She disappeared in July last year. And *you're* the only person I know to have seen her since." She said it as if it was an accusation or a challenge to him.

Mitchell closed his eyes, trying to make sense of this. "Disappeared?" he repeated.

"Walked out of her life without a word. Didn't let Mum, Naomi or me know about it."

He searched for something to say. "Do the police know about this?"

She sighed, exasperated. "The police won't treat her as a missing person because she writes to me sometimes. So, they wouldn't be interested that you saw her. Too busy with burglars and petty theft and fights in bars…"

"Liza, *Liza.*" A voice rang through from the back garden.

"Duty calls." Liza shrugged. "Will you get back in touch with me if you think of anything—" Her words choked up. "*Anything* at all that might help me find her again?"

"Of course, though I've told you all I know," he said.

She nodded slightly. "In two weeks, Yvette will have been missing for exactly twelve months. I want her home by then. I promised Mum. A year is too long without my sister. We've got to get her back."

Mitchell's head ached as he tried to think what he could possibly offer. "Yvette attached a padlock… There could be something written on it."

Her eyes lit with hope. "Really?"

"Sometimes there are only initials on the locks, or nothing at all," he reconsidered out loud, not wanting to raise her hopes.

"But if there is, it could be a clue."

"Finding it again will be like looking for a needle in a haystack."

Liza rubbed under her eye. "Will it even still be there?"

"It may have been cut off," Mitchell said. Then he thought about how slowly Barry worked. "But yes, it probably is."

"Then I need to see it." Liza sat upright. "You've brought us a fresh lead, Mitchell. Will you help me to find that lock?"

Mitchell shifted uncomfortably at her ask, a knot forming in his stomach. He didn't need any more complications in his life. But when he looked over at Poppy, her eyes urged him to say yes. Her words about no one being there to help her mum felt branded into his brain. Maybe he *could* do something this time around.

"Okay," he said reluctantly. "I'll see what I can do."

7

MESSAGE

Mitchell was usually like a coiled spring, ready to take up his bolt cutters and get to work. However, today his movements were slower because of his sore back and aching limbs. He felt glum rather than determined when he saw all the locks stretching out in front of him. When he trudged over to Redford, he found Barry working there.

Barry cut through a shackle and kicked the lock across the pavement. He rubbed his neck and stared at his mobile phone before he noticed Mitchell. "I can't work in this heat," he groaned. "Just look at the amount of locks now. We need a drastic solution here."

Mitchell surveyed the railings and for the first time ever, the size of the task removing the locks felt overwhelming. "A stick of dynamite might be the only option," he said.

"It's all down to you and me, mate. Russ isn't going to help us."

The word *impossible* appeared in Mitchell's head and he ordered it to go away. All he could do was set to work and keep going. "Do you have any spare bolt cutters I can use?" he asked.

"Yeah, but they're a bit rusty. I've asked around about your missing toolbox, too, but no luck. We could stick a note to the railing and see if anyone replies. I've got paper, a pen and sticky tape."

"That's very organized, for you."

Barry shrugged self-consciously. "Tina the artist said I should try out some landscape drawing, but that's not going to happen."

As the two men walked along Redford, Mitchell glanced at the river, and a shiver ran down his spine. The water wasn't gushing as quickly today, but it looked cold and gunmetal gray. He thought of Yvette Bradfield's smile and the gold heart-shaped padlock glinting in her hands.

We did share a connection, didn't we? How does she know me?

"I found out the woman I helped is Liza Bradfield's sister Yvette," he told Barry. "But she's been missing for almost a year, and the family have no idea where she is."

Barry blew from the corner of his mouth. "Wow. Mind blown."

"I know. And now Liza wants me to find Yvette's lock. She hopes it might provide a clue to her sister's whereabouts."

"Can't they put something on Facebook?"

"I think they want to keep things in the family."

Barry stared at the thousands of locks on the railings. "Hmph, you've got no chance." He picked up a thick black pen and wrote on a piece of paper "Lost toolbox (shiny metal). Award for safe return." "We should add your phone number to this," he said.

"My mobile's not working, and I don't want to put my home number."

Barry rooted around in his toolbox and handed a gnarled plastic mobile to Mitchell. "It's a spare one, a bit bashed, but it works okay. You may get calls from random women looking for dates. Not that it's a bad thing."

"Yes, it is. And I'm still going to look for Yvette's lock."

Barry put his hand on his hip and looked around. "I'll help you," he said. "It's easier than cutting them off, and I'll tell you about Enid."

"Another lucky woman?"

Barry nodded proudly. "A dog stylist."

"I thought you didn't like dogs."

"I like cats better, but she looks great in her photo."

Mitchell moved the conversation on by describing Yvette's lock to Barry. He tried to remember roughly where she'd fastened it.

"At least it's a different shape to the norm," Barry said as the two men crouched down on the pavement. They worked methodically, examining locks on a stretch of railing, one by one.

"Are you sure we've got the right place?" he asked after a while when they failed to find it.

Mitchell was beginning to doubt himself, too. "Let's try farther along."

As he picked up another padlock, he became aware of someone standing behind him.

"Are you *him*?" a voice said. "The Hero on the Bridge? You *look* like him."

Mitchell and Barry looked up to see a young woman clutching a fake Mulberry mustard-colored satchel. She had an ice-blond straight bob and wore a white blouse with a large bow at the neck. Plasters were stuck to the back of her heels, where her half-size-too-small designer court shoes had chafed.

Barry stood up and smoothed his hair. "Barry Waters," he said. "Pleased to meet you."

She gave him a withering look. "I meant *him*." She held her hand out toward Mitchell. "I'm Susan Smythe."

Mitchell recognized her name from the online article. He straightened himself up and tentatively returned her handshake.

"I'm a journalist," she said. "Well, in training."

He retracted his hand. "We don't know anything about Word Up," he said dismissively. "We get asked about them all the time."

"That's not why I'm here." Susan's eyes glistened as she took a tissue out of her satchel, giving her nose a blow.

"Hay fever?" Mitchell asked warily.

"I'm gathering myself. I'm a bit, um… I'm rather upset."

Barry took a step to the side. "Time for my break," he said and sidled away. "Catch you later."

Mitchell waited for Susan's sniffling to stop. She stuffed her tissue back into her satchel and moved the strap higher on her shoulder. "I wrote a piece about you for the Upchester News channel. Your name is Mitchell Fisher, right?"

He nodded reluctantly.

"I recognized your, um…" She eyed his face.

"My *courageous* and *dashing* nature?" he quoted from her article.

"I was about to say your eyes. I came to give you something." She opened her satchel again and took out a batch of ten or so letters fastened together with a purple rubber band. "These. They arrived this morning. I, um…" Her tissue reappeared, and she spoke to herself through clenched teeth. "All I want to do is come up with a great story, and I messed up. *Again*."

Mitchell was surprised to feel a touch of paternal-like concern toward her. There was something about her determined demeanor that reminded him of Poppy. "I'm sure you've done nothing of the sort."

She gave him a self-deprecating smile. "My first week on the job, I spilled coffee on a politician. During the second week I got stuck in a traffic jam and missed an interview with Brad Beatty."

"Brad who?"

"The lead singer of Word Up. For my triple whammy I wrote an article about you jumping from the bridge and didn't include your name. I asked the general public to submit their stories and didn't publish an email address. The news channel address was printed online, so people sent letters instead. And, here they are." She proffered them to him.

Mitchell thought of all the envelopes stuffed in his night-stand drawer and he raised a palm. "Thank you, but I have plenty of my own."

Susan kept her hand outstretched. "My boss warned me not to mess up again. I thought you could help me out."

"Um, how?"

"Perhaps by reading these letters and selecting a winner for the competition? They're all addressed to you, anyway."

He shook his head. "Sorry, I want to move on from what happened."

She gave a defeated sigh. "I suppose I'll just throw them away, then. Or leave them on my boss's desk, where he'll use them as coasters. He's more interested in the sport and crime stories."

Mitchell glanced at the letters in her hand. He'd so enjoyed receiving the ones Anita sent him in the past. He wished he'd kept them to remind himself that she did love him, once. With some reluctance, he took the letters from Susan and hoped there weren't any featuring red hearts among them.

The top envelope was textured and white, already opened, so he slid out the letter and read it.

Dear Sir/Madam,

My neighbor read your story about the heroic man on the red-brick bridge, and I felt compelled to write and tell you mine.

I was nineteen when I met Douglas and he was twenty-two. We met on the same red bridge, many years ago. The Second World War had just ended and the streets rang with cheering and laughter, as the entire city celebrated. Strangers kissed strangers and didn't care who watched.

I first saw him standing in the middle of the bridge in his army uniform. He looked so handsome and tall, like a matinee idol. Our eyes met. He said hello and I smiled back. For a while we were like small birds, a little shy of each other. But then he took off his hat and scooped me into his arms. I'd never kissed a man before and my first time was definitely the most memorable.

Afterward, Douglas apologized. "I got caught up in the moment," he said. "I usually treat ladies with respect." But I really didn't mind. He insisted on walking me home and shook my father's hand. "May I request your permission to take your daughter out one afternoon for tea, sir?" he asked, and I tried not to smile, for we were already acquainted well.

My father was a kind man and he liked Douglas straightaway. When we eventually got engaged and married, he was delighted to have a new gentleman addition to the family. I wonder if he'd have felt the same if he had seen us kissing on the bridge!

My father died many years ago and Douglas passed on six months ago, God rest his soul. Today, I hung a padlock on the bridge in his memory. I'm almost blind now and use a cane, but I still felt Douglas beside me. "Chin up, old girl, give me a kiss," he said, and I laughed to myself. I suppose anyone who saw me must think me a foolish old woman, alone and chuck-

*ling. Yet inside I felt nineteen again, and there's nothing foolish
about that. At my age, it's really rather lovely.*

*With kind regards,
Annie Rogerson (Mrs.)*

The letter in Mitchell's hands felt heavy with a lifetime of love, something he and Anita would never get to experience. An ache rose in his chest that she'd never write to him again. She wouldn't get to read his own apologetic words and his throat tightened. "It's a fine letter," he managed to say. "What should I do with it?"

She shrugged at him. "It belongs to you now. You're its keeper."

"I told you I have enough of them," he said and slipped it back with the others under the rubber band. "I *am* really busy."

She looked at him sadly. "You jumped into the water to help someone. I thought you'd be a nice guy. It's up to you, but it would help me out immensely."

Mitchell thought of Anita again and shame bubbled inside him. She'd probably encourage him to do this. "This is only two days' worth of letters, right?" he confirmed. "More might arrive?"

"I expect so."

"And you'd like me to read them all?"

Susan fiddled with the fastening on her satchel. "Only if you want to."

Mitchell gave a small nod. "Well, okay then."

"See, I knew you'd be a good guy," she said. Bidding him goodbye, she grinned as she walked away.

When Barry returned from his break, he stared at the letters in Mitchell's hands. "Are you really going to read them?"

Mitchell nodded. "I told Susan I'd do it."

"She wouldn't know if you didn't."

"*I* would know."

The two men resumed their positions next to the railings and began to examine the padlocks again.

After a while, Mitchell picked up a lock and time stood still. It was gold, large and heart-shaped. "I think I've found it!" he said to Barry excitedly. He read the words engraved into the metal.

MY HEART IS ALWAYS YOURS.

"What does it say?" Barry asked.

When Mitchell told him, his voice cracked but he couldn't explain why. He ran a finger over the sharp ridges of the letters and read them over and over. It sounded stupid, but he felt the words could be meant for him.

Barry handed him the rusty bolt cutters. "Here you go."

Mitchell didn't take them. He had removed thousands of padlocks off the bridges of Upchester, but this one was different. "I can't cut it off," he admitted eventually.

"Why not?" Barry demanded. "You got a cramp or something?"

"No, I just think Yvette's lock should stay on the bridge, where she wanted it to be. The message must mean something, and I don't want the lock to be broken. Liza will want to see this, too."

Barry scoffed at him. "When you go back to hospital, you should get your head checked out, mate. That bump is doing weird things to your mind."

Mitchell touched the plaster above his ear. "I've got an appointment soon." When he stared at Yvette's padlock again, he felt like wrapping his fingers around it to keep it safe.

As he looked around him, at all the locks fastened to the

bridge, he thought of how others saw them as love tokens. He tried to resist but couldn't stop himself from glancing at a few padlocks and reading their words.

TM. MARRY ME? PV
TRISH AND PETE XXX
WORD UP, FOREVER
HONEYBEE LOVES WASP

An unnerving picture flashed into his head, of a mountain of locks abandoned on a scrap heap with their messages rusting and flaking away. He found himself wondering if *Honeybee* might be a beekeeper. Were they a man or a woman? What kind of person called themselves *Wasp*?

He reminded himself he was being paid to remove the locks, not consider the people who hung them there. However, as he reached out for Barry's bolt cutters, his fingers were stiff and unresponsive. The locks had always been an irritant to him, just a way to earn a living, but now he wondered if his job cutting them off was like removing flowers from a grave. He thought about Annie's letter and how her eyes met with Douglas's on the bridge. Just as his own had done with Yvette's.

Get a grip. They're only chunks of metal.

Before he carried on working, Mitchell tried to call Liza to tell her he thought he'd found Yvette's lock. When she didn't pick up, he presumed she was busy at work and left her a brief message.

He tried to get on with his job, but with each padlock that broke and fell to the pavement, his mood shifted lower. The stitches above his ear itched and Barry's rusty cutters took double the time to cut through the lock shackles. He didn't feel his usual sense of satisfaction.

When 4:15 p.m. came, he'd had enough of work for the

day. He wanted to see Poppy and try to catch Liza at Hinch-ward if she was working there. "I'm finishing now," he said, shoving the bolt cutters back into Barry's toolbox.

Barry stared at him. "You're forty-five minutes early."

"It won't make much difference."

Barry's mouth fell open.

Mitchell kicked his padlocks into a heap and stuck the batch of letters into his back pocket. He wished Barry a good date with Enid, and when he walked away from the locks on the pave-ment, a strange sense of attachment to them washed over him.

As he made his way toward the school, Mitchell opened a few more of the envelopes and read snippets of the letters in-side them along the way.

Dear Man on the Bridge,
My wife and I read about your courageous act, jumping from the bridge, and we both think you deserve a medal. We have two teenage sons and hope they grow up to be as helpful as you are. There are so few role models these days…

He opened a very short one from an eight-year-old named Matthew, which started:

Dear Sir,
I am writing to you because you are very brave and because my mum says I have to learn my writing more because I need to write better or I can't have a phone…

Another came in a flowery envelope with a thank-you card inside.

My name is Alicia and I'm writing to say the Hero on the Bridge has restored my faith in men. Well, almost. Four months ago, my husband took our dog for a walk and never returned. I've had a downer on him and all blokes since, but this guy has shown maybe there are some decent people still out there in the world. Do you know if he's single? I've got the dog back and am MOVING ON with my life.

As Mitchell read their words, an unexpected warmth spread over his body that his impromptu act had initiated this outpour of support. People were opening up and sharing their stories with him, a stranger, and the molecule of pride it sparked inside him was something he hadn't felt for a long time.

Finding it tricky to read and walk at the same time, he pushed the letters back into his pocket and promised himself he'd read the rest of them later.

Mitchell exited the city center and noticed how the sun sparkled crystal-like on the surface of the river. He smiled at a couple of teenagers who shyly held hands.

And, as he walked on, he wondered where Yvette Bradfield could possibly be, and why his pulse quickened whenever he thought about her.

8

CHOCOLATES

Mitchell arrived thirty minutes before the end of Poppy's club, so there would be no disapproving looks from Miss Heathcliff today. He headed along the main school corridor, which smelled like baked bread and crayons. The scent of schools always made him feel uneasy. He and his childhood friend Graham had once been discovered smoking behind the PE block and hauled into the head teacher's office. In fact, it had only been Graham trying out a cigarette for the first time. Mitchell had followed him to quote statistics on lung disease in an attempt to stop him from doing it. The long anticipatory wait outside the head teacher's office had been far worse than the lines and detention doled out to them both.

Thinking about his friend reminded Mitchell he hadn't been in touch with Graham for a long time, and he made a mental note to do it soon.

As he glanced at Miss Heathcliff's office door, he heard feet clipping along the corridor and saw Liza walking toward him. She wore a fuchsia-colored summer dress, a necklace with glass beads that looked like marbles and pink pointed shoes. She was holding an armful of tambourines.

"Mitchell?" Liza cocked her head at him. "Are you here to get Poppy? She's in the middle of a quiz and probably won't appreciate you showing up early. End of term games are very competitive, you know?"

"Miniature chocolates at stake?"

"A huge box of them. I'm rather jealous."

They smiled at each other. "Did you get my message?" Mitchell asked, their pleasantries out of the way. "I called you earlier."

"No, sorry, I've been here all day. Not even had a chance to check my phone. Not that anyone rings me these days apart from Mum." Her face grew serious. "Have you found Yvette's lock?"

"I think so. And there *are* words engraved into the metal."

Liza took a sharp intake of breath. "What did they say?"

Mitchell wished he'd taken a photo of the padlock to show her. "The message said, 'My heart is—'"

There was a sound of wood scuffing against carpet as Miss Heathcliff's door opened outward, creating a barrier between Mitchell and Liza. A parent scuttled out, her head bowed.

"Please see Miss Penfold on your way out," the head teacher said to the parent. "She'll give you the offending item back." She turned to Mitchell and the hairs on her top lip glowed in a shaft of daylight. "Mr. Fisher," she said. "Have you recovered from your ordeal?"

"Just about," he said. "Thanks for asking, and for looking after Poppy until my friend collected her."

"It's our role to care," she said. "Might you have a small moment to converse?"

Mitchell glanced at Liza apologetically.

"It's okay, I'll catch you later," she said and moved away.

Miss Heathcliff led the way into her office. "Please take a seat."

Mitchell followed her inside. Individual black sports shoes, broken trophies and lost sweaters were piled everywhere. She picked up a couple of pieces of paperwork, shook her head at them and set them back down again. "The last day of term is always such a kerfuffle," she said.

"Poppy was excited by the idea of not doing much work today."

She didn't smile at his joke. "The children have been working on some notes for their school holiday project," she said. "I'm expecting to see some excellent pieces."

"I'll make sure she does her best."

"Good. I do suppose her end of year results came as a surprise to you?"

Mitchell clasped his hands together in his lap. "Um, end of year results?"

"You might have noticed Poppy's grades in her report are noticeably lower this time around?"

His blank expression must have told her what she needed to know.

"Ah. Another missing report situation." Miss Heathcliff tutted. "Please remain seated." She left the room.

Mitchell felt like he was fourteen and sitting alongside Graham again, waiting for his punishment. He cursed himself for forgetting to ask Poppy about her report when she undoubtedly had it noted down in his hallway.

When Miss Heathcliff returned, she passed him two sheets of paper.

Mitchell scanned over them and saw Poppy's grades had dropped across her subjects. He read parts of the comments.

Not meeting her full potential...mind appears to be elsewhere...more effort needed.

"Oh." He screwed his eyes shut, feeling instantly responsible. This was all his fault. It had to be. Perhaps she needed even more planning and structure to help her.

He couldn't stop from babbling things Miss Heathcliff already knew. "Poppy's mum died and I switched jobs to look after her. She's been coping with everything really well. Or, so I thought."

Miss Heathcliff observed him kindly. "The latter primary school years can be a time of great change for children and they all manage it differently. We're here to give Poppy all the support she needs. I suggest we put this aside for now, Mr. Fisher, and start afresh in the next school year."

"Thank you."

"Notwithstanding, my expectations are high for Poppy's holiday project. Perhaps it's something you can work on together."

"She says my ideas are boring," he mused, but then mentally added it to their schedule of things to do together. "We'll give it a go, though."

"Good. And there is another important thing for Poppy to do during her break."

"Yes?"

"She should have plenty of fun, Mr. Fisher. You only have one childhood, and we adults are a strong influence on that. Encourage Poppy to work hard, but to enjoy her time off, too. I understand she's booked into the activity club here, during the school holidays?"

"Yes, and I'll be spending time with her, too."

"Well, that sounds just splendid. I'm sure she'll have a great time."

Mitchell left Miss Heathcliff's office and still had several minutes until the after-school club finished. He peeked into Poppy's classroom and the quiz was still in full swing. Twenty or so kids sat to attention, waiting for the next question. The box of miniature chocolates sat on tantalizing display on the teacher's desk.

Mitchell patrolled the corridor, glancing into the classrooms, looking for Liza. The lilting, sorrowful sound of a violin came from the Year Six room and he stuck his head around the door to see Liza sitting on a child's chair with her eyes closed, lost in the music. He tried to step quietly into the room but kicked a tambourine on the floor.

Startled, she stopped playing and lowered her violin. "Oh, hi. Did you mean to creep up on me like that?"

"Sorry to disturb you. It sounded...beautiful."

"Thanks. It's one of my favorite pieces." She placed her violin in its case and closed it. "Did you know that listening to music increases the neurotransmitter dopamine? It makes you feel better."

"I didn't know that."

"You can get it from eating chocolate, too. Though that's more fattening. I can't imagine life without it."

"Music or chocolate?"

"Both." She gave him a quick smile. "Look, can we talk about Yvette's lock? What was written on it?"

Mitchell took a child's seat at the table opposite her, his knees jutting out like frog's legs. He hoped he'd found the right padlock. "It said, 'My heart is always yours.' Does that mean anything to you?"

Liza jerked her head back as if struck. "'My heart is always yours?'" she repeated. "Those words exactly?"

"Yes. Do you know them?"

"Uh-huh. They're a song title," she said. "Our Auntie Jean was a singer in the 1970s. She had a few hit songs in Germany, but nothing big here. I don't know why because she was really good, like Stevie Nicks or something. Even better in my opinion. That song was her most popular one."

"I don't think I know it."

She glanced shyly at him then began to sing, her voice sweet and mesmeric. The hairs on the back of Mitchell's neck stood up to attention.

"The days ahead might be long, my friend,
Sometimes we'll think they'll never end,
But together we'll make it, we'll be strong,
My heart is always yours."

She shook her head, embarrassed. "Auntie Jean sings it much better than me. She's got soul, that woman. She wrote it after a doomed love affair, when she hit rock bottom. The emotion in her voice, when she sings, cuts you to the core. So, why would Yvette use it? She's an accountant and married to her job. I've never known her to bother much with relationships."

Mitchell shrugged. "It sounded, um—" He struggled to find the right word. "Otherworldly, in a good way. I think I might have heard it before."

Lisa gave him a quick smile of thanks. "I have *so* many questions running around in my head about Yvette," she said. "They won't keep still. I don't know where to start."

"Well, what happened on the day she went missing?"

She clasped her hands together tightly. "Everything was so normal. It was hot, like today. That nice kind of heat when everyone is happy, not the sticky type. The three of us were supposed to go to Mum's house for tea, the four Bradfield ladies together. Naomi was going to drive and pick up Yvette first, and then call for me. Except when Naomi got to Yvette's apartment, she wasn't home. Then she didn't pick up our calls.

After a while, Naomi drove over to my place. She was already really worried. We phoned Mum in case Yvette had gone straight there, but she hadn't turned up. And we all waited and waited. I remember looking out of the window and watching the sun dipping lower and lower. The sky grew red, like fire, and she still didn't arrive. Naomi had to get back to her kids…" Liza looked down and fiddled with a ring on her little finger. "Later that night, I called the police."

"What did they say?"

She clenched her jaw. "They asked for Yvette's details, a photo of her, stuff like that. They suggested I phone around her friends and relatives, obvious stuff I'd already done. I spoke to people she worked with, too. I let myself into her apartment, but couldn't spot anything untoward. Yvette's a bit of a minimalist, can't stand clutter, and everything looked tidy and normal. I think some clothes were missing from her wardrobe and a few bits and pieces.

"She'd been missing for a couple of days when a letter from her arrived." She patted her purse. "I was so relieved to get it. I mean, you hear these stories, don't you? About people disappearing, and you worry that something bad has happened to them. I still carry it around with me. Would you like to read it?"

Reluctant, Mitchell chewed his lip. Annie Rogerson's letter had stirred a myriad of emotions inside him. He wanted to know Yvette was safe, not be privy to her private correspondence.

In the few seconds he deliberated, Liza took the letter from her purse anyway. It was pale blue and the paper looked delicate, like it might fall apart when handled.

She held it out to him. "You read it," she said firmly, though the letter shook in her hand. "You might see something I haven't."

Mitchell felt he had to take it from her. When he opened it up, the fold lines were almost transparent. Still full of apprehension, he started to read.

Dear Liza,

I'm sorry. I know you, Naomi and Mum will be worried about me. I felt I had no choice but to escape from everything. I've done something I can't undo. Please believe me, that I searched deep in my heart and couldn't find another way forward.

I've hidden things from you all for a while. I've plastered on a smile, so please don't berate yourself if you didn't notice it was fake. It's my fault, not yours.

My head is full of things I want to say to you, and everything I can't.

Please don't try to find me. It will make things so much more difficult. One day soon, I hope I can tell you everything.

Love,
Yvette x

As Mitchell handed the letter back to Liza, she wiped a finger hastily underneath her eye. "She said to not try to find her?" he questioned.

"Yes, and I've tried my best to resist, but it's been *so* long," Liza said. She placed the letter back in her purse. "I've had other things from her, too, another letter and a couple of postcards. But they didn't have postmarks to indicate where she might be. I told the police about them, but because Yvette's disappearance sounds voluntary they won't set up a search. The thing is, Yvette isn't a mysterious type of person. She's the serious sister, the straightforward one. I worry myself sick about her being gone, keep running over in my mind what might have happened. I don't like the things I invent. Then

I get something in the mail from her, and I tell myself she's okay. But she still doesn't come home or say where she is."

Mitchell tried to think of different scenarios in his head about where Yvette could be and why she left, but he found himself at a loss. He had no idea what might have gone on within the Bradfield family. And he wasn't sure if he wanted to know. While he and Yvette had shared a dramatic experience together, she was still a stranger to him.

"Does your mum know I saw Yvette on the bridge?" he asked.

She shook her head. "Not yet. Not from me. If she knew, she'd inundate me with questions, and I won't know the answer to any of them. I don't want to raise her hopes, either. She gets these nasty anxiety attacks, a racing heart and dizziness, and they're getting worse. I worry she'll keel over one day."

"Won't she see Yvette's image online?" Mitchell said. He felt like he was morphing into Carl, asking too many questions.

"She refuses to learn how to use a computer. She says the news depresses her and will only watch the national updates at teatime and the fun stories at the end of the report. Naomi is usually up to her eyes in nappies and toys. She probably watches kids' TV more than the local news. I doubt anyone else would recognize Yvette from the footage. Just me, because of her earring. Maybe Auntie Jean will know something about the song on the padlock…"

"Will you ask her?"

"Hmm, she's really difficult to reach. When she's not on tour, she runs a retreat for musicians in North Yorkshire. A kind of hippie place. She insists that phones and the internet are banned, so they don't disrupt the flow of creativity. If you ever want to see Jean, you have to go and find her. She has some show dates coming up soon in Germany.

"Jean said she hadn't seen Yvette for a couple of months before she went missing, but she can be a bit *unreliable* sometimes. I'll probably have to drive up there to see her." She placed her purse back in her bag then suddenly grew more animated as an idea seemed to form in her head. "Hey, maybe you could join me? You could tell Jean how you saw Yvette in person... It could be a day out."

Her suggestion caught him off guard, and he wasn't sure if she was joking or not. "The school holidays start tomorrow and I have Poppy to look after."

She pursed her lips a little sourly. "I understand. Poppy told me about your *intensive* itinerary."

"I wouldn't call it that, just a few plans. It's good to keep busy."

There was a sound of a bell ringing. Doors opened and children flooded into the corridor, chattering.

"I get it. Family time is important," Liza said, her voice loaded with disappointment.

Mitchell scraped back his chair. "Will you let me know if there's any progress with Jean?"

"Sure." Liza stood up and stiffly held out her hand.

He stared at it, wondering what she was doing.

She kept it outstretched. "Thanks for helping Yvette. She could have drowned, like that young man did last summer. It's good you were there, Mr. Fisher. I understand if you can't assist me further."

He noticed how she'd dropped his first name, and how her voice lost its lyrical quality. A handshake would signal they were about to become strangers once more. They might nod and smile at each other politely in the school corridor, or exchange small talk, if Poppy continued her guitar lessons. Mitchell would become the nice man who helped Liza's sister out once, but who wanted to keep his distance and not get involved any further.

But he could hardly drop everything and go on a trip with Liza to speak to her aunt, could he?

As he held out his own hand in return, Poppy popped her head around the door and stared at their awkward handshake. "I heard your voice, Dad. Are we going home?"

"Yes, Pops. Just a minute."

"How did the quiz go?" Liza asked her brightly.

"I won! I need to collect my prize."

"That's brilliant," Mitchell said. "Clever girl."

As Poppy turned on her heels and skipped out of the room, Mitchell thought about his plan of action for tomorrow—a visit to the library and baking healthy vegetable muffins together. He guessed his daughter would prefer a trip out someplace with Liza instead, and Miss Heathcliff said Poppy should have some fun.

Liza grabbed her violin case and stood. "Well, I should go, too. Have a truly fabulous summer," she said, walking toward the door.

Mitchell got to his feet and reached out a hand. He couldn't let her go, not like this. "Wait." His fingers brushed her elbow.

She turned, her expression questioning but hopeful.

"When you go to see your aunt, Poppy and I will join you. If you like?"

She eyed him, as if assessing whether he really meant it, before she broke into her usual smile. "*Yes.* Yes, please. That would be super. Then she can hear the story directly from you. If you text me your address, I'll pick you both up from your place in my car. How about tomorrow at noon?"

"Um, tomorrow?" he said.

Liza maneuvered her violin case through the classroom door. "It's urgent because of Jean's tour."

"Well, okay. We live in an apartment building, so we'll meet you in the lobby."

"Great. Oh," she added before she headed out into the corridor. "Bring an overnight bag. It's kind of a long drive up there."

When she'd gone, Mitchell stared after her. "Long drive?" he repeated to himself, wondering what he'd just agreed to. "Overnight bag?"

9

GREEN BOTTLES

Over supper of porridge that evening, Poppy's mouth fell open when Mitchell told her they were accompanying Liza on a trip the next day and staying overnight, too. He also told her about the letters Susan had given to him to read.

After rushing her last mouthfuls of food, Poppy sprinted to her bedroom where she rummaged in her drawers and wardrobe, gathering things to take with her.

"Slow down," he said, following her.

"You might change your mind."

He sighed to himself, hurt at how she perceived him. "I promise not to. Liza is picking us up at noon tomorrow."

She picked up a pajama top. "This will be great, Dad, won't it?"

He doubted she was right, but he nodded anyway. When he thought of his carefully mapped-out schedules in the hallway, he felt a pull toward them. "Of course, it will," he said.

"You can take the letters to read."

"Yes, I suppose I can." If he was going to be sitting in a car on a long journey, he didn't really have an excuse not to. And he did wonder what the unopened ones might reveal. "Now, don't pack too much stuff, and remember your toothbrush."

Poppy was still wearing her pajamas the next morning when a knock on the apartment door came at 11:10 a.m. Mitchell stood in the bathroom, mid-tooth clean, with white paste dribbling down his chin.

It can't be her, can it? Not this early. Perhaps it's Carl instead.

He spat into the sink, wiped his mouth on a towel and went to his front door to unlock it. He found Liza standing there, wearing lime-green-and-white pumps with pale jeans and an embroidered top. Her toadstool earrings had been replaced with pink Perspex triangles.

"You're extremely early," he said, rather annoyed.

"Hello to you, too," she laughed.

As she followed him into the hallway, she put her hands behind her back and examined the sheets pinned to the wall. "Hmm, interesting. So, are you planning a military operation or solving a crime? Or both?"

"What do you mean?"

"This is all so *regimented*. You've even written down times for taking out your rubbish." She squinted. "Do you schedule in watering your plants, too?"

"I don't have anything in the apartment that needs looking after, or that's nonessential," Mitchell replied tartly. "I thought we were meeting you in the lobby at twelve."

"I got here early and the blond caretaker guy told me your door number. When you walk up the stairs, do you like to look out of the windows and see the city getting smaller and smaller?" She didn't wait for his reply. "You'll never be burgled up here, will you? I mean, thieves would just target the lower floors. Unless the lift was working, of course. Which it's not. There's a sign on the doors."

Her talk made Mitchell feel weary. He never looked out of the stairwell windows. He concentrated on his feet and the bannister to avoid stumbling. Wouldn't anyone do the same? "Come into the sitting room," he said. "Poppy's getting ready."

When Poppy appeared from her bedroom, she was trying to stuff a scarf into her bag. He had already seen her packing her floppy cat, three lip balms and an atlas.

"We're only going away for a night," he said, sensing the excitement radiating from her. "It's too hot to take a scarf."

"It can protect me from the sun."

"That's good strategic thinking," Mitchell relented.

Liza looked around the room, at his sofa, coffee table and tiny TV. "Nice. Have you just moved into this place?"

"Dad's been here for ages," Poppy said.

"Really?" Liza looked at the bare light bulb hanging above the dining table. "It's…a bit naked."

Poppy giggled at her choice of word, and Mitchell picked up the batch of letters from his coffee table. "We have most things we need," he said.

"Except lightshades?" Liza shrugged.

"And a garden," Poppy added.

Mitchell managed a small wry smile as he picked up his overnight bag. "Hopefully, Jean's place will have both," he said.

Carl sat at his desk in the lobby, his head bent and his fingers working nimbly on a small square of white paper. Within seconds, he'd transformed it into a delicate lotus blossom. "Have you finished school for the summer holidays now?" he asked when he saw Poppy. He offered her the flower.

"Yep. And now we're going on a trip."

"Great. Where to?"

Mitchell and Poppy looked at each other. "I'm not completely sure," he said. "But we should be back by tomorrow afternoon."

"Righto." Carl's eyes drifted to the letters, still in Mitchell's hands. "Did you open the pink envelope I gave you, Mr. Fisher? I have my own here, too…" He patted his breast pocket where a turquoise envelope poked out. "Perhaps you could—?"

Outside, Liza beeped her car horn several times.

Mitchell spun Poppy around, so he could stuff the letters into the pocket of her bag. "Sorry, Carl. We really have to go. Let's talk when I get back."

They hurried out of the building and Mitchell got into the back seat of Liza's car, which was covered in dog hair. Poppy took the front seat because she often felt travel sick. There was a musty damp smell that Mitchell attributed to Sasha, who stared up at him with her amber eyes. When she repeatedly tried to put her head on his lap, he admired her perseverance.

Liza beeped her car horn again before pulling out into the road. A car behind her gave a long honk back and swerved around her. She screwed a finger into her temple. "Sawdust for brains," she shouted out of her window.

"You didn't indicate," Mitchell said.

"The sun is so bright, he wouldn't have seen my light anyway."

"The car manufacturer will have tested it, to make sure it's visible in all weather conditions."

"You're probably right," she said as she drove along the road and turned onto the Victorian bridge. "You look like the kind of guy who knows things like that. I bet you even iron your socks."

Poppy looked over her shoulder and gave him a knowing smile.

Mitchell laughed defiantly. "Don't be silly."

"You clip them together in the wash," Poppy said. "With small pegs."

"Now *that* is organized," Liza said.

Mitchell cleared his throat and looked down at the dog. "It's a communal laundry area," he replied defensively. "They can get lost easily."

When Liza pulled onto the motorway after leaving the city, she shifted in her seat. "Shall we all sing a song? It will make the journey go quicker. How about ten green bottles?"

"That's for babies," Poppy said. "Mum used to sing one hundred green bottles."

"Now that's a challenge. What about Taylor Swift or Ariana Grande instead?"

Poppy's eyes widened. "You know their songs?"

"Yep."

"I certainly don't," Mitchell said.

"Would you join in, anyway? Really?" Liza asked him.

Mitchell rubbed his chin, pretending to consider. "Do you like the sound of cats fighting? That's what my singing is like."

Liza laughed. "Let's not risk that while I'm driving—I need to concentrate on the road. I'll put the radio on instead."

After they'd been on the road for an hour, Mitchell felt himself dozing off in the back. Poppy and Liza chatted away in the front.

"I've got a *brilliant* idea for my school project." Poppy wriggled excitedly in her seat. "I could do a PowerPoint about the padlocks on the bridges."

"That sounds really great," Liza said.

Tuning into their conversation, Mitchell rubbed his eyes and leaned forward to speak through the gap between the front seats. "Isn't it supposed to be a historical project?"

"The locks are part of the city's *recent* history," Liza remarked.

Mitchell ignored her and addressed Poppy. "Why don't you research the city bridges like I suggested?"

She sucked in a breath. "Because they're *old*. *Mum* would say that's not creative."

Liza smiled to herself.

Mitchell sat back again. Anita had loved being creative. She used to keep plastic crates of wool, sequins, old buttons and string stacked in the attic. He thought of her now, with a lap full of glittery stuff, smiling up at him and telling him it would all come in handy one day. He smiled rather sadly at the memory.

"I could ask people for their stories," Poppy said to both him and Liza.

"You can't approach strangers," Mitchell argued. "They shouldn't be hanging padlocks on the bridges in the first place."

Poppy scowled. "It's a good idea."

"Can't you think of something else?"

"No. And it's *my* project, not yours."

Mitchell found it hard trying not to take charge of things, a throwback to years of working in management, and the level of organization required from being a single-parent family. "Well, I suppose I could help you," he said, after a while.

Poppy's lips thawed into a smile. "Thanks, Dad."

Mitchell looked out of the window, then pulled Poppy's bag toward him. After unzipping it, he took out the batch of letters and selected one to read. The first one was in a slim manila envelope.

Dear Sir,

Your request for stories has inspired my letter. It helps me immensely to finally set my words free. Despite being in my thirties with a good career and own house, I still wake at night full of dread from my bad memories, about leaving the country of my birth.

It was there I participated in an arranged marriage to a stranger. I told my mother repeatedly and respectfully that my heart belonged to someone else. However, my father insisted the honor of our family would lie in tatters if I did not acquiesce, and so I obliged his demands.

I only have fleeting memories of my wedding day. I gave my body to my husband but my heart couldn't follow. Eventually, I had to choose between losing my family, or my own sanity, and I fled.

I am now with the person who loved and waited for me. Love is an organic thing between us, never forced and always understanding. We fastened a padlock to the bridge as a symbol of our strength and togetherness. I am pregnant and if I should have a daughter, I shall raise her to be proud and the queen of her own desires and thoughts. I believe families should listen to and cherish each other. Now it is time to create my own, and to no longer look back.

I thank you sincerely for taking the time to read my letter.

Bless you,
Aisha

Mitchell wiped away an unexpected tear from the corner of his eye at how one page could contain such love and loss. He fumbled for another letter to chase away his emotions. It had been sent by a teacher from another local primary school.

Dear Mr. Fisher,
We wondered if you might be available to officially open our
school fete in September? There'll be face painting, a coconut
shy, stalls run by local businesses, and all proceeds will go to-
ward repairing the school roof...

The thought of being regarded as some kind of celebrity made Mitchell shiver. He didn't want to draw attention to himself, even if it did help the school. He folded the letter back into its envelope.

The next one had an artsy card inside. It featured a small line drawing of the new white bridge, and his nostrils flared when he saw it. He recognized the drawing style and knew who it was from before he opened it up.

Mitchell!
Salutations. I heard through the grapevine you leaped from the
old red bridge to help someone. That's so incredibly selfless of
you and I hope you're doing well.
Look, it's been on my mind since you left Foster and Hard-
man that you and I didn't part on the best terms. My creative
vision has always been both my gift and Achilles' heel. Though,
I do think the centenary bridge is looking totally wondrous, don't
you? The opening ceremony should be sublime.

No hard feelings, huh?
Jas

A ball of anger grew and burned inside him. Mitchell had to hold his breath until it subsided as a hiss through his teeth, so Poppy and Liza didn't notice. Jas hadn't even mentioned Anita, only thought of herself, as usual.

He crumpled her card in his fist, pushed it into his pocket

and stuffed the remaining letters he hadn't read back into Poppy's bag.

Then he folded his arms, stared out of the window and allowed himself to think of Jasmine Trencher, and her contribution to him losing Anita.

10

OFFICE

Three years ago

Increasingly, as weekends approached, Mitchell felt like he was a parched man crawling toward an oasis in the desert, desperate for water. Seeing his family was the only way to quench his thirst, a brief reprieve from the intense pressure of his job.

Staying in his city apartment was losing its attraction. He'd been here for a year and was fed up with his weekday life of loneliness. The eighty-mile distance from home felt like an ocean.

Although Anita tried to support his long hours, he knew deep down she was growing disillusioned with their splintered family life. As his workload on the centenary bridge project intensified, his letters home dwindled. He was sluggish and tired, and didn't want to bore Anita with details about pedestrians, traffic flow, safety and maintenance issues he had to address.

His once-healthy eating habits slid into a rota of cereal and takeaway pizza. He no longer had the zesty morning feeling of excitement he got from rushing around to help Poppy to pack her schoolbag and walking her to school. His mates gave up asking him to play football, after he missed out on too many matches. All he saw were the insides of his apartment and office.

Disappointed that he wrote home less often, Anita's letters to him fizzled out, too.

One day, when Mitchell was home for the weekend, he and Anita stood drying dishes in the kitchen. "I have to work away next weekend," he said miserably.

"Again?" Anita placed a glass down heavily on the draining board.

"I'm so sorry. I have to entertain some overseas suppliers."

"I don't know why you don't just move into that bloody apartment permanently," she snapped.

They stared at each other, both taken aback by her words. Mitchell picked up a plate to dry and Anita put it back in the cupboard. The air was sharp with tension as they carried on the task in silence.

"You're right. It's too much," Mitchell said when they'd finished. He placed his hand on her back. "I took the job to help our family, but it's no good if I don't see you."

"I *know* you try your best." Anita softened. "But things aren't working, Mitchell. You're stressed and I am, too, trying to work full-time *and* look after Pops. She's growing up so quickly, and you're missing out."

Since he was last home, she'd lost two teeth, and was a centimeter taller on the height chart in the kitchen. "I'll do something about it," he said firmly. "I promise you. I just need to find the right time to speak to Don."

Two weeks later, as Anita's birthday approached, Mitchell still hadn't spoken to his boss about his workload. Don Hardman was difficult to pin down, flitting between the office, entertaining clients in posh restaurants, and his holiday home in Marbella.

One night, Mitchell woke in the apartment in the early hours of the morning. He'd had a nightmare about a bridge collapsing down on his family. He had managed to dash to safety, but in the dream, Anita and Poppy were buried under the rubble. He dug at it frantically, debris caking under his nails and bloodying his skin, but he couldn't reach them.

The screech of twisting metal and falling stone had sounded so real in his head that Mitchell's pajamas clung to his body in a fearful sweat. He staggered out of bed and into the bathroom where he gulped a glass of water. After entering Poppy's empty bedroom, he clambered up onto her mattress, opened her window and thrust his head outside.

His brain was muggy, as if stuffed with cotton wool, and a pain pierced his chest that he hoped wasn't serious. His own father had died of a heart attack, aged just forty-five. He didn't want to go the same way.

As Mitchell's pulse eventually slowed, and he shivered in his perspiration-soaked top, he knew he had to do *something*. Enough was enough.

The next day at work, Mitchell tried to speak to Don again, but he was out of the office. So, Mitchell took matters into his own hands. He decided to take Anita's birthday off work, that coming Friday, whether Don liked it or not.

"Are you sure about this?" Anita asked when Mitchell phoned and invited her out for lunch.

He heard the warning tone in her voice. There had been

a few occasions he'd said he'd be home for the weekend, but then had to work. "Absolutely," he said. "We need some time together and I want to treat you. I'll call into the office on Friday morning to pick up my emails, then drive straight home. Shall I book a table for two at Mazzo's, for twelve thirty?"

"I've always wanted to try there," Anita said cautiously. "The tiramisu is supposed to be amazing."

"We can spend all afternoon at the restaurant, then pick up Poppy together from school. The three of us will spend the entire weekend together."

"And you're *sure* you can take the time off?"

"Yes," he said resolutely. "I know things have been difficult for us all, but things will change. I need to put you and Poppy first."

"Okay," she said, a fresh lilt to her voice. "I'll wear my new green dress. I'm looking forward to it already."

"Me, too."

Mitchell felt almost as giddy as when they'd first dated. But he would always remember Anita's last words to him, before they said goodbye.

"Please don't let me down, Mitchell."

"Of course, I won't," he said.

And, at the time, he really meant it.

Jasmine Trencher joined Foster and Hardman seemingly intent on stirring things up at the firm. She was all platinum hair, piercings and scarlet lipstick and the granddaughter of an esteemed architect, Norman Trencher. She tottered around in studded boots and schmoozed Don. She announced she had a new vision for the centenary bridge that was the antithesis of Mitchell's existing design.

His plan was to construct it from local steel and quarried stone. It would be solid and steeped in history, a representation of Upchester and its heritage. Whereas, Jasmine's vision was a modernist creation, all shiny white struts and dramatic angles. To Mitchell, it was a kind of fantasy design.

On Friday morning, Don arrived with a large roll of paper under his arm. He was a small, nervous man with a tiny head and jutting ears. "Jasmine has some very interesting ideas," he said. "They're refreshingly ambitious."

Mitchell closed his laptop. He'd made good progress with his emails and was ready to leave. He'd booked the full day off as a holiday, his first time off in months, and he was desperate to see Anita for her birthday lunch. "I know and that's great. The company needs fresh perspectives."

Don nodded his head too many times. "She's, um, taken an interest in the new centenary bridge, and has a few fascinating observations to share."

"My door is always open. I'm happy to chat." Mitchell zipped his laptop into its bag. He turned in his chair to pick up his jacket.

"Good, because I have her ideas, here..."

A metallic taste appeared in Mitchell's mouth. Jasmine was encroaching on his project without asking him. She had bypassed him and gone directly to Don. He glanced at his watch.

Don unrolled the paper and spread it out on Mitchell's drawing bench. It wasn't a computer-generated design, but a hand-drawn one, not particularly detailed. It was stylish, though, all swoops of ink pen and watercolor washes, the kind of design that might accompany a travel feature in *Vogue*.

"It's a nice piece of work," Mitchell said. "I'll take a proper look at it on Monday."

Don clicked his tongue. "There are rumors that Norman Trencher is going to be awarded a knighthood soon."

Mitchell frowned, not understanding. He slipped an arm into his jacket. "Um, am I missing something here?"

"Foster and Hardman, as a whole, need to decide if we stay committed to the existing design for the bridge, or if we look at more modern ideas, too."

Mitchell worked his jaw. "My initial concept has been approved by the council's centenary committee," he said tensely. "I've been working on it for months."

Don's Adam's apple rose and fell as he swallowed. "It's not had the final sign-off, so there's still time for, um, tweaks. I'm calling an urgent meeting, today at one thirty. Everyone is expected to be there."

Mitchell's blood cooled in his veins. "This afternoon?"

"Yes."

"Sorry, I can't make it," Mitchell protested. He couldn't let Anita down and he cursed himself for coming into the office at all, when he should have driven straight home. "I'm finishing work now. I tried to see you, to book the time off..."

Don let go of the paper and it curled back into its roll with a snap. "You'll have to cancel."

"No, you don't understand. I need to—"

"Jas has canceled going to her best friend's wedding, and *no one* else here has a problem with attending. In fact, it's obligatory." Don fixed him with a steely glare. "See you in the boardroom at one thirty, Mitchell. And keep your weekend free, too."

Mitchell paced in circles around his office. He thumped his desk with both hands and resisted tearing Jasmine's design to shreds. When he stumbled over his wastepaper basket, he booted it across the room.

He knew he didn't have a choice.

His mouth was bone-dry as he called Anita's mobile. He got through to her voice mail, urgently wanting to speak to her in person. He tried a further four times and knew she must have seen his missed calls.

She called him back thirty minutes later.

"This had better not be about our lunch today, Mitchell," she said, her voice flat and cool.

"I'm so sorry," he blurted. "Don has called an urgent meeting and I have to be there, everyone does. This new architect, Jasmine, is questioning the design of the new bridge, and she holds a lot of sway. I have *got* to be there, to put my case forward."

His explanation was met with a ghostly silence.

"You could keep the reservation at Mazzo's and go with a friend," Mitchell tried. "I'll take time off next week instead."

Again, there was nothing.

"Anita, please," he pleaded. "This is out of my control. I'm so sorry."

When she eventually spoke, her voice was so small and hurt he could hardly hear it. "I know, but you've not even wished me happy birthday…"

Mitchell's entire body sagged. He'd bought her a pair of beautiful platinum earrings that were already wrapped in his jacket pocket. He'd taken the time to write a long note in her card, to tell her how much she meant to him.

"Will you be home this evening?" she said before he could apologize again.

"I'm not sure." He screwed his eyes shut. "I can't promise, but I'll try. I have your present here and…"

She interrupted with the deepest sigh, like a wave crashing against rocks. The quiet that fell between them felt deafening. "I'll write to you," she said, and hung up.

Mitchell stared at his mobile. "Happy birthday, Anita," he whispered. He tried to call her back, but she wouldn't pick up.

When Mitchell exited the four-hour-long meeting, he felt like he'd been crushed underfoot by a buffalo stampede.

Jasmine had systematically pulled apart his ideas and design.

She'd questioned the research he'd done, discussions he'd had and decisions he'd made. Mitchell fought for his own vision of the bridge, the one the entire team had previously agreed on. His words were fired up by the anger and passion he felt at letting Anita down.

Don attempted to appear as if he was considering both cases impartially. But Mitchell could see, in the glances between him and Jasmine, that he'd already decided to back her. Her grandfather's influence was too important to Foster and Hardman for Don not to take her ideas seriously.

After taking a vote, the decision of the team had been unanimous. Jasmine was going to work up her design for the bridge further and present it to the centenary committee as a priority. Her design fit the new council vision of Upchester being seen as a modern city, rather than one living on past glories.

The team would all reconvene the next day to work on an urgent plan of action.

Mitchell could barely muster the will to walk back to his office. His colleagues averted their eyes and flocked to congratulate Jasmine on her design. She wore a smug smile.

Mitchell closed his office door and banged his back angrily against it. The clock on his wall showed six o'clock. After letting Anita down, and the blow he'd had to his ego, he just wanted to hold her and beg for forgiveness.

He traced a finger around the edge of her present in his pocket.

I could still make it home, he thought. *I want to be with my family.*

If the traffic wasn't too heavy, he might get there before eight thirty. He could say happy birthday to Anita and kiss Poppy before she went to sleep. If he set off at six the next morning, he could make it back to work for Saturday's meeting.

When he took out his mobile and switched it back on, he

saw three missed calls on his screen. All were from the same number, one he didn't recognize. When he rang it back, it belonged to a hospital.

Anita had been involved in a car crash and could he get there quickly?

Mitchell knocked over his chair in his rush to flee out of the building. He left his wallet and laptop on his desk.

He dove into his car and slammed the door shut, beating his palms against the dashboard before he tried to compose himself.

Throughout his two-hour drive to be by Anita's side, he yelled at the traffic lights, his knuckles white from gripping the steering wheel.

When he got to the hospital, Mitchell ran blindly through anonymous gray corridors to find her ward. Dread coursed through his veins.

Except he was too late.

When he and Poppy returned home, later that night, they were like two soldiers returning from war, defeated and devastated, never to be the same whole people ever again.

A lilac envelope had been waiting for Mitchell, propped up against a pepper pot on the dining room table.

He picked it up, clutched it to his heart and cried.

SHEET MUSIC

It took three and a half hours for Liza to eventually pull up outside a compact Victorian folly in the middle of the countryside. The small castle with turrets stood proudly at the edge of green fields. Several tents dotted around them, like a badly promoted music festival.

"I feel a bit sick, Dad." Poppy tumbled out of the car, her face pale, and Mitchell gave her a mint. He was still smarting after reading Jasmine's letter, and his heart pounded as he tried to blank out the fateful events that led him to losing Anita.

"Take some deep breaths," he told Poppy, holding her tightly until his pain felt less raw. "You'll be okay."

A woman who could only be Jean stood on the front step of the property. She wore tight black jeans and an off-the-shoulder white T-shirt. Her feet were bare and a large silver crescent moon pendant sat on her chest. Her lips were overplump and Mitchell guessed she was in her mid-to-late sixties, though her bleached long hair made her look younger.

"Hey, why didn't you tell me you were coming?" She threw open her arms and swooped on Liza, kissing her on alternate cheeks twice over. Her accent was a mishmash with hints of London, the US and Yorkshire mixed in.

Mitchell shrank back as he received a big hug, too. Poppy sidestepped out of Jean's range.

"You refuse to use a phone, Auntie Jean. How anyone hears about this place, I don't know," Liza said with a laugh.

"Good news travels fast. My gang arranges all the humdrum stuff for me. Come on in."

Mitchell followed Jean, Liza and Poppy into the house, and Sasha scampered after them. The spacious square room was light and airy, painted all white, with arched windows. A tiled floor, patterned rugs and cushions gave it a Moroccan riad feel, at odds with its Victorian exterior. Gold disks in frames hung on the walls, with the name Jean Jamieson featured over and over. A tall shelf displayed lots of dolls in national costumes from around the world, and a banjo lay on the sofa.

"It's like a posh restaurant!" Poppy brightened up.

Mitchell gave her a small nudge. "Manners, young lady."

Jean laughed. "The room's got a cool vibe, hasn't it? I don't stay here much, prefer life on the open road." She turned to Liza and winked. "Are you here to introduce me to your new beau?"

Mitchell felt like he'd been plunged into icy water. "Oh no, sorry, we're just—"

Liza appeared to enjoy his discomfort. "Auntie Jean, you've always been a troublemaker. This is Mitchell, and we're *not* together. The lovely Poppy is his daughter."

"Darn it. I relish a good love story," Jean laughed as she moved closer to him. She examined his face, as if he was an old master in an art gallery. "Nope." She clicked her teeth. "Not your type of dude at all. Let me guess. Hmm, you're an accountant like our Yvette?"

Mitchell felt strangely offended by this. "I work in maintenance for Upchester council. I cut padlocks off the bridges."

"Hmm, interesting." Her expression said the opposite. "So, what's the groove between you and Liza?"

Liza's smile slipped. "This isn't about us. Not that there's an *us* at all. We're here to speak to you about Yvette."

"Oh." Jean's face crumpled with sadness. "And here I am joshing and all. Is there any news?"

Liza rubbed the top of her aunt's arm. "Can we sit down?" she asked.

Mitchell headed for a blue velvet armchair so Jean, Liza and Poppy could share a small sofa. Sasha lay down with her head on his foot.

When they had all settled, Liza spoke. "Mitchell saw Yvette on a bridge in Upchester."

"When?" Jean gasped, her black winged eyeliner creasing.

"Four days ago," Mitchell said.

"Are you sure it was her?" Jean said urgently. "Where is she?"

Liza's and Mitchell's eyes met. She nodded at him to tell his story.

Mitchell leaned forward and told Jean about Yvette falling from the bridge, and the padlock she'd hung there. Poppy busied herself by looking at the shelves full of dolls.

"That all sounds crazy," Jean said after listening. "Why would Yvette use the name of my song on a lock?"

Liza stood up. She unhooked a photo frame from the wall and handed it to Mitchell. In it, Jean was much younger and had flowers in her blond hair as she strummed a mandolin.

Three girls sat by her feet. They each wore white dresses in contrast to their dark hair.

"Naomi, Liza and Yvette loved my songs when they were small," Jean told him. "They used to dress up like me and sing them, my own little girl gang. I wonder if there's something in the lyrics that could tell us more…" Her lips worked as she sang quietly, her voice guttural with age and cigarettes. When she'd finished, she shook her head. "I really don't know."

Liza held on to her hand. "Please think about it some more, Auntie Jean. It could be a clue, our only one."

"I'll try. Um," she added cautiously. "Have you spoken to your mother and Naomi about this?"

"No. Naomi is always rushed off her feet with the kids, so I want to try to find out more first. And as for Mum…"

The two women's eyes met in an intense, knowing stare.

Jean moved her moon pendant along its chain and back again. "I need space to think about this. Clear my mind. I'll make us some apple tea, okay?" She stood up and padded out of the room.

Liza continued to stare at the photo. She gripped the frame tightly, lost in her thoughts. Mitchell gave Poppy a brief apologetic smile.

When Jean reappeared, she held a trayful of small colored glasses and a slim jug. They clinked together as she sat down and Mitchell saw her hands shaking. "Here we are," she said lightly, but he heard the catch in her voice.

"The glasses are pretty," Poppy said.

"They're from Morocco, a present from a fan."

Poppy held a blue one up to her eye and peered through it. "I've never been there, but I like Spain." She didn't pause for breath as she continued. "I went with Mum and Dad. I had paella and bought some maracas." She mimed a motion of using them. "Olé."

Jean smiled and set the tray down on the floor. She took a Spanish doll off a shelf. Her voluminous black hair was pinned into a bun and she wore a red lacy dress.

"Wow. She's beautiful."

"You can keep her, if you like. I don't have anyone to give the dolls to, now the girls are grown up."

"*Really?* Thanks. I'm too old for dolls now, but I'll look after her. I've kept ones Mum bought for me."

"You can show this little lady to her."

Poppy moved the doll's arms up and down. "Um, no. Mum died."

Jean and Liza shared a look, heavy with sympathy.

"Me and Dad live in an apartment together in the city," Poppy gabbled. "You can look out of my bedroom window at the stars, and I sometimes think Mum is up there, looking down on me. That's the best thing about it. Oh, and pigeons have built a nest in the gutter. I hope they have babies."

Mitchell didn't know where to look. He gulped at his apple tea.

Jean reached out and squeezed Poppy's knee. "If you like the stars, you should wander into the forest, just over there, at night. Everything is so clear. The moonlight makes everything beautiful, even the darkest things." She sat there for a few seconds, rocking back and forth, before she focused on Liza. "I need to tell you something," she said. "It's about Yvette. Please don't be crazy mad at me…"

Liza lifted her eyes. "What is it?"

Jean fidgeted with her pendant again and didn't speak.

Poppy looked around at the adults. "Shall I take Sasha for another walk?" she asked awkwardly. "She might need a wee."

"That's a great idea," Liza said. She took the dog's lead from her handbag and attached it. "Take her for a wander around the garden. She'll like that."

Jean waited until Poppy had led Sasha outside and cleared her throat. "Yvette came to see me, the week before she disappeared," she confided.

Liza frowned. "But when she vanished, I drove up here to ask when you'd last seen her. You said it was a couple of *months* before. And now you're telling me it was the *week* before? Don't go all flaky on me, Auntie Jean. This is important. When actually was it?"

Jean picked up a fringed paisley shawl and draped it over her shoulders as if she was cold. "It was six nights before she disappeared, *not* two months. She stayed with me for a couple of days and didn't seem like herself. She was quiet and I could sense there was something on her mind, but she clammed up when I asked her. She told me she'd been seeing this guy, Victor, and showed me a photo of him."

Mitchell's ears pricked. Liza had said Yvette wasn't in a relationship. He tried to catch her eye, but she looked away.

"I told Yvette he had a dark aura. It was gray, with no glow. I can sense these things, smell them out. He was bad news. Yvette went all pale and said she'd broke things off with him recently. She'd done something and said he was going to be furious with her when he found out. But she wouldn't tell me anything else. Then she left the next morning without saying goodbye." Jean trailed her hand down her neck and held it at her throat. "I've not seen her since."

Liza's eyes flared with anger. "Why on earth didn't you tell me this before?"

Jean shrank back. "Your mum has always seen me as a rabble-rouser. She'd probably blame me for Yvette leaving. I kept hoping she'd come back—then everything would be okay. I've been torturing myself for months over where she is. I don't think anything I said was enough to make Yvette disappear."

Liza stood up. "*Bloody hell*, Jean." She clenched her fists and stormed out the door, slamming it shut behind her so hard the frames on the wall jumped.

Jean turned to Mitchell, her eyes wide with shame. "Oh, mercy, what have I done? I was only trying to help."

Mitchell struggled to think of what to say. Through the window, he could see Liza pacing around in the garden with a set jaw and hands thrust into her pockets. "Let's give her some time alone and I'll pour you another apple tea."

"Thank you, Mitchell," Jean said meekly.

After a few minutes, Liza returned. "Sorry," she said, sitting back down. She ran a hand quickly through her hair. "I just want to find Yvette, okay?"

"We all do," Jean whispered. "We need to be strong and be here for each other. Family."

Liza took a few long breaths and the atmosphere in the room calmed. She picked up the banjo and strummed a few strings before she turned to Mitchell. "You know, Mum and Auntie Jean are both musical, but have very different tastes. Mum's interests were always more orchestral. She only played instruments from sheet music and practiced pieces over and over, striving for perfection."

"I was more experimental than Sheila," Jean said. "I liked to mess around and create my own songs."

"Mum insisted Naomi, Yvette and I learned the guitar after school each day, and on weekends," Liza continued. "I was the only one of us to keep it up. When I was ten, Mum got arthritis in her fingers and she grew even more obsessed with us doing well. She pushed us to play the music she could no longer perform herself. Except Naomi had no interest in learning instruments, could never remember the notes. Yvette was older, so she got away with saying *no* more. Which left me."

Jean cleared her throat. "I remember Sheila rapping the back of your hands once because you got a note wrong."

Liza distractedly rubbed her knuckles. "She apologized afterward. She got carried away."

"My sister is an amazing woman, Mitchell." Jean nodded at him. "But she has super high expectations about everything and everyone. I've never been able to meet her standards, musically or personally."

Mitchell looked around at all the framed disks on the walls. "But you have all these awards and hits."

"They're for folk and pop music, so they don't count to her."

Liza pursed her lips. "It's more than *that*, Auntie Jean..."

A strange silence settled in the room until Jean eventually found Mitchell's eyes with hers. "In a nutshell," she said, "Sheila and I fell for the same man—more than forty years ago now. It caused a huge rift between us.

"When I was a young woman, before I had my hits, I performed my music in clubs across Europe. One night, in a jazz bar in Germany, I met a man called Luther and fell head over heels for him. He was charismatic and talented, the leader of a top orchestra. We hooked up that night and from then on, if we ever found ourselves in the same city, we met up and had fun. We kept things simple, didn't talk about our families, so I never asked him if he knew Sheila.

"Anyway, after a year or so, Sheila confided to me that she'd fallen for someone special, and his name was Luther. She hoped it was serious between them. My heart stung when I realized we were both seeing the same man at the same time." She took a moment to gather her thoughts. "I tried to break it to her gently that Luther and I had a thing going on, but Sheila refused to listen. I think she knew deep down I must be telling the truth, but she didn't want to believe it."

Liza picked up her story. "Mum accused Auntie Jean of making it all up because she was jealous."

"But what did Luther say?" Mitchell asked.

Jean grimaced. "He totally denied our relationship and told Sheila he'd only met me a couple of times. He always thrived on lies and drama. I could see she was in love with him and I tried to warn her. But Sheila chose to believe him over me. My sister and I didn't speak a word to each other for a couple of years after that."

Liza nodded sympathetically. "Eventually Mum found out the truth—that Luther lied to her about Jean, and other women, too. Mum was devastated, but she met my dad not long afterward. He was lovely, and another musician, a clarinet player. They got married within months and had me and my two sisters."

"I moved to Germany and shacked up with a record producer," Jean said. "I wrote 'My Heart is Always Yours' about Luther. But my relationship with Sheila never fully recovered." She gazed out of the window. "We don't speak much, though I send her tickets to my concerts for her birthday, and she sends me Brahms sheet music for mine. We're different people and keep our separate ways.

"That's why I was flabbergasted when Yvette told me about this Victor. He sounded very controlling, telling her what to do. After living with your mother, I thought she'd have had enough of that type of behavior. I'm glad she split up with him."

"Hmm." Liza looked down, studying the floor. "That still doesn't explain why Yvette used your song lyric on her padlock."

"I know Yvette's been in touch with us from time to time, but I'm still really worried," Jean said. "I'm supposed to be hosting my campfire jamboree tonight, but I don't feel in the mood for it now."

Mitchell shifted in his seat, not sure there could be two

worse words bolted together in the English language than *campfire* and *jamboree*.

"Don't let this spoil things for you, Auntie Jean," Liza said. "I thought Yvette's padlock would be good news for you."

"The young musicians have been working hard and I don't want to let them down." Jean shook her head. "I've not even asked if you've had something to eat."

"Oh, don't worry about us. We're fine."

"You *must* stay," Jean insisted. "I've made some parmesan and dill scones just this morning, and you've always loved the jamboree. *Please*, Liza, I don't see you very often. Perhaps I'll think of something else about Yvette or Victor to tell you."

Liza looked at Mitchell. "Okay," she said, her voice subdued. "Do you have spare tents we can use?"

"Those are all full, I'm afraid. But you can always sleep in your old room."

Liza found a small smile for her aunt. "I think Poppy will love that."

Mitchell felt a pulse of alarm at the thought of him, Liza, Poppy and Sasha having to share a space. "Poppy and I can get a hotel," he offered quickly. "Are there any around here?"

"We're in the middle of nowhere," Liza said. "Sorry."

Jean patted his leg. "Don't look so horrified, Mitchell. Liza's old room is under the stars. Sleeping bags on the floor of the forest."

12

CAMPFIRE

After they'd all eaten the strange parmesan and dill scones, Mitchell, Liza and Poppy walked across a field toward a small green hut. A young man wearing a black woolen hat and a khaki army jacket handed over three sleeping bags. Each was tied with a string bow.

"Maybe we could drive home," Mitchell said as he tucked a bag under his arm. "I'd prefer to go back and get a good night's sleep. If we set off now, we shouldn't be too late."

Liza and Poppy fixed him with a stare. They didn't reply and headed out of the hut without waiting for him.

Mitchell reluctantly followed them. He wondered what Anita would make of Poppy sleeping on the ground of a forest. There might be earwigs, and were scorpions ever found in the North Yorkshire countryside? However, he suspected she might have shared Poppy's excitement.

A couple of hours later, after Jean had given them a tour of her house and recording studio, Mitchell found himself sitting on a tree stump around a small fire with Liza, Poppy and a straggly group of young musicians.

The evening sky was still denim blue and the air was thick and hot, so he wasn't sure why a fire was necessary in this weather. However, tinfoil-covered potatoes baking on the end of sticks, poking into the fire, made his stomach groan with hunger. The paltry scones felt like ages ago.

"This is the life," Poppy said, peeling off her socks. She wriggled her toes in the soil on the ground.

"You're getting your feet mucky," Mitchell scolded. "You have a smear of dirt on your cheek, too."

"Try it, Dad." Poppy giggled. "It tickles your toes."

Jean stood up. She had changed into a short black dress with tassels around the hem. "And now, what you're all here for…our musical jamboree! Each musician will perform a song they've been working on. Be fearless and have fun. Let's welcome Delilah first. Come on up, sweet pea."

Mitchell fought the desire to get into his sleeping bag and zip it up over his head. Anita had loved going to the theater and any kind of performance, but creativity and putting yourself on display were not his type of thing.

A pointy-faced girl sporting a cream night slip and peacock feather earrings waved her arm. The guitar sitting on her lap was almost as big as she was.

"Just listen, Dad," Poppy whispered to him. "You might enjoy it."

Delilah crooned a song about her boyfriend leaving her for a forty-year-old woman. It went on for around five minutes and felt much longer. The best way Mitchell could describe it was *experimental*.

"Astonishing." Jean clapped her hands together. "Delicious. Next up, let's bang our drums for Ian."

Ian wore a hat with bunny ears attached to it. He strummed a ukulele and sang out of tune about never finding true love, even though he looked to be in his early twenties.

"Maybe if he wore a different hat…" Mitchell whispered to Poppy.

She hiccuped a laugh. "Shhh, Dad."

After each subsequent song about unrequited love, or relationships that had gone terribly wrong, there was clapping and whooping, and shouts of, "Nailed that!" and "Awesome!"

Poppy sat cross-legged, swaying to the music. She cupped her hands to her mouth and cheered. Mitchell relished watching her. Nine was such a bittersweet age. She was still so young, his little girl. Last year, she could still convince herself the Tooth Fairy existed, but he increasingly saw glimpses of the young woman she was going to become. Her youth felt like sand slipping through his fingers.

The sky turned dusky pink and then sapphire, and the next turn fell upon Poppy.

"You don't have to do it," Mitchell assured her.

Sometimes she retreated into herself, her body shrinking like a wool sweater in a hot wash. In her last school pantomime, she'd hidden behind all the other kids onstage.

Delilah held out her guitar. Poppy gnawed her bottom lip and Mitchell felt sure she'd refuse it. However, her eyes became determined and she set the instrument on her knee. When she strummed it, an out-of-tune note rung around the forest and Poppy smiled apologetically. After putting the instrument back down, she sang without it.

Her song was about how flowers in a garden need sunshine and water to make them grow. She stumbled with her words, but somehow it was innocently beautiful.

When she'd finished, rapturous applause rippled around

the fire and she swooped her arm across her middle and bent into a shy bow.

Mitchell clapped his hands furiously. "Encore," he said, as she returned to his side. "I've never heard that one before."

"I made it up." She shrugged.

He stared at her, not sure if she was kidding. "Really?"

"Yep. We had to write songs at school ages ago. I remembered some of it."

"It's beautiful."

"I sang it in a concert, before Mum…" She looked away, her face in the shadows. "She was there."

He frowned, trying to remember. "When?"

"I don't know. You were *probably* in work anyway."

"Oh, Pops, I'm sorry," he started. His body deflated, as he wondered what else he might have missed while he worked and lived in the city. He imagined Anita sitting proudly in the school audience as Poppy performed her song, and himself staring at his computer screen, calculating dimensions and measurements for the new bridge instead. Regret was a heavy burden to bear.

"She said you were busy." Poppy sniffed, as if trying to show she didn't care. "Anyway, it's your turn next."

"But I want to talk about—"

She interrupted his words. "I don't."

Jean stood up in front of them and waved her hand in his direction. "And now," she said, her voice full of drama. "All the way from Upchester city, for one night only, we have Mr. Mitchell Fisher."

Mitchell just wanted to wrap his arms around Poppy and apologize again for not being there to hear her song at school. "Move on to the next person," he told Jean. "I'm not musical."

Poppy gave him a small smile and Mitchell couldn't tell if she was angry or sad with him. "Go on, Dad," she said.

Everyone started to chant his name, and he couldn't think how to wriggle out of joining in. He took a deep breath, and held his hands up to refuse again, but someone shoved a guitar into his arms.

He gulped and tried to think of a song that he wouldn't totally murder. The only time he'd ever sung was to Poppy when she was smaller, or to Anita if he was trying to tell her about a song on the radio.

Finally, he settled on an old favorite, the first one that came to mind and probably older than most of the people around the campfire, "Yesterday" by The Beatles. He placed the guitar on the ground—he didn't know how to play—and started to sing softly, not thinking of how the words might resonate with him personally.

At first it was just an old song to him, and he sang about troubles, and someone saying goodbye, and a shadow hanging over him, and not being the man he once was. An image of him holding Anita's hand in the hospital and whispering goodbye to her dropped into his mind and wouldn't leave. It stayed there like a footprint in setting concrete.

A sadness rushed through him, and his throat grew smaller. An ember rose from the fire and he thought of how Anita sometimes sent him signs. Silly, he knew, but a red admiral butterfly, a rainbow, the pop of cider bubbles on the tip of his nose, could make him feel she was still with him. He could sense her now, and each word became harder to squeeze out. As Mitchell reached the final verse, he reduced the song to a rasp.

When he felt his tears swelling, fuzzing his vision, he bailed out before he reached the last couple of lines. He held a cupped hand to his mouth. "Damn campfire smoke," he muttered.

When he sat back down, Poppy had surprise in her eyes. "Not bad."

"That's charitable of you."

"It was nice. Was it about Mum?"

He nodded slightly. "It won't be a regular thing." He shuffled back from the fire and stared into the flames for a while. When he turned to face Liza to ask if it was her turn next, she wasn't there.

"She went for a walk in the woods," Poppy said.

"Did my singing scare her away?"

"Maybe. She said she was too hot, and she had watery eyes."

Mitchell looked over toward the trees, wondering if she'd heard his emotion breaking through in the song. "The smoke can do that," he said. "I need to stretch my legs, too. Do you want to join me?"

"Nope. Can I stay here? I like the music."

Jean appeared and sat down beside her. She took off her shawl and draped it around Poppy's shoulders. "I'll sit with you, if you like?"

"Is that okay, Dad?"

"Well, all right," he said. It was good to see Poppy relaxed and happy, and he wanted to move away from all the lovelorn anxiety for a while. "I won't be long."

As Mitchell headed into the trees, their trunks glowed orange from the reflection of the fire. He didn't believe in ghosts or werewolves or the like, but it was easy to spook yourself when twigs cracked underfoot and the full moon beamed through the branches.

With each step, his skin cooled and his surroundings fell darker. The clapping around the campfire grew faint and the music faded away. Within a hundred meters, he suddenly felt far away from everything. He couldn't hear anything but nature, and when he looked up he could see the stars shining brightly through the canopy of trees. There wasn't any smoke from catering chimneys or chugs of car gas to smog up the sky.

He reached a clearing in the woods and, when his eyes adjusted to the moonlight, he detected the shape of a large fallen log and then the silhouette of a person sitting on it.

He stepped backward to move away and let them be alone, just as he needed to be. A twig snapped under his shoe and he heard a sharp intake of breath.

"Who's there?" a woman's voice called out.

Mitchell's pulse sounded in his ears. He walked to the center of the clearing. "Sorry to disturb you."

"Mitchell, is that you? It's Liza."

"Oh." He stood motionless, not sure what else to say because he couldn't see her properly. Something scampered across the ground in front of him and he thought it might be Sasha, but it was small and rodent-like. "I'll leave you in peace," he said. "Are you okay out here on your own?"

"Sure." She didn't speak for a while and her silence was strange to him. "I'm okay. You go back."

"I don't like to leave you alone in the forest."

"I'm used to it here, and you don't want to miss Jean's marshmallow toasting session. She buys these really big fluffy ones."

"That sounds good." He stepped in the opposite direction, then moved back again. "You should come, too."

"I need more time to myself. A song reminded me of Yvette and it triggered a few memories. I need to run through them in my head."

"Okay, well…if you're sure."

"Yes. Please go, I'm fine."

As Mitchell stepped away and back into the trees, he wasn't sure if he heard a forest animal, or a small sob ringing out from behind him. He battled a strong urge to go back toward Liza. But Poppy had been on her own for long enough and, with some hesitation, he made his way back to the campfire.

Poppy thought toasting marshmallows was the most exciting thing in the world. She gave a small yelp when Jean handed one to her.

"Is it still hot?" she asked, lifting the stick to her mouth.

"Yes, so make sure you blow on it," Mitchell said. He wondered if there was anywhere to clean your teeth out here.

Poppy cupped her hand under the marshmallow and ate it. "Dad, it's yum," she said and offered one to him. "You've *got* to try it."

He reluctantly took a bite and wasn't expecting the taste to be so wonderful. The goo warmed his mouth and left a powder coating on his lips. He ate the rest of it and hoped there'd be some marshmallows left for Liza to eat.

"Told you it's nice," Poppy said, before she skipped off and sat down beside Delilah.

Mitchell became aware of Jean closing in on him. She sat down next to him with her legs crossed.

"Okay?" She smelled of vanilla with a hint of patchouli oil, and her eyes looked tired.

"Surprisingly, yes."

"This isn't your thing?"

"I'm more of a city person."

She studied him. "Why?"

He thought about it for a while. "Nature is too unpredictable. Things sprout wherever they want, and where you don't expect them. The city is more solid and contained."

"That's the kind of thing Yvette would say, too, but she loved it here. She came at least twice a year to escape the rat race."

"From what you said about Sheila, I'm surprised she allowed the girls to come here at all."

Jean lifted her face and reflections of the flames flickered on her cheeks. "Sheila used to play in musical tournaments, at

grand hotels and venues across Europe. She liked to compete
and show she was the best. Without me returning to the UK
to help out with the girls, she wouldn't have been able to do
that. Liza, Yvette and Naomi all loved staying here with me.
They could leave their cares behind and run free. Maybe that's
why Yvette came here that last time I saw her." She looked
over at Poppy. "Kids should be allowed to roam free and have
an adventure, don't you think? The grown-up world can wait."

Mitchell thought of how Poppy had to grow up too quickly
after Anita died. There was nothing intrinsically wrong with
his plans and strategies pinned in the hallway, even if a diversion now and again was good. "Perhaps if it's done in a struc-
tured way," he admitted.

Jean reached into the pocket of her dress. "I've got something to show you. It's a postcard Yvette sent to me after she
disappeared. Liza's already seen it."

Mitchell looked at the glossy photo of a group of flamin-
gos on the card. He turned it over and held it up to read, by
the firelight.

Darling Auntie Jean,
I'm so sorry we quarreled. You've always understood me the
most. If anyone would sense how I'm feeling, it's you. I'm more
like you than you know and I don't know if that's a good or
a bad thing.

Yvette x

"Why does Yvette say she's like you?" he asked.

Jean took the card from him. "That's what I'm worried
about. When Sheila and I fell out, I ran away to Germany
without a word. I suppose I was punishing her. Even though
it was a long time ago, Yvette knew about it. I'm afraid I've

not set a good example to her. Maybe she's gotten back with this Victor, especially if she knows Sheila wouldn't approve. He's dreadful, I can feel it." Without warning, she clamped her hand on to his wrist, her fingernails digging into his skin. "You'll help find her, won't you, Mitchell? Bring her home safely. I'm worried sick about her."

He shifted uncomfortably, unable to make a firm promise. "I'll do what I can."

"Good, good. I *know* you won't let us down."

When Poppy rejoined him, the fire was dying down. She sat next to him and rested her head on his shoulder. "Have you seen the sky, Dad? It's so black out here."

"We should get some sleep," he said, feeling worn-out after his conversation with Jean. "Do you know where your sleeping bag is?"

"Yep. Um, are you okay?"

"Just a bit tired, that's all."

They shook out their bags and clambered inside them, fully clothed. Poppy pulled her floppy cat out from her bag.

As they lay there, Mitchell listened to her breathing growing slower. He saw the silhouette of her arm reach up. "Do you think Mum is up there in the stars?" she asked sleepily.

He didn't answer, in case his voice faltered. "Pull up your sleeping bag," he said. "So that bugs don't crawl on your face in the night."

"Okay."

He watched Poppy's eyes blink in the darkness as she looked up at the stars for a while, and then as they closed.

"Good night, Poppy," he whispered. "Sleep tight."

"Night, Dad. Love you."

"Love you, double that," he said.

Mitchell wasn't sure what time it was when he next woke up. The fire was low, and he could make out the dark shapes of guitars propped against tree trunks. People looked like giant caterpillars in their sleeping bags. The outline of someone moved toward him and his limbs stiffened. Fingers prodded his shoulder.

"Mitchell," Liza whispered. "Are you awake?"

"I am now."

She shook out her sleeping bag beside him, then sat down on it and cradled her knees. "I can't sleep."

"I'm not surprised. There's probably foxes around here, maybe even wild boars." He raised himself up onto one arm. "Are you okay?"

"I told you I was fine, but I'm not really." She paused. "I don't want to load stuff onto you."

"If it helps us find Yvette…"

"Thanks," she said, relieved. "I just don't know what's going on. Everything seems to be falling apart. I used to be so close to Naomi and Yvette, but when Jean told us about Victor…"

"You told me Yvette wasn't in a relationship," Mitchell confirmed.

"That's right. She never mentioned Victor to me. And why did Jean get such a bad feeling about him? Why would he be furious with Yvette?"

He could tell she needed reassurance, but he had never been good at that kind of thing. "I don't know," he said. "Maybe everything will look clearer in the morning. Jean said the forest makes everything look beautiful, even the darkest things."

Liza didn't speak. She unzipped her sleeping bag, climbed inside and lay down a few inches away from him. He could feel the heat from her body.

There was a rustle and she clumsily reached down and took hold of his hand. His fingers tensed and, not sure if he'd offend her by moving them away, he let them stay. Burnt wood cracked and a few embers danced upward from the dying fire and, as time slipped by, Mitchell felt his eyes closing.

He was keenly aware of Liza's hand still lying loosely in his own. But as he slowly drifted off to sleep, he decided he liked the comfort of it there.

CARL'S LETTER

The sound of yawning filled the car as Mitchell, Liza and Poppy traveled back to Upchester. They were too tired to speak to each other properly and communicated in a series of small sporadic sentences, hums and okays.

Poppy insisted she wouldn't get sick if she sat in the back with Sasha and, within half an hour, she had fallen asleep and her snores punctuated the quietness. After reading Jasmine's letter yesterday, Mitchell wasn't in the mood for looking at the other letters Susan had given to him.

Liza focused on the road, occasionally taking one hand off the steering wheel to rub the corners of her eyes. She pressed the button on her CD player and Madonna's *Immaculate Collection* started up.

"Madonna?" he said, surprised.

"Um, yeah?"

"I thought you liked serious music."

"I like most of it, except head-banging stuff. Did you know music stimulates oxytocin, a brain hormone known as the trust molecule? It helps people bond with others?"

"I didn't know that," Mitchell said.

After "Express Yourself" played, the gauze on the side of his head fell off onto his lap. He surreptitiously rolled it into a ball.

"What was that?" Liza asked. "Something dropped down."

"My plaster," he said, grimacing at it. "My stitches are due out tomorrow."

"Gross." She mused upon this. "You're going to the hospital?"

"Yes. They gave me an appointment for six days after the accident."

"Hmm." She indicated to turn onto the motorway. "Do you think you might see the doctor who helped Yvette?"

Mitchell frowned. "The hospital is a huge place, and he might not even work there. He could be a GP, or have been passing by from somewhere else."

"Yeah, but you can ask, right?"

"Sure, except I'll have Poppy with me. I can't do much hunting around."

Liza didn't speak for a while. She leaned forward in her seat with her face closer to the windscreen. "I'm going clothes shopping tomorrow. I need some emerald green shoes. I have all the other colors. Do you think Poppy would want to come with me, instead?"

Mitchell had noticed some of Poppy's skirts were looking shorter, and one of her T-shirts was a bit tight. He usually took her to the supermarket, where she pointed at things in the sale and he put them in his trolley. "She'd love that," he said. "Thank you."

"Great. It will be fun. She can help me choose."

He thought about it for a while. "Let's not tell her in advance, though, or she might explode with excitement."

"It can be my way of apologizing for last night."

Mitchell paused, not sure if Liza meant waking him up from his sleep, or falling asleep beside him. "Absolutely none needed," he said, anyway.

When Liza pulled up outside Angel House, Poppy woke up. "Oh, are we home?" she asked with a yawn.

"You slept all the way."

"It's kind of like time travel," she said.

Liza and Mitchell shared a secret smile.

Even though he longed to jump straight into a shower, he felt obliged to invite Liza inside. "Do you want to come up for a tea or coffee?" he asked lightly.

"Oh, thanks, but I should get home and—"

Poppy perked up. "You can read Dad's letters. People have written to him."

"They're from strangers," Mitchell added. "Nothing important."

"Well," Liza smiled sympathetically at Poppy. "I'm sure your dad will be *really* tired after the long car journey."

Mitchell bristled, how she made him sound like an old man. "You're more than welcome to join us," he reasserted.

"Well…okay. In that case, I'd love a brew."

After Liza found a car parking spot, she, Mitchell and Poppy walked into the lobby.

Carl looked up from his desk, his eyes alert to the sight of Mitchell with Liza. His wastepaper basket overflowed with snowballs of scrunched-up paper and his fingers worked as if he was crumbling bread. When he moved his hands back, he had created a small paper boat. "I'm better at making things than writing letters." He tutted. "Did you have a good trip?"

Poppy grinned. "We slept in a forest and toasted marshmallows on a fire."

"That sounds awesome."

"It was."

"You had a visitor this morning, Mr. Fisher. She left something for you." Carl reached down and placed an overstuffed plastic shopping bag in front of him on the desk.

Through the translucent white plastic, Mitchell could see brown envelopes and yellow padded bags, postcards and even something with polka dots. He estimated there must be at least fifty pieces of mail in there.

Carl eyed it. "Are you sure it isn't your birthday?"

"Are all those for you?" Liza laughed. "You're *very* popular."

"They're a mistake," Mitchell said tetchily. "A journalist published a competition asking people in Upchester to write in. She asked me to read some letters, but not this many."

Carl pushed the bag toward Mitchell. "She said her name was Susan Smite, or something like that. She had light blonde hair and a big yellow bag. I told her you'd be back this afternoon, and I'd look after these for you."

"How on earth did she trace me here?" Mitchell wondered aloud.

"She's a journalist, a clever person. I bet she can find out things like that," Carl said. "I told her I was trying to write a letter, too. She said there were some open ones in the bag that I could read for inspiration." He fiddled with his tie. "I thought you'd want to read them first, right?"

When he looked at them, Mitchell clenched his jaw. "I said I'd help her, but this number of letters is ridiculous. I need to call her." He tugged Barry's mobile out of his pocket.

"Um." Carl bit his lip. "I said you'd meet her in the Dala café at four."

Mitchell stared at him in disbelief. "Me?"

Carl nodded meekly. "She was quite adamant."

"Well, I'm not going to—" Mitchell raised his voice.

"*Dad.*" Poppy's eyes urged him not to kick up a fuss in front of Liza.

"I *need* to end this."

An awkward silence fell between the four of them until Liza broke the tension. "Gosh, I could do with that cup of tea," she said.

"I'll make you one." Carl jumped up. "Can't write letters but I make a great cuppa."

"Oh, I wasn't hinting…" Liza began, but Carl hurried off and disappeared through the door to the basement.

Mitchell calmed down and lowered the phone. "I suppose I could meet Susan," he relented. "Very briefly."

They stood together uneasily until Carl reappeared holding a silver tray with a flowery teapot, jug of milk and four dinky cups and saucers. He carried over a few chairs and they all sat down around his desk. After pouring the tea for each of them, he fumbled for a piece of paper in his drawer. "I found someone to read my friend's letter for me," he said. "I want to write back to her, but don't know what to say. I'm not very good with words. Can you help me, Mr. Fisher?"

"I'm not the best person to ask…"

"You have a big bag full of letters," Carl noted.

"They're not mine."

Liza sipped her tea. "I can help you, if you like? I'm not bad with words."

Carl nodded gratefully. "I don't know where to start, or what to say."

"Just be yourself. Write to the person as you'd usually talk to them. You don't have to start it with *Dear* or *Dearest. Hi,* is fine, or *Hello.*"

Carl wrote, *Hi Donna*, at the top of his page, and Liza smiled with encouragement.

"Writing a letter is a bit like building a bridge," Mitchell joined in. "Now you need to think about your foundations, the groundwork, the things you really want to lay down. Maybe use a pencil first. Then you can add your building blocks, the words you want to purvey and the sentences and paragraphs to give your letter structure."

Poppy shook her head slowly at him.

"That sounds complicated," Carl said.

Liza leaned in closer, ignoring Mitchell. "What do you want to say to your friend?"

Carl thought for a while. "Just that she's a beautiful person. I'd tell her I won't be a concierge forever and that my uncle is helping me out with this job, because I get really nervous when I apply for other ones. And I know there are lots of people with more qualifications and experience than me, but I try hard. I want to ask her if she wants to go on a date with me, and if she'd prefer the cinema, or a picnic in the park."

"Well, that sounds ideal. Just write that."

Carl dubiously picked up his pen. "I'm not confident with these things."

Mitchell thought about Annie's letter about Douglas, and Yvette's letter to Liza. He pictured the drawer in his bedside cabinet, stuffed with his own letters to Anita, and her sealed lilac envelope to him.

"It doesn't have to be perfect," he said. "You taking the time to write something is sometimes as important as the words you use."

"That makes more sense," Carl said. "I'll take my time and, when I finish it, will one of you read it for me? I want to get it right."

"Sure," Liza said. "Anytime."

"Give me a shout when you're ready," Mitchell added.

After they'd drank their tea together, Liza picked up her bag. "I should go. I'm a busy person, you know."

"You haven't read any of Dad's letters," Poppy said.

"He has lots more now. Maybe I can look at his favorite ones after he's looked at them. And I have to get ready for my night out."

Mitchell felt a strange prickle on the back of his neck that he couldn't identify. "Going anywhere nice?" he asked.

"I think Henry has got us tickets for the Comedy Store. I'm a bit tired and groggy, but a shower should wake me up."

Mitchell stood still. *Henry*, he thought to himself. *Who's he?* But he didn't like to ask. He didn't know Liza that well and it was none of his business. "Great. Well, have a good time," he said as casually as he could.

"Thanks. We always do."

The Dala café was supposed to resemble a Swedish log cabin. The menu had a wooden cover and its contents consisted of mainly pickled things or fish.

When Mitchell and Poppy met Susan at four o'clock, they found her at a table sipping from a tiny coffee cup and nibbling on a piece of rye bread.

After sitting down opposite her, Mitchell made a show of giving the plastic bag full of letters a chair of its own.

Susan eyed it nervously. "I know there's a lot of them, so I wanted to explain face-to-face," she said. "I spoke to another journo from the channel and he told me that some stories attract just a few responses, but others really capture people's imaginations. This is quite unusual."

"They're probably just interested in the prize money," Mitchell said with a snort.

"Why not read them and see?" she said hopefully.

"Because *that* will take forever."

"Can't you just read them a few at a time?"

Mitchell stared at the letters. "Surely, other stuff must be going on in the city? The story of me and the woman on the bridge must have died down by now."

She glanced at him over the top of her coffee cup. "Unless you want it to keep going…?"

"Why on earth would I want to do that?"

"That's why I wanted to meet you in person, to ask you the question."

"Absolutely not," he said.

Susan placed her satchel on her knee, as if using it as a shield against him. "People love stories about other people, especially if they've done something heroic, or different, or lovely. The bridges are a hot topic, too, because of Word Up, and the new bridge opening soon. Add the prize money into the mix and it's sparked some kind of synergy." She clicked her fingers together. "I'd like to write a piece about how your act of bravery influenced people in the city to write letters. In the computerized age, it's a dying art."

"But they've only written them because of a mistake, because you didn't publish an email address," he protested.

"Every cloud has a silver lining."

Poppy had remained quiet throughout their conversation. "I'm doing a school project about the padlocks on the bridges," she said.

Mitchell stared at her. "You were going to change it."

"*I* didn't say that."

Susan nodded at the bag on the chair. "A few envelopes were open, and I read the letters. They were from people who hung padlocks, saying why they did it."

Poppy's eyes shone. "*Dad*, can I read them?"

"I want to give them back," Mitchell said firmly. "I didn't ask to be part of this. People don't even know my name."

Susan pursed her lips. "Um, I might have updated my article to, um, include it."

"What?" Mitchell's pulse shot up. "Don't you need my permission to do that? Don't I have to sign something?"

She gave him a small smile and shook her head. "Nope."

A frosty silence descended between them, and Mitchell briefly snatched a postcard from the top of the bag.

I hope this card brings you an eternity of joy and that your life is sweetened with the richness you give others. Rejoice in the beauty of today and forever.

He showed it to Susan. "What does this even mean?"

"There are better ones," she admitted.

Their conversation was broken when a set of cowbells jingled over the door as it opened. Carl dug his hands into his overall pockets and walked up to the counter. He studied the blackboard menu for a long time before requesting, "Just a white coffee, please." His gaze fell upon Mitchell, Poppy and Susan and, after getting his drink, he walked over to join them.

"Hello. We meet again." He shook Susan's hand. "Are you talking about all the letters? It's usually all bills and fast-food menus in the mailbox of Angel House. Isn't it wonderful to see so many people writing like that?"

Susan smiled triumphantly at Mitchell. "Join us," she said. She picked up the bag of letters off the chair and held it out toward Mitchell.

He reluctantly took them and placed them on his lap.

"Any luck with *your* letter, Carl?" Susan asked.

"Mr. Fisher's friend, Liza, was helpful. And Mr. Fisher is

going to read it when I've finished, but I'm probably going to make a gigantic fool of myself." He shrugged.

"Don't say that. I can help you more now, if you like? I'm between stories."

Carl touched his tie. "Are you sure? I'm allowing myself a small break."

Susan put her notepad back into her bag. "Quite."

"Um, there's something I should tell you..."

Mitchell felt a small strange lurch that he could only identify as envy. "I said that I'd help you with your letter, Carl," he interrupted.

"Yes, but I know you're always busy, Mr. Fisher. And you have all those other ones to read, don't you? Also, Susan is a proper writer."

Susan beamed at this. "Mr. Fisher and I are just finishing our conversation anyway."

Mitchell stood up and circled his arms around the bag of letters in a hug. "Well, I—"

Susan ignored him and looked at Poppy. "If I can help with your school project in any way, please let me know," she said. "I'm good with ideas, so don't be shy. It can be my way of saying thanks to your dad, for *helping* me out."

"Wow, thanks," Poppy said.

Mitchell squeezed the letters tighter to his chest. "It's my job to help her," he said more territorially than he meant to. "We're working on her project *together*."

14

STITCHES

Mitchell steeled himself before he walked into the hospital building. Only six days had passed since he helped Yvette, met Liza, slept in a forest and attracted a hoard of strangers to write to him. Although he'd learned more about the Bradfield family, spoken to Jean and found Yvette's lock, he didn't feel much closer to finding her.

He wondered where she was and if she might be thinking about him, too.

He made his way along several gray corridors to reach and report to the clinic. The male nurse who checked his stitches had a retro-flick hairstyle and a chirpy attitude. "This is healing nicely," he said with a satisfied nod.

Mitchell thought of Liza's plea to try to find the doctor who helped Yvette. Before he left the room, he asked, "Is there a doctor who works here, who's bald, has a thin mustache and wears round horn-rimmed glasses?"

"Is this a riddle?" The nurse laughed. "What's his name? Department?"

"I don't know."

"There are almost two hundred doctors working here, you know? Fifty percent probably look like the one you describe, except for the ladies." He grinned at his own joke. "Good luck with your detective work, Sherlock."

As Mitchell traipsed along many corridors and several linked buildings, he became more despondent that he was going to fail his task. His stomach rumbled with hunger and he stopped at the hospital shop.

A white-bearded man stood in the middle of the confectionary aisle. He wore a crumpled cream linen suit with a blue velvet bow tie, and his left cheek was creased, so the skin looked like a drawn-back curtain. He painstakingly peered at each chocolate bar on a shelf before stooping lower to assess the next ones down.

When Mitchell approached, the man straightened his back. "Sleeping in this place does nothing for one's style," he said.

Mitchell smiled quickly and picked up a Mars Bar. He imagined the man curled up in the corner of the shop, under a duvet.

"I'm buying chocolate for my partner, Harold. He likes Maltesers. I'm trying to persuade him to try something new, but..." The man stopped and narrowed his eyes. He pointed a finger at Mitchell's nose. "You have a very strong profile, noble, like Julius Caesar."

"Um, thank you."

"I was a photographer for forty years and I notice these things. Now, I just live here."

Mitchell frowned. "What, actually *in* the hospital?"

"It certainly feels that way. Harold's got the whole shebang, everything you can think of. I tell him he's a greedy git and should save some ailments for other people, but he's intent of having them all." He fiddled with his bow tie. "I do hope you don't mind me telling you this. You must let me buy you that Mars Bar."

Mitchell found he'd lost his appetite at the thought of poor Harold. "It's fine, I—"

"Maltesers are the only chocolates Harold can eat now, because they melt in his mouth. He says other small ones, for example Smarties or M&M's, get stuck. I keep looking for others, but there's a limited choice here. Maltesers are the only thing he truly enjoys." His eyes glistened and he stuck out his hand. "By the way, I'm Alan."

Mitchell put his Mars Bar back on the shelf and returned Alan's handshake. "I'm Mitchell," he said.

"I sit next to Harold's bed all day, playing sudoku and reading the paper. So, buying that chocolate bar for you would mean a great deal to me."

Mitchell felt lucky he only had a minor injury. "I'm sorry to hear about your friend."

"There's no point in apologizing, that won't do anything," Alan said. "Harold says the worst part about dying is remembering how good it feels to be alive, but I'm not sure there's any positive bit. What are you in hospital for, anyway?"

"I've had stitches taken out, and now I'm trying to track down a doctor." He looked around him helplessly. "This is such a big place."

"What's his name or specialty? Harold might know him. He's encountered a lot of them."

"I only know what he looks like. He might not even work here."

"Hmm. Well, pass me the chocolate. I'll pay and we can talk as we walk."

When they reached Ward F21, Alan turned around. "Why

do you want to find this doctor? Harold will ask me. He likes to hear stories about other people being ill. Makes him feel less alone."

"It's not about me. It's about a woman. I'm trying to find her again…"

"Aha." Alan tapped his nose. "You're in love. I understand."

"No, I—"

"I can see it in your eyes. Harold and I have been together for thirty-nine years," he said knowingly before heading into the ward.

Mitchell paced up and down the corridor. He looked at the paintings on the walls done by schoolchildren, of people in hospital beds with watermelon slice smiles. He caught sight of himself in a mirror and studied his own face. He didn't have love in his eyes, that was ridiculous. He just looked a bit brighter after having his stitches removed.

After a few minutes, Alan returned. "Harold says to try the General Surgery department. There's a consultant called Grey who works there who fits your description. If it's not him, it's a good place to start, anyway."

Mitchell thought this sounded a good step forward. "Thank you. I hope Harold gets better soon."

Alan gave a small nod. "Love can be a great healer. Or so I try to convince myself."

Mitchell made his way to the General Surgery department, where he found photographs of twelve doctors on the wall. The nurse with the hair flick was right, that there was much of a sameness about their appearances. However, the third photograph down was of the man who had helped Yvette on the riverbank. His name was printed below his image, consultant Ernest Grey.

Mitchell made his way to the consultant's waiting room where he loitered for a while, unsure of his next move.

When the receptionist called out, "Mr. Pinkerton to see Mr. Grey, please," Mitchell looked furtively around. After there was no response, he held up his hand. "Um, here."

"Second door on the left," the receptionist told him. "Ask Mr. Grey to check your hearing, while you're in there."

Mitchell entered the room and the doctor who helped Yvette on the grass verge sat before him. He felt like he was encountering a film or TV star, that he couldn't quite believe was here in the flesh.

"Take a seat."

"Thank you." Mitchell sat down and pressed his fingers together in his lap.

Mr. Grey pushed his horn-rimmed glasses up his nose and studied some papers. "What can I do for you, Mr. Pinkerton? How have you been since your hernia op?"

"I've not had one," Mitchell said. "I'm not actually your patient."

Mr. Grey lowered the papers and stared at him intently. "Do you have the wrong room?" He reached to pick up the phone receiver on his desk. "I'll ask the—"

Mitchell leaned forward. "My name is Mitchell Fisher and I helped a woman who had fallen into the river six days ago. She wore a yellow dress and you came to her assistance."

Mr. Grey moved his hand away from the phone. He slid his glasses farther up his nose. "Oh, *yes*, I recognize you now. Didn't you bump your head on the pavement afterward?"

"Yes," Mitchell said with a whoosh of relief that he had found the right man. "A cyclist rode into me. I woke up in hospital and I'm trying to find out what happened to the woman we helped. Was she admitted into hospital?"

"I recommended she come with me to get checked out, but she insisted she was fine. She was in a hurry, said she had to leave straightaway. She used my phone to make a call."

"So, the last time you saw her was on the bridge?"

Mr. Grey nodded.

"Do you have a record of what number she rang?"

"Sorry, no. I got a new phone two days ago."

Mitchell knew that Liza wouldn't mind if he shared more information, if it helped to trace Yvette. "I found out the woman in question, Yvette Bradfield, walked away from her family, and I'm helping them to trace her. I'm the first person to see her for almost a year, and you saw her, too. Did she say anything to you that might help us to find her?"

"That is a distressing situation," Mr. Grey said softly. "I'm presuming you've covered off all other options, spoke to her friends and family, etcetera."

"I think the family have tried everything. Yvette gets in touch from time to time, they just don't know where she is, or why she won't come home."

Mr. Grey thought for a while. "I overheard some of the call, and she said Connor was waiting for her."

"Connor?" Mitchell repeated. "Not Victor?"

"She definitely said Connor. And that's all I can tell you, I'm afraid. Our conversation was very short. I think she was rather stunned by what happened."

"It's a good piece of information," Mitchell said, pleased he had found out something to share with Liza. "Thank you."

"Very glad to be of assistance. Though, I suggest you don't try to impersonate other patients in future."

"Sorry," Mitchell said. "Now I'm here, may I ask you a medical question?"

"Is it about a hernia?"

"No. After I bumped my head in the accident, I've been feeling, well—different."

"Can you be more specific?"

Mitchell hmm'd, thinking about his strange emotional pull

when it came to the locks on the bridge and the strangers' letters. "Since my accident, I'm *feeling* everything more deeply," he said.

"And you had checks when you came in?"

He nodded. "Everything looked fine."

"Well," Mr. Grey said, "saving Yvette could certainly have triggered your emotions. It's a big thing you did, jumping in the river to help her. Your mind and body will have experienced stress, anxiety and relief. It's totally natural to feel emotional after going through something like that. Even minor injuries can disrupt the brain function, changing the way a person thinks, acts or feels. They don't always show up straightaway. Perhaps you should make an appointment to see your own doctor and ask to be referred to a neurologist. Or there's something else to consider..."

"What?"

Mr. Grey smiled. "Maybe you're a nice guy who cares about others."

Mitchell looked away, embarrassed. "It's good to hear I'm not going mad."

"You did a courageous thing, and exposure to cold water can cause hypothermia, even on a hot day. You should give yourself a pat on the back. Make sure you take care of yourself, as well as looking for Yvette."

"Hmm, I'll try," Mitchell said before leaving the consultancy room.

While Mitchell sat on the bus, heading into Upchester center, he called Liza a couple of times but got her voice mail. He left a message saying he was heading into the city and would be on the redbrick bridge at one o'clock, if she and Poppy wanted to meet him there.

When he reached and walked along Redford, he again felt

the unlikely tug toward the padlocks hanging there and the stories they held. At least Mr. Grey had given him a reason why his emotions might be playing up.

Mitchell spotted Barry working on the other side of the road. Or at least, he thought it was Barry. The person crouched next to a toolbox and brandishing bolt cutters had close-cropped hair.

Mitchell crossed over and stood behind him. "Um, Barry?" he said.

His friend looked up sheepishly. His chest curls were missing, as well as the hair on his head. "Yes, it's me."

"That's a drastic haircut."

Barry's cheeks flushed. "Enid bought some new dog grooming equipment and wanted to try it out."

"On you?"

"A trial run," he said. "The electronic clippers worked well, but I think she preferred dogs to me. I've been messaging a lady called Amanda and she wants to go ice skating."

"It sounds less risky than grooming."

"I hope so." Barry smiled tightly. "How did things go at the hospital?"

Mitchell touched his head. "All fine. I've had my stitches out and a doctor confirmed I'm not going crazy, so now it's official. Any news on my toolbox?"

"Not a thing. Any luck in your search for Yvette?"

Mitchell gave him a very brief update, not mentioning Connor's name until he'd spoken to Liza. "And how's work?"

"The usual. Locks and more locks." Barry nodded toward the new white bridge. "The celebration preparations are all well underway, so Russ's stress levels are sky-high. Stay away from him."

Mitchell looked upriver toward the Yacht bridge and saw

Liza walking and Poppy half skipping along the street toward Redford. They met him in the middle of the bridge.

"I got a new dress, and a headband and shoes," Poppy said before he could even say hello. "And a necklace with a pug dog pendant."

"That sounds like a productive morning."

"It was," Liza said. "We had lots of fun in the sales, trying stuff on, and I got my green shoes, though maybe not quite the shade I was looking for. Poppy and I went for a burger, after our debate about whether Burger King or McDonald's is better."

"Burger King," Poppy said.

"Who won?" Mitchell asked.

"Who do you think?" Liza fixed Poppy with a pretend glare. She then turned her attention to Barry and squinted at him. "Oh, hi, it's you. You look so different without your hair."

"It's a long story," he said. "Don't ask."

"How did your appointment go?" Liza asked Mitchell. "All good?"

"It was okay. I had my stitches out." It was too awkward to talk further, with Barry and Poppy being here. "Do you still have the paper and pens Megan gave you?" he asked Barry.

Barry nodded. "Yeah, in my toolbox."

"Poppy, do you fancy doing a bit of drawing while I tell Liza about the hospital?" Mitchell asked.

She nodded readily and jumped over to Barry's side.

Mitchell and Liza walked over to the spot Yvette fell from the bridge. He bent down and located her heart-shaped lock again, among all the ones hanging there. He thought of Yvette in her yellow dress and again felt a connection to her somehow.

Liza crouched down. "My heart is always yours," she whispered as the noise of the gushing river almost drowned out her words. She peered through the railing at the water, then up at him. "Yvette was so lucky you were here. I dread to think what might have happened to her if you weren't."

Mitchell looked over the railing, too. "I managed to track down the doctor who attended to Yvette at the river edge," he said.

Liza sucked in a breath as she stood up. "You did?"

"His name is Ernest Grey. He tried to persuade Yvette to get checked out at hospital, but she was in a hurry to leave." He cleared his throat. "She said a man called Connor was waiting for her."

Liza frowned, as if she had a migraine setting in. "*Connor*? Are you absolutely sure about that?"

"That's definitely the name he gave me. Does it mean anything to you?"

Liza chewed her bottom lip for a while, before nodding. "It's my father's name."

"So, *he* might have been waiting for her?"

She gave the smallest laugh. "It's highly unlikely, Mitchell. My dad died five years ago."

They glanced at each then away again, confused.

Mitchell's mind went momentarily blank. "Could Connor perhaps be a friend, or Yvette's boyfriend?" he tried.

"But he was *supposed* to be called Victor," Liza said wildly, the color in her cheeks draining. "It sounds like Yvette was confused. She thought she knew you, and then said Dad was waiting for her. Maybe she has some kind of amnesia. It'd explain why she went missing. She might not know who she is any longer. A friend of mine had early onset dementia. Perhaps it's that… Oh, I just don't know."

Mitchell spoke calmly to reassure her. "Yvette wrote to you, and to Jean. If she had amnesia or dementia, I doubt she'd remember your addresses."

Liza took a moment to think about this. "Yes, yes, you're right." She placed her hand over his on the railing. "She wrote to Naomi, too. I just can't make sense of all this."

She looked so lost Mitchell gently slid his hand out from under hers and slipped it around her shoulder. She leaned in toward him and tucked her head under his chin for a while. When he breathed in, her hair tickled his nose. A warmth filtered through him and he wondered if she felt it, as well. He wasn't sure if he liked it or not, but that didn't matter. She needed him and, for a few moments, he needed her, too.

A couple of girls' voices sounded behind them, and Mitchell smelled violets in the air. It made him think of Anita, and his arm fell suddenly away from Liza's shoulder. He inched awkwardly away from her.

Liza picked at a piece of paint flaking off the railing. "I think I need to speak to Mum and Naomi," she said. "I need to tell them you saw Yvette, especially if she mentioned Dad. I can't keep this to myself any longer. Perhaps I could invite them over to dinner. I can tell them all about you and come clean about what I know."

"Let me know how you get on," Mitchell said.

She pursed her lips, considering. "Will you join us? I bet they'd like to talk to the man who helped Yvette."

A family meal, Mitchell thought to himself. When was the last time he, Anita and Poppy ate together? It was probably a sandwich in front of the TV, or even McDonald's. He wished he could say it had been significant and lovely, but he couldn't remember what it was.

Anita always said her last meal on earth would be warm crusty bread, lots of cheese and a glass of cider. He didn't even know what she'd eaten at Mazzo's. Had she had tiramisu without him?

The thought made his chest tighten and he curled his fingers over the railing, like he was clinging on.

Dinner parties had never been his thing. He hated smiling stiffly, eating fancy food and the one-upmanship of snobbery as conversation turned to who had seen the most obscure theater production. He supposed Liza's family gathering would be different than that. "I have met them already, at your house," he reminded her.

"So, is that a *yes*?"

Mitchell thought how it was easier to agree to her invitation, rather than excuse himself. "Sure," he said. "I'll come along."

"Great."

Her face was still and he felt the need to reassure her again. "We'll keep trying to find Yvette, okay? We won't give up."

"Thank you."

Footsteps approached them and Poppy arrived, waving a piece of paper. "I drew the new white bridge, Dad."

He looked at it. "That's wonderful. Very detailed."

"Are we going home yet? I can show you my new dress."

"Yes. I'm ready to go. Liza and I were just, um, talking."

"Ah, yes, I saw *that*." Poppy smiled knowingly.

15

MOSAIC

That evening, after Mitchell and Poppy had eaten, he tugged his coffee table to the side of the sitting room and shook out all the letters from the plastic shopping bag onto the floor. Poppy insisted on lining them up to make a large mosaic square of colorful correspondence. He welcomed the opportunity to focus on something else while Liza spoke to her family. And he could spend time with Poppy, too.

A few envelopes were addressed to Mitchell by name, some to the *Hero on the Bridge*, and others to Upchester News. Several were blank, but were of a nature (pink paper, stickers, doodles of padlocks) to suggest they weren't official.

"Cool," Poppy said and she walked around them in a circle.

Mitchell scratched his head as he looked down at them. The thoughts, ideas and secrets of strangers were all laid out on his stripped floorboards.

Poppy stooped down and picked up a zebra-striped orange envelope from the middle of the square. "Can I read this one, Dad?"

"Let me take a look first, just in case." He took it from her and slid out a peach sheet of paper.

Dear Man on the Bridge,

What a good person you are! I was close by when I heard the fracas of the woman falling into the water. I was rushing home to take delivery of a parcel—a new hairdryer for my wife's birthday! I was so impressed by your kind deed and wish I'd performed such a demonstrative act of love in my past. You see, my lovely wife wasn't my first choice because I was secretly in love with someone else. I tried to tell my wife, before we married, but my words shriveled up.

My wife and I have now been married for over twenty-five years and, although we've enjoyed many happy times together, I know she isn't the love of my life. I still see and admire the other lady from afar and hung a padlock on the bridge for her. It made me feel like a schoolboy carving initials into a tree and I feel better for sharing my story with you. Congratulations on taking a leap of faith for your own lady friend. All the very best to you both!

Best wishes,
Mr. Smith
PS: My wife loved her new hairdryer!

Mitchell frowned, unable to tell if this was a story with a happy ending or if he'd just read something extremely sad. How awful it must be to keep such a secret, a longing, to yourself. And for the wife, whose husband was in love with someone else. The letter was definitely not suitable for Poppy's project.

The next one came in a pale blue envelope with *Merci* printed on the flap. Mitchell opened it up and read the letter.

Dear Sir,
My name is Henri and I am a French exchange student, aged almost seventeen. I am present in your beautiful city to examine your magnificent buildings and to practice my English.

My teacher, Monsieur Ingres, brought our class to look at your bridges and I was very surprised to find so many padlocks hanging from them. I live in Paris and one of our bridges collapsed under the weight of locks. When they were removed, they came to forty-five tons in weight. It is likely there are thousands of keys in the river, which is dangerous to both fish and animals.

I understand why people would like to fasten their locks, but not why they would want to damage fine bridges or hurt living things.

Your friend from Paris,
Henri

Mitchell admired the boy's ethics and he handed the letter to Poppy. "This one would be good for your project," he said. "It has an environmental message and the writer is from France."

She took it from him. "So, people's stories *can* be part of history?"

"Yes," he laughed. "I admit you're right and I was wrong."

"Ha," she said triumphantly. "Do you know I kept some of yours, too?" Poppy said.

"Mine?" Mitchell frowned.

"The letters you sent to me and Mum."

Mitchell felt as if he'd stridden onto an escalator and missed his step. He'd sorted through all Poppy's things when she moved into the apartment, and he didn't recall seeing any letters. The only letter he'd kept from Anita was the one in the sealed lilac envelope.

"Do you want to see them?"

Before he could reply, Poppy sped off to her room. She returned and held out an old dictionary to him. "Open it," she said.

Mitchell did so and saw the pages inside had been hollowed out, a gift box dictionary rather than a real one. Inside it, a few letters were tied together with a thin red ribbon. Poppy took one out and handed it to him.

His words took up barely a quarter of the paper.

Dear Anita and Poppy,
Everything is very busy at work. I may have to stay over in the city again this weekend, so will let you know. I promise you the new bridge will be very exciting and I think you'll like it.

Love, Dad x

He read it again and a chill ran over him at its sparseness. There was no emotion, no asking how they were, and what they'd been up to. It was all about him and his work.

"Do you want to read another?" Poppy said.

Mitchell shook his head. He tried to inject lightness into his voice. "No, it's fine. I don't have much to say in this one, do I?"

"Nope, not really."

"Why did you keep them?"

She shrugged and took the letter from his hands to place it back inside the dictionary. "Mum said letters are important. They're like a diary and nice thoughts you can keep."

Mitchell wished he'd kept the letters Anita and Poppy sent

him. If he could go back in time, he'd cover whole pages with words and kisses. He'd never forget to send them.

Poppy kneeled back down on the floor. "Shall we read another one of Susan's letters? That pink one looks romantic."

"I think I'd had enough of them for one day. Let's look through your window before bedtime instead."

Half an hour later, they stood on her bed with their faces outside in the fresh air. Poppy's pajama top was inside out and she wore her new pug pendant.

"What would you like to do tomorrow?" Mitchell asked as he looked up at the moon. "Maybe the library, or a museum?"

Poppy threw a piece of her crust to three pigeons that were strutting around the rooftop. "Um, can I go to the park with Rachel instead?"

Mitchell tried to picture his plan in the hallway of what he'd scheduled in for the day. He'd have to readjust it. "I suppose I could take you both there."

"It'll be with Rachel's mum. There's giant inflatables and a hot dog stand. Rachel said the sausages are so big they hang out of their bun. They said they'd pick me up at ten thirty."

Mitchell raised an eyebrow at her. "So, this is already arranged?"

She nodded meekly. "I bumped into them in a shop. We made a plan."

Mitchell had looked forward to spending the day with her. However, if he was the same age and had a choice between a museum or bouncy castles and junk food, there'd be no contest. He liked how she'd inherited his planning gene.

"Okay, Dad?"

"Yes, it's fine," he replied. "But try to give me advance notice next time so I can readjust our schedules."

After tucking Poppy into bed for the night, Mitchell went into the sitting room and picked up the pink envelope that looked romantic. When he opened the flap, he was surprised to see a wedding invitation covered in pink heart-shaped sequins from his schoolmate, Graham. He assumed Carl must have taken delivery of the card and placed it in the bag of letters, among all the others.

Graham Gates and Rosie Gillespie are getting married at 2:00 p.m., Jupiter Hotel, Upchester on 28th July. Please tick and complete the following,

☐ *I will/won't be there*
☐ *I like cake*
☐ *I prefer cheese*

*If I could listen to any song while riding a dragon into battle it would be*_____

*I have a dietary requirement, which is*_____

PS: We know it's very short notice, so if you can't reply in time, just show up on the day!

Mitchell frowned at it, not having known Graham was even dating. He hadn't seen his friend for ages, and it wasn't like him to send such a sparkly, silly-looking invite. The wedding was in just over two weeks' time.

Graham had lived with his mother for many years until she'd died a couple of years ago. When he wasn't glued to his PlayStation, Graham had dedicated his time to taking her out to garden centers, and for afternoon tea. He called her *his best friend*, which didn't go down well with any women he sporadically dated.

Mitchell couldn't recall Graham having had a serious girlfriend for a long time, and he wondered if Rosie shared his friend's interests of gaming, graphic novels and sci-fi conventions.

As he traced a finger over the sequins, Mitchell felt a thickness in his throat that his friend's life had taken this major upturn without him realizing. He had been so wrapped up in his own grief over Anita that he hadn't checked in with Graham much after his mother's death. He had let their friendship slide.

When Mitchell picked up his pen, he thought back to the carefree times he and Graham spent together when they were kids and he knew he should have been a better friend. He guiltily filled in his reply.

☑ *I will be there*
☑ *I like cake* (AND CHEESE)
If I could listen to any song while riding a dragon into battle it would be "(K)NIGHTS IN WHITE SATIN"
I have a dietary requirement, which is LOTS OF GREAT FOOD

As Mitchell read over his answers, a smile twitched his lips. A feeling flooded over him of wanting to get away from his apartment and the city for a while and to try to make some amends. If Poppy was going out with Rachel tomorrow, and Liza was speaking to her family, he would enjoy his own spare time, too.

He decided to RSVP to Graham in person.

16

SWING

Back when they went to school together, Graham had been one of those kids who wore a hand-me-down uniform from his brother, so the sweater wool balled on the elbows and the sleeves hung down over his fingertips. "My mum says I'll grow into it," he said, when other kids laughed at him, and that was how he got the moniker Grow-Into-It-Graham.

There had been a hierarchy at the school, imposed by kids who had wealthy parents, were good-looking, or who passed their exams with ease. Graham was assigned to the group of outcast kids who were overweight, nerdy, poor or spotty.

Mitchell found himself positioned somewhere between the elite and the outcasts. He got stick for the size of his nose, but there were other pupils who attracted more malicious attention. Katie Broadbottom had a problem with both body odor and an unfortunate name, and Andy Timmons once peed on the floor of the sports hall by accident.

Mitchell and Graham didn't get to know each other properly until they were thirteen, when Mitchell happened across Graham in the woods close to their school. He was attempting to make a swing out of an old rubber tire and kept trying to toss the rope over a tree branch. He did it ten times before he lost his patience and kicked the tire.

Mitchell stepped out from behind the trees. "You need to add weight to the end of that rope, or get someone up the tree to catch it for you," he said.

Graham gawped, unused to other kids talking to him.

"I'll climb and you throw." Mitchell shimmied up the tree trunk with ease and caught the rope when Graham threw it. He looped it around the branch, pulled on it and tied a firm knot.

The two boys spent a fun afternoon pushing each other on the swing and spinning around, until two other boys from their school year approached them.

"Spider" Spencer and his friend, Birchy, shoved Graham clean off the swing. He landed flat on his back and breath wheezed out of his lungs. They laughed as he writhed in agony on the ground.

Mitchell quickly scaled a tree and stealthily spread himself along a high up branch, like a panther observing its prey. He weighed up the best course of action and dropped down onto Spider's back and clung on with gritted teeth, pummeling his fist into Spider's face. Spider spun around so Mitchell felt like he was on a bucking bronco, but he held on.

Finally, after several minutes of trying to shake him off, Spider yelled, "Okay, okay. Get *off* me."

"Promise you'll leave Graham alone."

"Yeah. Get off."

Mitchell jumped to the ground where Graham still lay

prostrate and groaning, one of his front teeth broken. Birchy had vanished.

"You'll pay for this, Fisher," Spider sneered as he stood panting with his hands on his knees.

"Yeah. And I'll tell everyone how Mitchell battered you," Graham lisped.

Spider glared at the two of them, before he tossed his head and ambled away.

"You okay?" Mitchell crouched down and helped Graham to his feet.

Graham nodded and dusted off his clothes. He stuck a finger through a fresh hole in his sweater. "I owe you one for this, Mitchell. I'll never forget it."

They had been best friends ever since.

Graham lived in a boxy house with pebble-dashed walls on a street full of similar houses. He was a bus driver by day and loved gaming on his Playstation at night with a wide network of friends.

Michell used to call around a few times a year, when the two men would revert to their teenage years and play computer games in Graham's bedroom. When she was alive, Mrs. Gates kept them supplied with toast, chocolate biscuits and cups of tea.

After Anita died, Graham kept in touch with phone calls and notes, telling him to call him anytime, day or night, if he needed to talk. But, too wrapped up in his own grief, Mitchell often didn't reply.

When Mitchell attended Mrs. Gates's funeral, memories of Anita's service brought on such a pain in his chest he found it hard to breathe. As the vicar spoke, he stared at his shoes and couldn't meet Graham's eyes for fear of dissolving into a quivering wreck. He had dashed off after the service, unable to face sandwiches and drinks in the local pub afterward and the two men hadn't met up properly since.

Mitchell took the wedding invitation out of his pocket and thought again of how sequined hearts were so unlike his friend. He hadn't been there for Graham for a long time, and it was time to change that.

He rang the doorbell and noticed Mrs. Gates's chintzy curtains had been replaced with red velvet ones.

"Mitchy Boy," Graham said when he opened the door. "Wasn't expecting to see you here." He wore a dark green Adidas tracksuit and white running shoes. His skin had the deathly pallor of someone who rarely ventured outside. He'd never had his broken tooth repaired so when he pronounced the letter *S* it sounded like a hiss. "It's good to see you."

The two men performed an awkward hug on the doorstep.

Mitchell waved the card. "It's amazing you're getting married. I'd love to accept your invitation."

"It'll be great to have you there, man. I mean it. Come on inside."

Mitchell followed Graham into his home. The flowery wallpaper, swirly carpets and burgundy tasseled lightshades that had been there since their childhoods were gone, along with the gold-colored sofa and photo frames that proclaimed *The World's Best Son*.

The room now resembled a fortune-teller's caravan. The walls were purple and tarot cards lay in a cross pattern on Graham's coffee table. There was a foot-tall wooden man standing on the mantelpiece that Mitchell assumed was a fertility statue due to the size of a certain appendage.

There were still definite hints of Graham around the place—a Lego Death Star displayed on a shelf, gaming trophies and piles of tech magazines everywhere—but the place looked very different.

"Tea?" Graham asked, gesturing for Mitchell to sit down.

"Please."

"We have oolong, green tea, matcha or lapsang souchong. And we may have Darjeeling."

Mitchell stared at him. "You really have a tea menu?"

"Rosie has opened my mind. I recommend the oolong, it's of a very fine quality."

"I'd prefer a plain old tea bag, if you have one."

"I think I still have a box of Mum's breakfast stuff somewhere," Graham said with a grin before ducking into the kitchen.

Mitchell moved a mirrored velvet throw off the sofa and sat down. He felt like he was attending a job interview but, when Graham returned, Mitchell recognized one of Mrs. Gates's cups, bone china with a tiny rose print. It made him feel instantly more at home. "This place looks very…um, bohemian."

Graham beamed with pride. "Rosie," he said, as if her name explained everything.

"Ah."

"When Mum died, I thought I was set to be a bachelor for life. I mean, I go to gaming conventions, but conversation usually revolves around wiggling your thumbs on a controller."

"Not a good dating environment?"

"Not really."

"So, where did you meet Rosie?"

"She works in a computer repair shop in the city. My PlayStation controller was playing up, so I took it to be fixed, and there she was, behind the counter." He smacked a fist into his hand. "I saw her violet hair and a twinkle in her eye and I was a goner. Just knew it. That woman knows everything about *Fortnite* and *Overwatch*. You should see her on *Call of Duty*." He sipped his tea. "I should tell you that she's pregnant, too. Seven months."

"Oh, congratulations." The speedy wedding date suddenly made more sense to Mitchell.

"I'm not the biological daddy, but I don't care. I want them both to be part of my life forever." He thumped his chest. "Can feel it here. When you know, you know, right? I'm ready to take that plunge. I'm not sure Mum would approve of Rosie, especially her interior design skills, but she was always a hard to please woman. I happen to think the house looks amazing."

Mitchell looked around him and noticed a dream catcher in the corner. "It's very striking."

"I kind of feel like I'm emerging from a cave, after living with Mum for so long. Rosie's helped to find the real *me* again. I know you're not a romantic kind of guy," Graham said as he clasped both hands around his teacup. "But will you be my best man?"

Mitchell's jaw dropped. He felt touched his friend wanted him to do this. "Me?"

"Yeah. You'll have to dig deep to find good stuff to say about me in your speech. No talk about computers or school detentions, but yeah, I want you to do it."

The crystals and chunks of amethyst on Graham's mantelpiece glittered in a shaft of sunlight, and Mitchell felt like he was shining, too. "I'd be honored. Really. I'm sorry I've not seen as much of you as I should have done. This is a big deal…"

"You can do it. Getting married feels like the easiest decision I've ever made." Graham laughed. "Never thought I'd be a lovey-dovey fool. And I always knew we'd be friends for good."

"Thank you." Mitchell smiled and held up the invitation. "This is definitely not the Graham Gates I know. Are you having a traditional ceremony?"

"Rosie's taking the reins and I'm going with the flow. I've got a PlayStation buddy, Brock, who owns the Jupiter Hotel in the city. He's setting it up as a wedding venue and says we can use the place. He's been ordained, too, so can officially marry us. That's my main contribution. Though, Rosie says we should do something really special for each other to demonstrate our love." He lowered his cup and gave a small shrug. "Any ideas?"

"Can I recommend *not* hanging a padlock on a bridge?"

"Yeah, we'll try not to. I need a bigger gesture, something worthy of her." He gazed off into the distance, lost in thought for a moment, before snapping out of it. "Ahem, anyway, how about you, Mitchy? Are you seeing anyone?"

"I'm definitely single," Mitchell replied quickly.

"Rosie has friends, lots of them. Interesting types."

Mitchell was quiet for a while. "There's still Anita…"

The two men sipped their tea. "She'd want you to be happy," Graham said eventually. "You going to stay single forever?"

To Mitchell, it felt like the simpler option. "Maybe."

"If you don't use it, you lose it," Graham said seriously.

Mitchell laughed into his tea, and a bit slopped onto his T-shirt.

"Good to see you smiling, mate." Graham stood up. "Come and see what Rosie's done with the garden. You won't recognize it."

The small rockery remained, but Mrs. Gates's concrete fairies and rabbits lay piled in a heap in the corner. The garden shed had been painted lilac, and the oak tree that stood in the middle of the lawn was decorated with wind chimes. Around the base of the tree lay a series of upturned milk crates and tires, to be used as seats.

"I got the tires from a gaming buddy, who's a farmer," Graham said.

"Remember Spider and Birchy in the woods?" Mitchell said. "When we made the swing that day."

"Yeah, Spider didn't know what hit him when you pounced. That was the day I knew we'd be best mates. Some people you meet and they drift in and out of your life, but others are like solid gold, precious." He shook his head slightly at his own words. "Ha, that was profound. I have no idea where that came from."

Mitchell smiled. "Rosie?"

"Must be."

Mitchell looked up into the tree. A curl of rope sat like a cobra on one of the branches. Thoughts of that day in the woods dropped back into his head, and he recalled how it felt to play outside until the sun went down. It was a youthful freedom you didn't realize you had, until it was gone. "We could make a swing now if you like?" he said.

The two men looked at each other. Unspoken thoughts transmitted between them, of how this wasn't a grown-up thing to do.

Graham stepped forward anyway. "Now you're talking," he said. "Let's do it."

Mitchell climbed the tree, much more slowly and carefully than he did when he was a teenager. He took hold of the rope and let it drop down into Graham's hands. The two men fashioned a swing and Mitchell took the first go. He swung and twirled, and the light twinkled through the leaves of the trees. He closed his eyes and felt his cheeks flush. The swooning feeling, peaking and dipping as he spiraled around, allowed him to escape to the past, a more innocent time for a while. He laughed and kicked his feet back against the tree trunk until he felt a little nauseous.

"I heard you've been busy saving damsels in distress," Graham said.

Mitchell groaned. "You know about that?"

"Rosie does. She always keeps an ear to the ground. So, what happened?"

Mitchell twirled around some more until his light-headedness made opening up feel easier. With some reluctance, he told Graham about how he had seen and helped Yvette, before finding out she was missing. He explained how he was forming a friendship with her sister Liza.

"You'll find her," Graham said as Mitchell slid off the tire and held it steady for his friend to climb on. "If I know you, you'll have already written a plan of action and devised a strategy. Have you got a map on your wall with pins sticking out of it?"

Mitchell sat down on a nearby milk crate and shook his head. "Not this time."

"I didn't even realize I was stuck in my life," Graham said. He pushed off the ground and leaned forward to gain momentum with his swinging. "I was so comfortable living with Mum, with her chatter and cups of tea and toast, I didn't notice I was missing out on stuff. I mean, I loved her, but I was kind of in a comfy nest, so I didn't even attempt to fly out of it. It's like Rosie's shown me my wings."

Mitchell picked up a twig and scratched it into the grass. "A lady in my apartment block, Vanessa, invited me over to her place to share a bottle of wine. I thought it was weird, and Poppy called me lonely. I disagreed with her, but now I'm not so sure. Vanessa was probably just being nice."

"Maybe it would be good for Poppy if you did meet someone new," Graham said. "Or were at least open to it. Maybe she's feeling stuck, too."

Mitchell hadn't considered things from Poppy's perspective before. He thought he was protecting her, offering stability, with just the two of them. She was opening up with Liza, and perhaps she might with someone else, too. "Maybe," he said.

"Could there be anything between you and Liza, or with Yvette?"

The question caught Mitchell off guard. Even though Yvette had caught his eye on the bridge, it felt wrong to admit to it, because she was missing. And Liza was, well, Liza. Sometimes he felt funny around her, and it was kind of nice and weird at the same time. He avoided answering Graham's question.

"You won't know until you try. What's your next step in your search for Yvette?" Graham pressed his feet to the ground to bring the swing to a stop.

"She left a padlock with a message on it, attached to a bridge in the city. Liza thinks it's a clue, though we haven't sussed out what it is yet. There are other leads, too, a couple of men's names." Wanting to forget about it all for a while longer, Mitchell took hold of the rope and pulled it toward him. "Now, it's my turn on the tire again."

At the end of his visit, Mitchell batted grass off the legs of his jeans and hung a wind chime back in the tree that had fallen onto the lawn. His cheeks were ruddy and the heels of his palms were green from pressing into the grass. He followed Graham back through the house.

"You know the drill by now, Mitchy Boy," Graham said as he opened the front door. "Here's where I remind you I still owe you for rescuing me from Spider."

"You don't need to do anything." Mitchell gave him a small push. "You're like a brother to me."

Graham gave him a rough hug. "I'll see you at my wedding, mate. Bring a lady friend, if you like…"

"One step at a time," Mitchell laughed as he walked away. "One step at a time."

Back at Angel House, Mitchell found Carl sitting at his desk, folding a tiny yellow crown out of a sticky note. "I'm still writing my letter, Mr. Fisher," he said. "Susan is being a great help to me, though."

"Good. It will be like a novel by the time you finish it," Mitchell joked.

Carl's face reddened. "Hopefully it won't be *that* long," he said. "Have you opened all the letters in the bag yet?"

Mitchell shook his head. "Not yet. I've not had time."

"Spending time with your girlfriend?"

"Um, girlfriend?" Mitchell swallowed uncomfortably.

"Liza. She's very nice."

"Oh, Liza isn't my—" Mitchell started to protest, but Carl stood up and picked up his mop. He whistled as he pushed it across the floor.

Later that night, Poppy sang loudly as she got ready for bed, and Mitchell couldn't ever recall her doing that in the apartment before. It was the song she'd performed around the campfire, but this time she injected it with more oomph and joy. She mimed picking up a watering can and sprinkling pretend flowers.

She'd been full of life since she returned from her day out with Rachel at the park. The Jackson Pollock-like splats of ketchup and ice cream on her skirt offered proof of her enjoyment.

"I'm glad you had a great time," Mitchell said.

"The bouncy castles were amazing, and we had hot dogs and candy floss and, oh, Rachel's mum invited me to sleep over tomorrow night. If it's okay, can you call her?"

"Sure, and we'll have to take Rachel out somewhere in return."

"Ice-skating would be great!" Poppy said.

Mitchell laughed. He agreed to ring Rachel's mum, and he told Poppy how he'd spent the day with Graham. "We're both going to his and Rosie's wedding, and he's invited me to be his best man."

"Cool," Poppy said. She jumped up onto her bed. "I can wear my new stuff."

Mitchell went to the kitchen and took a small bag of oats from the kitchen cupboard. Back in Poppy's room, he stepped up onto the mattress to join her, and opened the window in her ceiling.

They sprinkled the oats on the roof slates for the pigeons, and Poppy giggled as they cooed and pecked at them.

Mitchell watched, a pleasant feeling of happiness and well-being enveloping him. For once he felt things could be changing for the better. They were moving forward.

He didn't know what the future held and if he'd ever find Yvette, but when he looked up at the stars he swore they somehow looked brighter tonight, almost as clear as they did from Jean's forest habitat.

17

DINNER

The next morning, Mitchell received a text message from Liza inviting him and Poppy over that evening. I've told Mum and Naomi everything we know, she said. My place at 6, for dinner with us?

Her words made him feel nervous as he wondered how Sheila and Naomi would react to his and Liza's visit to see Jean, and to the names Connor and Victor.

Poppy has a sleepover, but I'll be there, he replied. See you later.

Mitchell phoned Rachel's mum and arranged for her to collect Poppy that afternoon. He offered to take the two girls ice-skating the day after that. When Mitchell told Poppy he was going to Liza's house without her, she was disappointed.

"You'll have a much better time staying over at your friend's place," he assured her. "Do you remember Liza's mum had lots of questions for you?"

"Yeah, she was a bit bossy."

"We'll be talking adult stuff."

"About Yvette?"

"Probably."

Poppy picked up her bag and looked inside it. It was still half packed after their trip to Jean's place. "You said you'd find Yvette…"

"It's only been eight days. I'm doing my best to help her whole family."

"I know, Dad. Do you think she'll come home?"

He didn't want to lie to her, but the more he got involved with the Bradfields, the more he worried he wasn't going to find Yvette after all.

"I hope so." He wrapped his arm around her. "I really do."

Liza appeared distracted when she opened her front door to him. She wore jeans with embroidered roses on the thighs, and a coral-colored T-shirt. Her hair was half in a ponytail and half out.

He handed her a bottle of chardonnay. "How's things?" he asked.

"Okay…well, not really. I called Mum and told her about Yvette mentioning Dad's name, Connor. It freaked her out that Yvette might think Dad's still alive, and she's not happy I went to see Jean. It brought on one of her anxiety attacks and I wish I hadn't said anything. I spent ages on the phone talking to her until she calmed down. I persuaded her to still come over tonight."

"You're only trying to help," Mitchell said.

"I know." Liza's voice wobbled. "And now I'm behind on cooking dinner. I haven't even started, and they'll be here in an hour."

"I can help you. I'm great at muesli," he said, trying to cheer her up.

"It might come to that. I'm not kidding."

Mitchell followed her into the kitchen, where the worktop was covered in utensils and open recipe books.

"I was going to make a cottage pie, but my potatoes are past their sell-by date and have all these sprouts coming out of them. I've tried to think of something else, but my mind keeps wandering off and I can't follow any recipes. Perhaps we'd be better going out to a restaurant or something?"

"Will that be okay if your mum is feeling stressed?"

"Hmm, yes, you're right. That's not a good idea. I'll have to try to rustle something up here. Or order in."

Mitchell thought for a while. "If you have all the other bits and pieces for cottage pie, you could make spaghetti Bolognese, or a vegetarian chili."

The worry wrinkles in her forehead dissolved. "Chili? That's a great idea. I can make it a bit milder than usual for Mum. I know it's July but I love to eat it all year round."

"Me, too. And I've made chili before, so I won't poison anyone."

"Thanks, you're a lifesaver."

Liza took more ingredients out of her cupboards and fridge and set them down on the worktop. Mitchell found a recipe in one of her cookbooks, then washed his hands and chopped a red chili pepper into tiny slivers. Liza donned her aviator sunglasses to tackle an onion.

Mitchell tried to think of something to talk about that wasn't to do with Yvette and her disappearance to keep conversation light before Naomi and Sheila arrived.

"I've heard a rumor that Word Up might be playing at the bridge opening ceremony," he said, thinking of something Barry told him.

"Oh, yes. I heard that, too. I bet Poppy will love it. I wouldn't mind seeing them myself. They use this chord in one of their songs and it reminds me of Beethoven's Ninth Symphony." She sang one note and held it. "Do you hear that?"

"I don't know their music," he admitted. Poppy had excitedly jumped up and down on her bed when she heard the boy band might be playing in Upchester. But whenever Mitchell looked across the river at the finishing touches being done to the Yacht bridge, memories flooded back of his late nights and meetings. He imagined Jasmine Trencher striding around with drawings clamped to her chest. "We might be busy that day," he said.

"Just let me know," Liza replied. She rubbed away tears under her sunglasses with the side of her wrist and tipped the chopped onions into a saucepan. "It's sure to be fun, whether the band plays or not. I bet there'll be food stalls and face painting, stuff like that, and I *love* the new bridge. Poppy told me you worked on its design."

"I did, for a while." He was about to change the subject, uncomfortable talking about the structure that contributed to his loss of Anita, but then he reconsidered. It was something he had been passionate about, once. Liza liked to explain about music and he wondered if she might be interested in architecture, too.

"It's a cable-stayed bridge," he told her. "Probably the most modern and elegant type. Cables span out from the two white masts and secure to the road, to hold the weight of pedestrians and traffic. The design is beautiful, responsive and flexible, but it can struggle in high winds. The cables need a lot of maintenance so they don't corrode."

"Impressive. You know a lot about it. And I think that's the most I've heard you say about anything." She cut the pepper in half. "Which is your favorite bridge?"

Mitchell knew his answer straightaway. "The old redbrick one. I call it Redford."

"What, after Robert Redford?"

"I never thought of that. I just give them all nicknames. Silly really."

"I think it's cute."

He blushed at her word choice. "Arch bridges have been around since Roman and Ancient Greek times, because their simple design works well. That old red bridge doesn't have ornate colorful panels, like the Victorian bridge, or showy white masts. People probably walk over it and don't even notice it's there. But if they took the time to look closely, they'd see how strong and durable it is. When you're rushing around, you don't always notice the thing beneath your feet that supports you."

Liza opened a can of kidney beans, drained off the water and tipped them into the saucepan. "It'd be boring if all the bridges were the same. I mean, they do the same job even if they look different, right? It's nice to have different designs—adds to the aesthetics of the city."

Mitchell used a knife to slide the chili pepper slices off the chopping board. "You've got to be open to change."

He took a moment to digest that he'd actually said *that*.

"When I was a girl, I couldn't play the piano because my hands are stocky," Liza said. She held up a hand, fingers splayed, that looked perfectly normal to him. "Mum said I'd be better learning the guitar and violin, because of my strong fingers. She never did know how to give a compliment. Instead of telling me I looked nice, or was kind, or clever, she said I had a guitar-player's fingers. I listened to her for ages, before teaching myself the piano."

Mitchell shrugged a shoulder, wondering what this had to do with the bridges. "You have nice hands."

"Thank you." She smiled. "When did you know you were interested in architecture?"

"I was always fascinated by buildings and used to make Lego constructions with my friend, Graham. I'd study those numbered diagrams for hours and I liked to create and test structures, to see which could take the most weight."

"Oh." She looked at him curiously. "That's, um, interesting."

"And nerdy?" he asked with a smile.

"Well, now you mention it. I didn't say it first."

They returned to sliding their ingredients into the pan.

"Everything's done now," Liza said. "I just need to add some water, stock and spices and let this simmer for a while, then we should have the perfect chili. Not too spicy but with a little kick. Good teamwork, eh?" She wiped her hands on a pot towel and raised her palm for a high five.

"Yes, we made this happen," Mitchell agreed, and his hand met hers.

They held them together midair for a couple of seconds longer than necessary and Mitchell felt an intriguing prickle in his fingertips. He clutched his hand away.

Liza cleared her throat and looked around her. "Mum and Naomi will be here soon," she said. "I'll set the table, and I need to think about drinks, too. I think I've got a nice bottle of merlot somewhere."

"I'll help," Mitchell offered, too quickly. "Where do you keep your knives and forks?"

Half an hour later, Sheila bustled into the dining room, Naomi trailing behind. Sheila wore a flowing purple dress and long white cardigan. She took a seat at the head of the table and her knobby knuckles looked like tree bark as she picked up a glass of water. "Oh, this is still, not sparkling?" She studied it, then peered up at Liza.

"Sorry, Mum. I ran out of the fizzy stuff. You've got Upchester's finest tap water there."

"That food smells very spicy."

Liza flitted around her mother, straightening a knife, setting down a plate of bread. "I made us a big pot of chili con carne. Nice and fresh."

"It tastes delicious," Mitchell told Sheila.

"But it's July—"

"Oh, Mum," Naomi interrupted. "We're all here, and we're all eating together. It's not easy for me to leave the kids behind and get out of the house." She pulled out a chair and sat down with a thump. Her hair was messy and she had a smudge of green paint on her cheek.

Liza eyed her with concern. "Are you feeling okay?"

"Yes. Why wouldn't I be?" Naomi replied sharply.

"We're not *all* together. *Yvette* isn't here," Sheila said. "I had no idea what had been going on, about her showing up on the bridge and then falling into the river like that. You've kept me in the dark."

"It was with the best intentions, Mum. You know how you get all worried and panicky," Liza said firmly. "Only eight days ago, we'd reached a dead end looking for Yvette. We now have a sighting and a couple of names as clues. It's a big leap forward, and it's a relief Mitchell was there to come to her rescue."

"I bet there's a lot more I still don't know about this," Sheila said.

Naomi glanced at her and toyed with her fork.

"Let's enjoy our food, then talk properly. It's great we're all here," Liza said with exaggerated cheeriness.

While the four of them chatted about the heat wave, Liza

spooned the chili out of a big bowl sitting in the center of the table.

Sheila made a show of looking around her. "No rice?" she asked.

"Just bread," Liza said.

"It looks delicious." Naomi attempted a smile. "A nice change. I swear I eat so many spaghetti hoops my skin is turning orange."

Sheila side-glanced at her. "You should feed those children properly. I managed it, even when I was working. It's all junk food these days."

Naomi's lips pinched. She stared at her plate.

There was silence until Sheila started up again. "Why on earth would Yvette use Jean's lyrics on a padlock anyway?" she asked. "It's not even a good song."

"It's a lovely song," Naomi replied. "Perhaps there's no meaning in her use of it. She might just like the words."

Mitchell noticed how Liza didn't tell her mother that Yvette had visited Jean before her disappearance. He wasn't sure if she was protecting Jean from her mum's wrath, or trying to prevent Sheila from having another panic attack.

"Is there anything else anyone wants to tell me?" Sheila asked.

Naomi dropped her fork onto her plate. Her hand shook as she picked it back up.

Sheila studied her. "What is it?" she demanded.

"Well, we know that Yvette had a boyfriend," Liza said slowly.

"I didn't know that." Sheila frowned. "Did you know, Naomi?"

Liza turned to her sister.

Naomi looked down at her coffee cup and hesitantly shrugged. "A couple of months before Yvette vanished,

I bumped into her in a café. When she waved at me, she knocked over the salt pot and this man she was with shot her a look, as if she was useless. She introduced him to me as Victor, someone she knew through work. There was something in the way he looked at her that was really intense, as if he owned her. I never saw him again after that, and Yvette never spoke about him. I didn't think to mention him to the police."

Liza studied her. "Is there anything else…?"

"Um, no."

"Are you sure?"

Naomi rubbed her chin. "Um, I don't know if…"

"If you know something, just say it," Sheila cut in. "Stop dillydallying."

Naomi shrank back. "I remember Yvette said Victor's surname was Sonetti. So last night, after I got off the phone to Liza, I looked him up online. It took a bit of searching around, but I found an article about him…"

"What was it?" Sheila asked.

Naomi took a deep breath. "Victor was sent to prison for embezzlement. He stole funds from the company he worked for. It was discovered just before Yvette vanished and, after a court case, he got sent down for six months."

"To prison?" Sheila gulped.

Naomi nodded.

Mitchell remembered Jean's words, about Victor's photograph having a bad aura. He was relieved his imprisonment wasn't for anything violent, but wondered why Jean was so worried about him.

Liza sat back in her chair. "Well, that's good. If he's been locked up, Yvette can't have been with him during that period of time."

Naomi frowned, seeming to wrestle with her thoughts. "I

believe Yvette was the one who discovered he was skimming off the funds."

Liza narrowed her eyes. "How on earth do you know *that*…?"

Naomi looked quickly away. "Um, I believe Victor was released two weeks ago," she mumbled.

"You didn't answer my question—"

Sheila let out a gasp and her cup fell, splashing coffee on the table and Mitchell's shirt. She clutched at her neck. "What if he finds Yvette?"

Liza rushed to get a cloth. Naomi dabbed her mother's place mat with a napkin and Mitchell patted his chest dry.

"Everything is probably okay," Naomi said quickly, though her face suggested she thought otherwise. "As I said, I only saw Yvette and Victor together the once."

"What if Yvette was trying to escape someone on the bridge?" Sheila's hands began to shake. "What if her fall wasn't an accident? Someone might have pushed her."

Mitchell remembered Yvette smiling at him and her trying to reach for something. "I'm sure that wasn't the case," he assured her. "I saw her fall, and she was alone."

"But her lock…those song lyrics…and Victor out of prison, too," Sheila stuttered.

"Please try to stay calm, Mum," Liza pleaded.

However, Sheila clamped a hand to her chest. Her breathing quickened until she was gulping for air. "My heart," she cried out.

Liza sprang up. "It's okay, Mum. Are you having one of your attacks?"

Sheila nodded, her head lolling.

Mitchell rushed to the kitchen to fill a jug with more water.

"My heart is breaking… I can't take this much longer," Sheila's words tumbled out.

"It's okay, Mum. Close your eyes and take long deep breaths," Liza said. "Remember what the doctor told you. Nice and gentle. Come on, you'll be okay."

"Her padlock. I want to see it for myself…"

"I'll take a photo of it for you," Liza said. "No problem. Just try to relax."

Naomi's face paled and Liza huddled up to her mum. Sheila began to cry, tears plopping onto her skirt.

Mitchell surveyed the scene and clenched his fists. He longed to do something to help. "I can bring Yvette's lock to you, Mrs. Bradfield," he said rashly. He filled her glass with water. "I'll find it. You don't have to worry about that."

Sheila met his eyes and nodded slightly. Her breathing eventually slowing. "Can you do that?" she asked.

"Yes, of course. I promise I'll find it for you."

She reached out to grasp his arm. "You're a good man," she said, her voice full of relief. "Thank you."

A little later on, when Mitchell helped Liza carry the empty plates to the kitchen, she whispered to him, "Mum will hold you to that. There'll be no getting out of it. I shouldn't have told her about Victor, especially as Naomi knew more than I did. I realize Mum's attacks are getting worse."

"I want to help," he said firmly. "I thought your mum was having a heart attack."

"They're really scary." Liza sipped a glass of water but it slipped from her hand and crashed to the floor. She dropped into a crouch and plucked at the shards on the lino. "What a mess. Ouch." She studied her palm as a tiny bead of blood appeared.

Mitchell knelt down beside her. "Is your hand okay?"

"It's fine, really. I think."

They both reached out for the same piece of glass, and the fronts of their heads brushed together. Mitchell felt a tickle through the roots of his hair and the air felt thick around him. He tentatively took her hand in his and examined it for glass splinters. "Don't risk cutting your fingers. You won't be able to play the guitar wearing plasters."

"You're right. That's really thoughtful of you. I had a bandage on my hand once, right across the middle, and it was very restrictive when I played the violin."

"Do you have a dustpan and brush?"

"Yes, and I'll get a cloth for the water."

Mitchell swept the floor. He slid the broken glass into a piece of newspaper and folded it up. His breath felt inexplicably short when he was close to Liza. He glimpsed his watch and realized how much time had gone by. "Sorry, but I have to go. I need to get home for Poppy."

"It's okay. Thanks for coming over. Apologies it's been so dismal."

"It's been fine," he fibbed. "I'll go and say goodbye to your mum and Naomi."

They stood up awkwardly together, as if there was a knee-high fence around them, hemming them in. Mitchell found he wanted to circle his arms around her waist and, disconcerted by this feeling, he held them stiffly by his side.

They walked together toward the dining room. "Tell Poppy I said hi." Liza made a crown behind her head with her hand. "It would have been nice to see her. But I'm glad she didn't witness our family drama."

He dawdled in the hallway. "I'm taking her ice-skating tomorrow."

"Ha, I've not been skating for years. I bent my little finger back once and Mum banned me, said it could mess up my entire music career. A bit overprotective, if you ask me."

"Join us?" Mitchell suggested, before he could think about it. He wanted to make amends for the upset of the evening, even though it wasn't his doing. "Poppy will be with her friend most of the time."

"Liza," Sheila called from the dining room.

Liza studied her fingers and her eyes flashed with defiance. "The small girl in me wants to rebel against Mum by going skating. Is that really childish?"

Mitchell shook his head. "Not after tonight."

"I could do with a break," she said. "We have clues about Yvette, but none are fitting together. The cool air at the rink might help me clear my head. They play music, too, while you skate and it's a bit like a daytime disco."

"Come with us," he said, really meaning it this time. "Poppy and I will be there tomorrow at noon. We can talk more then. Wear gloves to protect your hands."

In the dining room, he picked up his jacket and gave Sheila and Naomi a peck on their cheeks. For some reason, he avoided doing the same to Liza. "It's been lovely," he said as he headed back into the hallway. "Thank you."

"Thank *you* for coming." Liza performed a small curtsy. "And for offering to find Yvette's lock for Mum. I'm sure it will help her to feel a bit better."

"I said I'd get it for her," Mitchell said firmly. "I'll keep you posted."

18

ICE-SKATING

When Mitchell unpinned the next day's itinerary from the wall, the black rectangles of the spreadsheet looked rigid, like the bars of a cage.

He took a pen from his pocket to cross out his and Poppy's original planned trip to the library, intending to replace it with their outing to the ice rink. Instead, he stared at it for a while. He thought about Liza's words about defying her mother, and he felt a jolt of boldness that he didn't want to comply with his own rigid plans.

He ripped the paper into small pieces and, clutching them in his fist, he carried them into Poppy's room to show her.

She took them from him and stood on her bed. She let them flutter down inside her room, so they looked like blossom petals falling from a tree.

Mitchell stepped up, too, and the bed creaked as they both poked their heads out of the sloping window. Mitchell crooked his fingertips over its frame and felt the roof tiles were already warmed by the sun. There was cooing as five pigeons strutted around next to a nest in the gutter.

"Can we feed them again?" Poppy asked. "*Please*, Dad."

Mitchell brought another small bag of oats from the kitchen, that he'd planned to make healthy muffins with.

Poppy poured them onto the roof in a heap, so they looked like a melting snowman. The pigeons flocked toward it.

"Liza is joining us at the rink today," Mitchell said as casually as he could so Poppy wouldn't get too excited.

"Ace."

"The heat is making everyone want to cool off. Barry even mentioned meeting a date at the rink."

"If he's trying to find a girlfriend," Poppy said. "He might like Liza."

Mitchell took a moment to digest this thought.

He pictured Liza and Barry taking Sasha for a walk along Redford, chatting together and holding hands. He supposed they'd make an attractive couple, and they'd probably get along. It should give him a warm feeling to imagine two people he knew getting together, but somehow it made the back of his neck itch. "Maybe," he said, and left it at that. "Now find some extra socks, so your skates won't rub your ankles."

The temperature inside the ice rink provided welcome relief from the sticky air outside. The foyer smelled of old socks and strawberry slushies, and goose bumps formed on Mitchell's forearms.

A bored-looking girl behind the counter handed over three sets of skates to Mitchell, Poppy and her friend Rachel. They sat on the floor and fastened their laces up tight.

"What time is Liza coming?" Poppy asked.

"She should be here soon." His stomach skittered and he put it down to the apprehension of venturing onto the ice.

Holding hands, Poppy and Rachel teetered onto the rink and cautiously pushed off from the side. As they both performed a half skid, half walk, Mitchell shuffled behind them. He held back, not wanting to cramp their style, but trying to practice before Liza arrived.

He watched as Poppy fell down onto her backside, pulling Rachel over with her. The two girls lay on their backs on the ice and laughed so much they couldn't get up. Seeing his daughter having fun made him grin.

After checking they were okay, Mitchell skated on very slowly. He conducted an awkward two laps of the rink before he felt two hands clamp on to his shoulders. He almost lost his balance as he looked behind him.

Barry removed his hands and clung to the barrier instead. "Mitchell," he said. "What are you doing here?"

"I've brought Poppy and her friend skating. What about you?"

"Amanda wanted to come, remember? The speed dating session is just after lunch. I get to skate with six women for five minutes each. I've got a card to mark on who I like." He sighed as he peeled off a sticker with MAN No.4 printed on it and stuck it to his chest.

"Doesn't that mean Amanda will be skating with other men, too? It doesn't sound much like a date."

Barry rubbed his shorn head. "You're right. Never thought of that."

As they chatted, Liza arrived and glided over toward them. She was elegantly composed on the ice, and performed a graceful turn before she stopped beside them.

Mitchell and Barry stared at her, surprised. "I thought you hadn't been skating for ages," Mitchell said.

"Yes, but I had lessons until I was eleven." She grinned. "I think it's like riding a bike. Once you learn you have the skill forever."

"I think it's called cheating."

She laughed at him and skated over toward Poppy and Rachel.

Mitchell found a shuffle-walking-slipping way of getting around. The skates hurt his ankles and it wasn't very pleasurable. Liza slowed down to skate alongside him, but he felt she was humoring him. Everyone else on the ice held hands as they moved along, but he kept his to himself.

After he'd conducted several more circuits, a speaker crackled overhead. "It's our Skate and Date session in five minutes, people. Everyone else, clear the ice."

Barry tottered toward Mitchell. "Amanda hasn't shown up. Some date this is."

"You can still take part."

"If someone attached ice skates to a giraffe, its legs would be better coordinated than mine."

"It's a good excuse to hold hands with different women."

Barry perked up. "That's true."

Liza, Poppy and Rachel skated up to Mitchell and Barry.

"I've worked up an appetite," Liza said. "Anyone else fancy a hot dog?"

"Me," Poppy and Rachel chorused.

"I'll go and make a fool of myself." Barry jerked a thumb over his shoulder. "Please don't watch."

After Mitchell, Liza, Poppy and Rachel took off their skates and put their shoes back on, they headed toward the café. A girl with long auburn hair waved at them. "Hey, Poppy," she said. "You enjoying the school hols?"

"Hey, Eva. Yeah."

Eva mimed a weighing action with her hands. "I'm getting a slushie. Raspberry or strawberry? I can't decide." She lowered her voice to a whisper, but Mitchell overhead. "Did your dad *really* save someone?"

Poppy giggled nervously. "Um, yeah."

"So, he's famous? Can I get a selfie with him?"

Poppy shrugged as Eva handed her an iPhone.

Mitchell felt himself shrinking back as Rachel and Eva moved in on him, while Poppy glowered with embarrassment. Her two friends made peace signs with their fingers and peered through them. Poppy reluctantly took a few shots and Mitchell managed a rictus grin.

"Can we sit on our own, Dad?" Poppy said after handing Eva's phone back to her.

"Okay." He handed her some money. "I'll be just over here with Liza."

At the café counter, he bought two hot dogs and coffees and carried them across. His and Liza's table had a good view of the rink.

"I should be buying these instead to say sorry for last night," she said as she bit into her hot dog. "I can't believe I thought dinner was a good idea. Though that chili tasted really good."

He smiled sympathetically. "At least your mum and Naomi now know what's been going on. Though Naomi looks to be keeping something to herself..."

"She mentioned something about Yvette discovering Victor's misdemeanors." Liza pursed her lips. "I've been thinking about it all night. I'm going to head up to her apartment tomorrow and take another look around. I want to make sure Victor's not been there and to set my mind at rest. I feel spooked by what Naomi told us."

Mitchell imagined Liza on her own with a shadowy figure following her along lonely corridors. He felt an urge to protect her. "Maybe I should join you..."

"You've done enough. I'm fine doing this on my own."

He sipped his coffee, considering what to do. The shame of not being there for Anita had curdled inside him for three years, but he could be here for the Bradfields. He *wanted* to find Yvette and help make their family whole again, because he could never do it for his own. "I'll come with you," he insisted. "Poppy starts her activity club tomorrow. I've got one last day off before I go back into work."

"Henry's accompanied me there a couple of times. But if you don't mind?"

That man's name again. Mitchell didn't like how it made him feel, and she mentioned him so casually, as if he was part of her family. "I'll come with you," he said firmly. "I want to do it."

"And now, ladies and gentleman," the speaker sounded again. "Time for our Skate and Date. Five minutes with each partner, starting now."

A whistle sounded. Eleven people stood around the perimeter of the rink and didn't move.

"I said *now*," the voice repeated grumpily.

Mitchell watched as a woman, six inches taller than Barry, yanked his hand like a husky dog pulling a sled. She wore Princess Leia-style hair buns and a silver T-shirt. Barry's jaw dropped, petrified, as she tugged him out onto the ice.

Liza guffawed into her coffee. "I shouldn't laugh, but…"

Mitchell's lips twitched, too, and soon they were both giggling like schoolchildren at the back of a classroom.

They watched Barry until a whistle sounded again. A girl dressed all in orange approached him and they each skated a couple of steps before falling over. When one was up, the other was down, like the valves on a trumpet.

By the time Barry was on his fourth date, his eyes were so

full of terror that Liza couldn't look at him any longer. Tears of laughter rolled down her cheeks.

Mitchell tried to keep a straight face to show solidarity with his friend, but he couldn't help chortling, too. Whenever he and Liza caught each other's eyes, they triggered each other even more.

He couldn't remember the last time he'd found something so funny.

When the fifth whistle blew, Barry stumbled off the ice and hobbled into the café area still wearing his skates. "Thanks for your support." He grimaced.

"You're not finished. You have one date left," Mitchell said. "Unless Amanda has shown up."

"No, she hasn't." Barry tore the number sticker off his shirt. "And I've had *enough*."

Couples stop-started, skating hopelessly around the rink. One lady stood at the side, closest to the café, all alone. She was petite with short-cropped blonde hair and wore jeans and a bubblegum pink T-shirt. Her lips were straight as she looked around for her date.

"You can't leave her there," Mitchell said.

"I said I've had enou—" Barry stopped, and his eyes focused on the lone skater.

She smiled sadly over at him.

"Barry?" Mitchell said, but his friend was transfixed.

Barry edged back toward the rink, as if in a trance. He skated over to the woman and held out his hand. She took it and they set off together, their feet hesitant but in perfect unison.

Poppy and Rachel joined Mitchell and Liza at their table. "Aw," the two girls gushed as they watched Barry, too.

Mitchell's laughter had subsided, leaving him with glowing cheeks and a sore throat. He glanced over at the fridge behind the café counter, to see what cold drinks were on offer. When he saw a woman standing in the queue, his spine straightened up.

She had her back to him and her coppery curls bobbed as she chatted to a friend. Her jacket was tomato red.

Mitchell's surroundings and everyone around him vanished, until he could see only *her.*

Surely, it's not…

He wondered if she had seen him laughing with another woman, and an urge to explain to her who he was with and what he was doing here surged inside him.

He stood up and banged his leg against the table. A pepper pot toppled over, but he didn't notice.

He was vaguely aware of Poppy saying, "Dad?" and Liza uttering his name, as he stepped blindly away from them.

He could hardly swallow as he got closer to her. What was she doing here? Why now?

As he drew nearer, her hair was coarser than he remembered, and she was shorter. He tried to breath in her violet scent, but could only smell strawberry slushies.

But he still reached out a hand anyway and laid it gently on her shoulder. "Anita?" he said.

She turned and a woman he didn't recognize, a stranger, gave him a bewildered smile. She was in her fifties and suddenly bore no resemblance to Anita at all.

Mitchell snatched his hand away, as if burned. "Sorry, I thought you were someone else."

"S'okay." She shrugged, before returning to talk to her friend.

And smack, Mitchell was suddenly back in the ice rink café, fully aware of what he was doing and who he was really with. His vision of Anita shot away.

His face shone crimson as he excused himself away from the café counter, and he returned to Liza and the girls.

"Dad?" Poppy said. Her eyes flicked over to the red-coated woman. "Did you think that—"

"No," he replied too quickly. "I thought it was someone from work. That's all."

She looked at him with questioning eyes.

Liza bit her lip. "Perhaps I should head off home… Do you still want to join me tomorrow?"

"Um, tomorrow?" Mitchell frowned.

"Yes, to go to Yvette's place. You don't have to come with me if you don't want to…" she said cautiously.

Mitchell glanced over at the vacant spot in front of the café counter where he thought he saw Anita. Sadness washed over him. "It's fine. I'll still join you."

Liza smiled and tugged on Poppy's plait. "Great, I'm pleased," she said, and then was gone.

Poppy stared after her before she spoke to Rachel. "Shall we go home, too? I'm fed up now."

Mitchell sloped after the two girls toward the locker area. As he waited for them to collect their belongings, his phone pinged with a text. He thought it might be from Liza, but the number was withheld.

I think my brother has your toolbox. If you want it back come to 23 Somerset House, Whitby Street, on Wednesday at 11:00 a.m.

Mitchell knew he should feel heartened by the news that he might get his tools back, even though it was a strange message. But as he left the rink and walked out into the blinding sunshine, he felt himself reeling at his confused feelings.

Anita's imagined presence was often a comfort to him, but today, it had felt like an intrusion.

★ ★ ★

That night, after Mitchell had changed out of his clothes and cleaned his teeth, thoughts of Anita still nagged his brain and he lay down in bed holding on to her lilac envelope. He wondered if seeing her at the ice rink was a sign for him to finally open it, but he couldn't bring himself to break its seal.

Instead, Mitchell took the pad of Basildon Bond notepaper out from under his bed. It had been over a week since he last wrote to Anita, and he had the urge to do it now.

Dearest Anita,

So much has happened over the last nine days, I feel guilty for not writing to you sooner. A woman fell into a river and I jumped in to help her. (You know I don't usually do anything without a plan.) Her name is Yvette and she's been missing from her family for a year. I understand how they must feel, because you're gone from my life, too. I'm helping Yvette's sister Liza to find her.

Poppy has taken a shine to Liza and the two of them have formed quite a bond. They went out shopping for clothes, which Poppy will wear to Graham's wedding (yes, he's really getting married).

It's good to see her smiling, but I worry about her getting too attached. I'm ashamed to admit it but I've had certain feelings for Liza. She's nothing like you, though. She talks too much, and wears garish clothes, and I sometimes feel like I've stumbled out of a nightclub, woozy in the early hours of the morning, after I spend time with her. She's not calm and together, like you. I'm not sure I can ever move on. Being with anyone other than you would just be a compromise too far.

Love always,
Mitchell x

He stared at his words, noticing how, this time, they had slipped out. When he read over them, they stated exactly what he wanted to say. He had managed to share moments in his life with Anita, without his usual feeling of remorse and regret.

After folding his letter once, he searched inside his night-stand drawer for a spare envelope, but they were all used up. So, he placed it on top of the stand with the others Susan had given him, and he settled down to sleep.

GHOSTS

Mitchell sat stiffly in Liza's car as she played a series of classical tunes. The atmosphere between them was uncomfortable after their awkward goodbye at the ice rink the day before. Both their moods only lifted when Liza inserted a Crowded House CD instead.

"You thought you saw Anita yesterday, didn't you?" she said as she drove onto the motorway. "I saw you go pale, like you'd seen a ghost."

"I don't believe in ghosts," he replied quickly.

"That's not what I asked. You've evaded my question."

He thought about denying it, but felt he owed her better than that. "Yes," he admitted. "I see her sometimes, in crowds or walking down the street. She's usually out of reach, so I can't call to her. But I thought I saw her at the café yesterday, right in front of me. I know it's not her, but it's like my brain doesn't accept that."

"Because you *want* her to be real?"

"What I *want* doesn't really matter, because it can't actually *be*." He felt prickly at this conversation.

Liza thought for a while. "A lot of people think ghosts are these see-through things, or covered in a white sheet with eyeholes cut out, but I think they're sometimes glimpses of the past to reassure us in the future."

He didn't reply, not sure if his sightings of Anita particularly comforted him. Contradictory feelings of anticipation and sadness overwhelmed him, that she wasn't really there.

"When my dad died, I used to pretend it hadn't happened," Liza explained. "He loved his shed, used to sit inside it and practice his clarinet for hours. I sometimes find his favorite pieces on my iPad and let them play in a different room, so I think he's still here. Even after five years, it's hard to accept he's gone. Do you think that sounds stupid?"

"No. I can understand it, and I'm sorry about yesterday," Mitchell said eventually, during the track "Don't Dream It's Over." "I wasn't thinking straight."

Liza fixed her eyes on the road. "Things must have been difficult after, you know...for Poppy especially."

Mitchell felt something shutting down inside him, a portcullis of privacy that often appeared to cut himself from other people's words. He could leave it there as a barrier against Liza, but there was something telling him to try to let her through. He just wasn't sure how.

"Did Poppy have any counseling?" Liza asked when he didn't respond. "It's good to talk things through so they're not going around in your head like a hamster wheel all the time."

Mitchell couldn't stop himself from thinking back to those days.

After Anita died, Poppy had weekly sessions at school. He'd attended a couple of them with her. Katerina the therapist wore lizard earrings and had a pierced nose. She had advised him to "just keep talking" to Poppy.

He had hooked on this, too vigorously, for months. Whenever the apartment was quiet, he punctured it with a stream of chatter about school, the weather, packed lunches, whatever he could think of, to break the silence. Until one day, Poppy had clapped her hands to her ears.

"Just shut up, Dad. I can't think straight."

And then he hadn't known how much to say, and how much not to.

He focused on answering Liza's question. "She saw someone for a while, but said it wouldn't bring her mum back. She's pragmatic like that, and I told her she can always pick it back up. I left my architect job to be there for her more, though nothing can replace her mother. I concentrated on keeping busy, making lots of plans for the two of us." He thought of the papers fluttering on corkboards in his hallway. "I may have taken it too far."

"Hmm, they did look rather regimented," she said softly. "Most people use a diary or their phone these days. Just a thought."

He considered the simplicity of this and decided it might be less restrictive. "Maybe I'll start," he said.

"There's hope for you yet."

When they arrived at Yvette's place, Liza led the way. An old warehouse at the side of a canal had been converted into luxury apartments and the sun glinted off their glass balconies. The building was double the height of Angel House, ten stories tall.

Liza took out a key. "Here we are, where the beautiful people live. All together in one place." She smiled wryly.

He heard the hint of something sad in her words and wanted to tell her she was a beautiful person, too, but he didn't say anything. When she put her shoulder against the door and held it open for him, he swallowed his thoughts and walked through.

The lobby looked like a posh waiting room, all brilliant white walls and marble flooring.

Liza headed to a row of mailboxes and took out a key for number thirty-six. "Yvette bought this place a couple of years ago. I pay the management company to collect and send Yvette's post to me," she said. "Sometimes they miss stuff." She picked out a few pieces of mail from the metal box, a couple of pizza menus among them. "See?"

She stuffed them into her bag and they took a lift up three floors. The stretch of blue carpet along a hallway reminded him of a hotel. When Liza unlocked Yvette's door, the apartment smelled of lemon air freshener and musty cardboard. The room was bright but soulless, with a designer leather sofa and interior design books on a low coffee table. He had expected it to be bursting with color, like Yvette's yellow dress.

"I'd offer you a coffee, but there's no milk," Liza said. "The tap water doesn't taste good. If I were you, I'd skip having a drink completely."

"It's fine."

"Maybe we could get one later?"

Mitchell paused, not sure if she meant going to a pub together, or not. "Sure, if we have time. I need to be home for Poppy when she returns from school."

"Right," Liza said briskly. She took the mail from her bag and dropped it onto the coffee table. "I'll take another look around, probably my tenth time here. Feel free to browse, too. I keep thinking I might have missed something—a letter or a note, anything, really. I want to make sure there are no signs Victor has been here."

She walked into Yvette's bedroom and he felt awkward

about following her. "God knows I've done this so many times already," she called to him. "Luckily, Yvette's the neatest person I know—can't stand any clutter. Not like Naomi's place. That resembles a fight in a toy shop."

Mitchell circled the room and spotted a year-old copy of *Vogue* on the coffee table. He loosely flicked through it and set it down again. The leather sofa squeaked as he sat down and picked up another magazine. He could hear Liza opening and shutting drawers and the wardrobe doors in the other room, but he felt uncomfortable about searching around, too.

After a while, Liza reentered the sitting room and flopped down on the sofa beside him. "There's nothing," she said, squeezing her eyes shut. "There never is. *How* could she just leave all this behind? She had everything going for her."

"Her place is beautiful," he agreed. "She must have a good job to live here."

Liza nodded. "There was only one year at high school, when all three of us overlapped. Yvette in the last year, Naomi in the first, and me in the middle. The older lads loved Yvette, with her high cheekbones and pencil skirts. She bought sweets and chocolates to sell at school, always business minded. When she was sixteen, she could already afford to buy designer perfume and dated this divorced businessman in his thirties. He had two kids and Mum was not happy. Yvette never wanted kids, though, and dumped him pretty quickly. She loves her single life.

"Naomi had these gorgeous puppy dog eyes and men always wanted to protect her. All she ever wanted was to have her own family."

"You must have had a lot of attention, too," he said.

"Well, thank you, kind sir," she said, then shook her head. "No, not really. I was the one in the middle, cursed by the greasy hair fairy and generally invisible. Boys only spoke to me to ask about Naomi or Yvette. I could play the guitar, though, joined a rock band when I was fourteen, to Mum's dismay. Not one of those band members ever hit on me. Saw me as one of them. I had snogs at parties, but no one ever asked me to dance with them. That's all I ever wanted, to feel good enough for some guy to ask me… What about you? Did you have girls lining up for you?"

"Ha, not at all. I suppose I was a late developer. I had a few girlfriends before Anita but, well, she was the *one*."

Liza lifted her chin. "I've never been anyone's *numero uno*," she said defiantly. "I don't mind, really."

But she sounded as if she did.

He cleared his throat, wanting to ask the question that had been on his mind for a while. "What about Henry?" he said, these new surroundings making him feel braver.

"Ah, Henry's my friend." Liza's eyes misted. "I met him at a support group for relatives and friends of missing people. He hasn't seen his brother for five years, since he didn't return from a night out. It's just so awful. You try to function as normal, then feel guilty when you have good times. You're always wondering if they're safe, why they left and what you could be doing to help them. At least Yvette has kept in touch, albeit only sporadically."

Unless the letters aren't from her at all, Mitchell thought, but he kept this to himself.

He knew these feelings well, of having to try to function normally while your world was falling apart. The fact that Henry wasn't Liza's boyfriend sparked the smallest flame inside him, even if he felt sorry for his situation.

Liza leaned over and picked Yvette's mail up off the coffee table. She leafed through the letters and flyers, shaking her head as she went. Except when she came to the final one. "Handwritten," she said, holding it up to show Mitchell. "Let-

ters are quite rare these days. Everyone emails or texts instead."
She slipped a finger under the flap and took out a small piece
of lined paper.

Mitchell watched the color drain from her cheeks as she
read it. Her eyes filled with worried tears.

"What is it?" he asked and gently eased it from her fingers.
When he read the words, his own throat tightened.

Hello Darling,
Miss me? Sounds like we've both been gone a while. Heard
what you did behind my back, then I find out about you and
Connor, too.
Don't worry, I'll find you. Won't be long. I have eyes and
ears everywhere.

V x

"V for Victor," Mitchell said solemnly.

Liza held a hand to her chest. "It sounds like it. How could
Yvette be mixed up with someone like that? He sounds so
angry. You don't think he'd do anything to harm her, do
you…?"

Mitchell couldn't be sure. "Perhaps you should contact the
police. It sounds like Yvette could be in trouble. Maybe get
in touch with her workmates, too, if Yvette knew Victor
through her job."

"Yes, I will do it. Though, I can't tell Mum about this. Not
with her health. It would send her over the edge."

"You should share it with Naomi, though. Don't do this
alone."

She took the letter from him and placed it in her bag. "Yes,
and I'm lucky to have you, too. We may have to take a rain
check on that drink."

Mitchell nodded. "I'm glad I could help," he said awkwardly.

As they left the apartment building together, all he could think about was what Victor might be capable of, if he got to Yvette before they did.

CHAINS

Dear Idiot,
It's people like you who set a bad example. You try telling my
kid it's not a cool idea to jump off a bridge, when there are peo-
ple like you doing it, in broad daylight. You should be ashamed
of yourself. And as for the prize money, that's bribery, plain
and simple, to detract from your stupidity. I hope you have a
shitty life.

The next day, Mitchell had picked a postcard up from the
mosaic of correspondence on his floor and read it after his
breakfast. It had a baboon on the front. Poppy tried to take it
from him to read, but he folded it in half and stuffed it into
his pocket before she could see it.

He dropped her off at the school activity club and walked
across the city to return to work. The thought of being back
on the bridges cutting off the padlocks made him feel like he

was wading through tar. Victor's ominous words swarmed in his head.

Liza had texted him that morning to say she was going to the police station and to call into Yvette's workplace, and he wished he could be there to support her.

The only contribution he felt he could make today was finding Yvette's padlock again, and retrieving it for Sheila, especially if it might prevent another of her panic attacks.

As he walked, the air felt hot and heavy with a closeness that made it difficult to breathe. He couldn't spot Barry on Archie, the Slab or Vicky, so he walked along the street at the side of the river toward Redford.

A juddering noise came, like a pneumatic drill digging up the road, and a flock of birds bolted from a tree into the sky. Mitchell walked on and found red stop signs had been positioned across the mouth of the bridge. A yellow sign said Road Ahead Closed. Follow Diversion Signs. His mouth slackened as a truck with a winch on the back thundered past him onto the bridge, bashing against one of the signs and toppling it over. He followed it through the gap and saw that a tall wire fence had been erected around a section of the railings, the twenty-meter-long rectangular zone looking like a cage. The truck billowed out thick gray smoke as it pulled up on the pavement, and two men wearing neon yellow bibs and orange hard hats climbed out of the cab. Another man already stood behind the fence, and the three men proceeded to open up two sections of the fence outward, into the road, like the gates of a stately home.

Mitchell's legs felt shaky as he walked closer to this unsettling scene. Yvette's lock was totally out of reach. A young couple joined him, and the three of them stared through the fence together at the padlocks, as if they were observing poorly animals at the zoo.

"What are they doing?" the woman asked. She stared at the council logo on Mitchell's chest, as if he was responsible for the situation. "We only hung a lock here yesterday."

Besides them, the truck choked out a plume of smoke and one of the hard-hatted men headed their way, a clipboard in his hand.

"Stand back," he bellowed. "Use the other pavement."

The couple muttered to each other and reluctantly walked away, but Mitchell stayed put. He looked up at the metal bar and chunky chains that hung down from the truck's winch. The chains were fastened to one of the bridge's panels, and the bolts that originally held it in place lay loose on the pavement.

Mitchell jumped as the winch suddenly turned and screeched. The chains tightened and the panel groaned and jerked upward. The padlocks hanging from it clanked and creaked as they swung. The panel levitated higher until two of the hard-hatted men grabbed hold of it to stop it swaying around in the air.

Mitchell hooked his fingers around the wire of the fence and watched helplessly. When he felt a tap on his shoulder, he spun around expecting someone wearing a yellow bib to order him to move away.

Instead, Barry grinned and stuck two thumbs up. "Bloody brilliant, isn't it?" he said above the crunch of the winch as it lowered the padlock-laden panel onto a large blue trolley.

"What's going on?"

Barry indicated they should move away to talk, and they found a spot at the end of the bridge. "Russ called the contractors in," he said excitedly. "A panel on the bridge has cracked, and he's worried someone else might fall into the river. The council media team says the padlocks are making the city look a mess. They want something done before the new white

bridge opens. It'll send out a clear message to anyone thinking about hanging a lock before or during the ceremony."

Mitchell's throat felt tight. "Are they going to remove the
locks?"

"Yeah, they're starting to. Russ found the budget to bring
in the big guys. That's temporary fencing they're setting up,
then they'll replace the railings with lock-proof ones."

"But they're part of the bridges, their design and heritage,"
Mitchell said. His gut cramped as he thought about Yvette's
heart-shaped lock being torn away. He had made his promise
to Sheila and Liza. "It's our job to remove them, not theirs."

"It's out of our control, mate. If the contractors step in,
it's less work from us. There's going to be bigger fines, too."

Mitchell thought about the messages and names on the
locks being taken away and destroyed. The padlocks weren't
just pieces of metal. They were parts of people's lives and love
letters to each other, and to the city. They were a modern-day
method of self-expression, and they were probably all going
to be mangled or smelted.

He'd made a promise to Sheila that he'd retrieve Yvette's
lock and he couldn't renege on that, especially when her health
was at risk. Mitchell curled his hands into fists.

"Um, you don't look very pleased," Barry said. "Rules are
usually right up your street."

Mitchell grunted. There was no worth in telling Barry
about his true feelings, only to be scoffed at. "What about
our jobs?" he said.

"Don't think about that now, mate." Barry patted him hard
on the back. "Let's see what happens when they've stripped
the first two bridges. Now, do you want to hear how my first
date with Trisha went?"

Mitchell clenched his teeth. "Sorry, Barry, but I've got to
do something."

Mitchell strode over to a man with a tufty black beard. He jutted out his chest and made sure the council logo on his T-shirt was on display. "Excuse me, mate. I need to get to one of those locks." He jabbed a finger toward the panel where Yvette's lock hung.

The man smirked at him. "Me, too. I just want to be rid of them."

"I need to remove one of them, intact if possible."

The man scratched under his hard hat with the end of his pen. "They're all being taken away."

"What will happen to them?"

"Who cares?" The man glanced at Mitchell's T-shirt logo but turned away.

Mitchell shot out his hand and gripped the man's arm. When the man glared at him, he awkwardly let go. "Sorry, I need to retrieve one of them. Just one."

The man slouched wearily. "Look. Those locks are a blight on this city. I don't know if they're going to be crushed, buried or blasted to high heaven, and I don't care. These manky chunks of metal will be history. Wiped out, like the dinosaurs."

Every word the man said felt like a knock on a stake through Mitchell's heart. He peered over the man's shoulder to the spot where Yvette had stood, where they shared their smiles. Now all he could see was fencing. "How long will it take to remove all these panels?"

The man shrugged. "We'll get half done today, the other half tomorrow."

Mitchell figured it would take them until at least tomorrow to get to Yvette's lock, but he didn't want to risk it. He lurched forward and tried to dart through a gap in the fencing. When a hand grabbed the back of his collar, he let out an, "Oof."

"*Leave* it," the bearded man snapped. "Move away, right now, or else I'll report you."

Mitchell batted his hand off. "Please," he tried again. "This one padlock is really important. I'm trying to find a woman…"

The man glared at him for a while before he let go. "Look, mate, I get it. I'm married. My wife and I came here and hung a lock, too. It was a nice thing to do. But they have to go. If you save one, you have to save them all."

"It will only take a few minutes—"

The man rolled his eyes and walked away, muttering.

Mitchell stared after him for a while, before he set his jaw. He turned and marched back to Barry.

"What's up?" his friend asked. "Your face is like thunder."

"Can you cover for me? I need to make a call."

Mitchell rang Liza and she answered straightaway. "I can't get to Yvette's lock and it's going to be removed," he said. "Make sure your mum doesn't come to the city center. The bridge is all cordoned off."

"Oh," Liza said. She sounded anxious.

"Are you okay?" he asked.

"Not really. I called into Yvette's workplace and asked about Victor but they said business matters are confidential. I went to see the police, too, and there's nothing they can do about his letter because it doesn't really contain a threat.

"I told Naomi all this, but then Mum kept phoning her for an update, and Naomi gave in. Mum had another panic attack and couldn't catch her breath, and now she's even more fixated about Yvette's padlock. If she doesn't see it for herself soon she's going to make herself really poorly."

"We don't want that." Mitchell thought quickly, and he could only come up with one solution. "I have an idea. Would you be free to look after Poppy this evening?"

"Um, yes, I'd love to. My last lesson is at seven thirty until eight. Is that okay?"

"Yes, thanks. I'll call you later to arrange things. I need to make another call. And in the meantime, you look after your mum."

Mitchell hung up and dialed another number.

He was finally ready to call in his long-standing favor from Graham.

When his friend answered, Mitchell explained how he wanted to save Yvette's padlock from destruction.

"Interesting one," Graham said. "Didn't see that one coming, Mitchy Boy. Out of all the things you could ask me for…"

"I know, but I can't let it be destroyed. It's a long story, but it's important. A removal operation is underway, so the bridge is all fenced off and I can't get close to the railings. The padlocks will probably all be gone in twenty-four hours."

"Let me think," Graham mused. "Yup. I've got a meeting at the Jupiter about the wedding plans this evening, but am free after that. We can do something tonight, near dark. Rosie can help, and you'll get to meet her."

"But Rosie's pregnant," Mitchell said.

"The woman is a dynamo—she'll want in on the action. She'll be good at keeping a lookout. I've got a team in mind, too."

Graham made the removal of one lock sound like a military operation, worthy of one of Mitchell's hallway spreadsheets. He worried that his favor was taking on bigger implications.

"Is Poppy coming along?" Graham asked. "She'll think it's cool, won't she? Roaming the streets of the city at night, like outlaws."

"Definitely not," Mitchell said, knowing how excited she was even buying her new necklace. "Let's keep this between ourselves."

After hanging up, Mitchell found Barry and told him he was going to finish work an hour early. He wanted to call Liza again and make proper arrangements for her coming over, before Poppy got home from the school club.

Barry pointed his bolt cutters at him. "If Russ finds out, you'll be dead meat."

Mitchell gave a small shrug. "I've worked through lots of my lunch hours in the past. I'll call Russ's PA and ask to book time off. Okay?"

"Whatever you're up to, keep under Russ's radar."

"Russ is the least of my worries," Mitchell mumbled as he hurried away.

21

PADLOCK

"Are you sure it's no trouble retrieving the lock?" Liza asked when she arrived at Mitchell's apartment to look after Poppy. "It all sounds a bit dodgy."

"It will be fine," he assured her.

Poppy bounced into the hallway. "Can I show Liza all the letters, Dad?"

Liza peered over his shoulder at his sitting room floor. "There looks to be a lot of them, now they're out of the bag. I thought you'd bought a new rug..."

"Now, does that sound like me?" Mitchell said.

She laughed and allowed Poppy to take her hand and tug her toward them. "Well, no, not really."

In his bedroom, Mitchell got dressed in a black pair of jeans and a black T-shirt. Poppy narrowed her eyes when he reentered the sitting room. "You look like a burglar, or like you're going on a date." She turned to Liza. "A lady called Vanessa wrote to Dad, and he reckons she *likes* him."

"It's nothing like that," Mitchell said hurriedly when Liza raised an eyebrow at him. "I need to see Graham about something, and will be back as soon as I can. Let Liza read through any letters first before you look at them."

"Okay," Poppy said in a singsong voice.

He grinned and kissed the top of her head. "See you later. Don't wait up for me."

In the middle of an alley close to the back of Angel House, Mitchell met Graham's fiancée, Rosie, for the first time. At nine thirty, the skies were darkening and, under the light glowing from the windows of an apartment above, he could see she was heavily pregnant.

Rosie wore flared jeans and a wide paisley scarf in her hair. Her faded T-shirt featured an illustrated PS4 handset and the slogan *Player 3, Coming Soon.*

"My wife-to-be." Graham proudly wrapped his arm around her shoulder.

They gave each other a loving glance before Rosie held out her hand to Mitchell. "He talks about you all the time. You're a legend in our household."

"He saved my life when we were kids," Graham said.

Mitchell shook his head. "Not really."

"I've still got my broken tooth as proof."

"It's brilliant to meet you. Thanks for being our best man," Rosie said. "Graham says you have a daughter, Poppy. Is she coming to the wedding?"

"Oh, yes. Just try to stop her," Mitchell laughed.

"Rosie is going to be on lookout duty tonight," Graham said. He laid a protective hand on her belly. "She'll keep her eyes peeled while we get busy. We're just waiting for reinforcements, then we can make a start. I've asked a couple of my gardening friends to help out with no questions asked."

"You really have *gardening* buddies?" Mitchell questioned.

"Yup, love plants almost as much as my PlayStation now. The lights are all turned off on the bridge, but we don't want to use a torch and be spotted. So, we'll strip the entire panel to make sure we get the right lock. My friends will bring a couple of wheelbarrows to transport them away."

Mitchell stared at him. "I only need to save the one lock."

"We're going to save a lot more than that," Graham said.

Rosie caught Mitchell's eye. "My beloved has got something planned, but won't tell me what it is. Can you give me a clue, Mitchell?"

"I haven't told him, so you'll just have to wait," Graham said teasingly. He held up a large key ring full of lockpicks. "I've brought these along, and I'll be onto those padlocks like vultures stripping a carcass."

"You've got this all planned out. I'm impressed," Mitchell said.

Graham nodded at him. "I learned from the master."

Mitchell, Graham and Rosie moved stealthily through the back streets of the city. Rosie led the way, leading them through alleys Mitchell didn't know existed. They witnessed an animated argument taking place in the backyard of a restaurant, and two teenage boys shared a furtive cigarette. A stray dog nuzzled inside a pizza box, and a motorbike roared past them.

They rendezvoused with two men who stood with wheelbarrows at the end of a backstreet close to Redford.

"This is Mason and Tony. Meet Mitchell, a great friend of mine," Graham said.

A man who had a scar running diagonally down his left cheek stuck out a huge hand. "Mason," he said gruffly.

Tony wore a grubby tracksuit with nothing underneath his top. His greasy hair shone in the darkness. He didn't offer his hand but chewed minty gum and nodded an acknowledgement.

"They'd do *anything* for me," Graham confided quietly to Mitchell. "Can turn their hand to everything, no questions asked. I'm glad they're my friends rather than enemies. Wouldn't want that."

Mitchell gulped. "Good."

Graham turned to Mason and Tony. "I've owed Mitchy Boy here a favor for years, and he's calling it in. There's a panel of padlocks on the redbrick bridge we want to clear off. We need to keep the locks intact, no cutting them off. Mitchell is on distraction duty and I'm on lockpicks with Mason. Rosie is keeping her eye out. Tony, you guard the barrows and be ready to move quickly when we need you. Everyone clear?"

The five of them nodded. The operation was underway.

The road signs were still in place, across the mouth of the bridge, acting as a barrier so it was closed to the traffic. The streetlamps that usually illuminated the bridge were switched off, casting the pavement and road in dark shadows.

Rosie stayed close to the mouth of the bridge. She held on to a dog lead. "If I anyone asks, I can say I'm looking for my dog, who escaped his leash," she said.

Graham kissed Rosie on the cheek. "*Now* you can see why I'm marrying this woman."

Mitchell smiled at the two of them and thought how perfect they were together. It had taken Graham a while to find his match, but he had got there in the end. When he recalled Barry's words about getting back into the wild to meet someone, it didn't seem such a scary prospect any longer. It was distinctly possible.

Mitchell's palms were sweaty as he walked along the bridge with Graham and Mason.

"Point out the panel, and we'll do all the work," Graham said.

"I'll help."

"Let's keep you out of this. You don't want to lose your job."

"There's no one around to see us."

"We can't be too sure."

Mason looked around him, lifting his chin high and low. "There might be security guys patrolling the city. Rosie will spot them."

Mitchell pointed to the area of railing that Yvette's lock was attached to behind the wire fencing. "It's in the middle somewhere."

"As I said, we'll get them all," Graham said.

"What will you do with them afterward?"

Graham laid a hand on Mitchell's shoulder. "Don't you worry about that. This is my favor to you. I'll sort everything out."

Mason stared at the padlocks and whistled through his teeth. "There's a lot of them hanging there."

"Then let's get started," Graham said.

Graham and Mason made light work of snipping through the fencing and squeezing through to the other side. Graham took out his picks and handed another set to Mason. They crouched and worked quickly, seeming to instinctively know which pick to use for which lock. They spread out a couple of blankets on the pavement, so there was no clatter of metal against the ground.

For forty-five minutes, Mitchell paced nervously up and down the bridge, looking out for any security guards. A police car sped toward him and its blue light swirled and siren screeched. He held his breath readying himself for it to halt alongside him.

When it sped on past, he exhaled with a gush of relief.

His body grew limper when he saw a figure heading toward him. It was the man with the tufty black beard and he was holding a torch.

Mitchell tried to find a posture that was nonchalant and unsuspicious. "Oh, all right?" he said.

The man shone his light at Mitchell. *"You?"*

"Um, yes."

"I told you to keep away from that lock."

Mitchell held up his hands. "I'm nowhere near it." He tried to speak calmly, though he felt light-headed. "I know I'm not allowed to remove it. I just wanted to walk over this bridge one last time, while most of the locks are still in place. I'm nostalgic like that. Sorry about earlier today, I know you're just doing your job."

The man crossed his arms, unconvinced.

"Look, it's my job to cut off the padlocks and when I saw the contractors, I grew anxious about losing my job," Mitchell chattered. "What are you doing here?"

The man shrugged. "Just checking out the bridges. It's too darn hot in my apartment and I had to get out for a while."

"I know the feeling."

Mitchell glanced over his shoulder to see Graham folding in the sides of one of the blankets. He could make out the dark mound of the padlock heaps. He grasped for something else to say to distract the man. "I have a daughter..."

"Yeah?" the man said. "How old?"

"She's nine and is Word Up crazy. That band has a lot to answer for, if you ask me."

The man tutted and relaxed his arms. "Tell me about it. I mean, their hit was crap. My girl is eleven and loves it, though.

I found out she'd gotten herself a bloody Instagram account to follow them. Friends of hers were on there already, posing and pouting. Eleven years old!"

"People in this city have gone padlock crazy," Mitchell agreed.

As the two men found a common bond, a clattering noise sounded from the middle of the bridge.

The man looked over Mitchell's shoulder and raised his torch. "Did you hear something?"

Mitchell swallowed. "Um, no."

"I'd better take a look."

"Stop—" Mitchell called after him. He could see the crouched silhouettes of Graham and Mason.

As the man strode away, Rosie appeared in front of him, like magic. She held out her dog lead. "Have you guys seen my dog?" She widened her eyes with worry, and rubbed her bump. "I can't find him anywhere."

Mitchell held his breath. He caught up with the man, who lowered his torch.

"What type is he?" The man alternated his gaze between Rosie and the middle of the bridge, where the noise came from.

"A Dalmatian. You'd think it'd make him easier to spot."

"Lovely dogs, those are. I'll take a look with you. I just need to go and—"

"Ooh." Rosie stooped over and rubbed her belly. She peered down at her bump. "I think I felt something then."

The man eyed her warily. "Are you okay? Should you be out walking your dog at this time of night?"

Rosie shook her head. "Probably not. I should get home. Could you take a look for my dog with me? Then I'll go."

"Maybe call a cab. It looks like that baby could arrive at any time."

Rosie circled her tummy again and pointed down the road. "Let's try over here first?"

Mitchell jerked his head. "I'm heading back over the bridge. I'll check everything looks okay on my way past."

"I'd appreciate that, mate," the man said.

Mitchell exhaled with relief as Rosie led the man away. He hurried over to the middle of the bridge where he found Mason and Graham still hunched over.

His friend looked up. "You gave me a fright then—thought we'd been caught."

"Rosie's just headed someone off."

"We're almost done, Mitchy. See you back in the alleyway in twenty minutes."

Mitchell took the long way around, walking across Redford in the opposite direction and then toward the Yacht bridge.

Preparations for the opening event were being ramped up. A small stage was being erected with floodlights around it. A line of three white vans were parked up. Mitchell stood and watched the reflection of the moon rippling on the surface of the river. He wondered what Anita would say if she could see him here, dressed all in black and rescuing a padlock. But this time he couldn't conjure up her copper curls and red coat in his mind. He saw Liza instead and he frowned, surprised.

What was *she* doing in his head?

A car horn sounded and, feeling flummoxed, he walked briskly away.

He made his way toward the alley as Graham had instructed until a noise came out of the darkness.

"Pssst, over here." Mason beckoned him over. He pointed to where the two wheelbarrows were parked up, level full of locks. Graham kneeled down on the ground, sifting through a pile of them while Tony pointed a torch at his hands.

Mitchell gasped at the amount of them. "How many are

there?" From his daily counting, he reckoned there must be a few hundred. "How am I going to move them?"

"I told you, Mitchy Boy," Graham said. "You don't have to worry about anything. And, here it is, voilà." He held out a heart-shaped lock in the palm of his hand.

Mitchell peered at it in the darkness. "That's not the right one," he said and crouched down to help his friend. "Yvette's is bigger and shinier."

"Oh, okay." They worked their way through more of the locks. "How about this one?" Graham said.

Mitchell saw the engraved words *my heart is always yours* glinting. His shoulders dropped, as if he'd slid into a hot bath at the end of a hard day. "That's it," he said, his voice full of relief.

Graham handed it over to Mitchell who wrapped his fingers around it. Although it was a cheap chunk of metal, in that moment it felt as precious as a diamond ring. Sheila could have Yvette's lock. "Thank you."

"Glad to pay you back. I hope Liza will be happy."

"I think she will be." Mitchell pushed the padlock into his back pocket. "Where are you taking the rest of the locks?"

Graham tapped the side of his nose. "You'll see soon enough." He picked a few padlocks off the ground and dropped them back into the wheelbarrows.

Tony and Mason heaved on the handles, turned the barrows around and wheeled them off down the dark alley without saying a word.

"Later," Graham said to Mitchell. He and Rosie wrapped their arms around each other's waists and stepped out of the alleyway back onto the road. "See you at our wedding, best man."

It had gone past eleven o'clock when Mitchell got back to Angel House. The lobby was dark without Carl's desk lamp turned on. There was a neat stack of papers and a set of origami hearts arranged in a line.

As Mitchell walked through the lobby, Carl appeared from the door to the basement. "Oh, Mr. Fisher," he said. He stood upright and smoothed down his tie.

There was giggling and Susan emerged behind him. The two of them shared an embarrassed smile. "Susan was helping with my, um—" Carl said.

"Letter writing," she said quickly and nudged Carl in his side. "It's going well."

Carl blushed.

Mitchell smiled to himself and stepped toward the lift. "Good night to you both."

"Sorry, Mr. Fisher, but it's out of order again," Carl said. "I did tell Liza. Susan brought some more letters for you and I dropped them off with her."

"*More* of them?"

"Only fifteen or so," Susan said with a smile. "That's all. People in Upchester have really caught the letter writing bug."

"It'll all stop soon," Mitchell said with fresh understanding. "The new bridge will open and the padlocks on the old bridges are going to be removed. There's a good story for you."

Susan frowned at him. "I heard about that. What will happen to them all? Are they going to be destroyed? What about all the peoples' messages?"

The same thoughts had also occurred to Mitchell. However, after lurking around on Redford tonight, and the effort it had taken to remove just one panel's worth of locks, there was really nothing he could do about it.

"I don't know," he said. "But I hope it takes people's thoughts away from writing letters."

After Mitchell had climbed the five flights of stairs and opened the door to his apartment, Liza met him in his hallway. She held her finger to her lips and pointed back over her shoulder. "Shhh, Poppy's asleep. She dropped off an hour ago."

"Oh, okay," he whispered back. "Thanks for looking after her."

Mitchell tiptoed after Liza into the sitting room where Poppy was curled up on the sofa. A small pile of letters lay by her feet.

"We've been chatting about her project and playing board games. She plays a mean game of Monopoly."

"Did she make you read lots of letters?"

"A few of them. Poppy was all excited about them at first, but then wanted to play instead. She's given me a small stack of them to look at." She stifled a yawn. "Sorry, I'm a bit tired. Can I take them with me to read?"

"If you don't mind?" he said.

"Some of them are really touching, and the things people are willing to share with a stranger rather than their own spouse is enlightening." Liza looked down and frowned. "Oh look, your hands are all dirty…"

Mitchell pushed a hand into his pocket and held out Yvette's padlock on his greasy palm. "My friend wanted to rescue more than just Yvette's lock. Many more."

"You got it?" Liza gasped. She took it from him and cupped it in both hands, as if it was water that might trickle away. "Thank you so much, Mitchell. It will mean so much to Mum, one less thing for her to fret about, and to me, too."

There was a fragility in her voice that made Mitchell want to wrap his arms around her. He wanted to tell her that everything would be okay. Instead, he said, "I'll wash my hands then call you a cab. The lift isn't working again, so I'll walk downstairs with you."

She picked up her bag. "It's okay, Carl said he'd hail a taxi for me. He knocked on your door earlier to drop off the letters and ask me lots of questions."

Mitchell groaned. "That sounds like Carl. Please let me do this for you instead, I'll only be a moment."

Liza smiled at him. "Okay, I'll wait."

Mitchell checked on Poppy, who was sleeping soundly, and washed his hands in the bathroom to get rid of the grease. He phoned for a taxi, then walked with Liza downstairs.

When they reached the lobby, the area was deserted again. The main lights were still turned off but Carl's lamp was now lit up. Mitchell picked up one of the origami hearts.

"What's that?" Liza asked.

"Carl makes things out of paper. He's really talented." He handed the heart to her so she could see. "Here."

She held it up and peered closely at it, before she held it to her chest. "Oh, it's so pretty. I don't want to squash it. Thank you," she said.

Mitchell hadn't meant for her to keep it and wasn't sure how to tell her this. A text message pinged through on his mobile to say that Liza's cab was ready outside. He let the heart go and led the way to the entrance. They stood outside on the front step together, self-consciously, like the start of a dance when you don't know how your partner is going to move.

"Thank you," he said. "I'm making a habit of saying that to you."

Liza tucked the letters under her arm. "I've enjoyed my evening and I really appreciate you retrieving Yvette's padlock. You're a star."

The taxi driver gave an impatient pip of his horn.

Liza leaned in and kissed Mitchell on his cheek. Her hand rested gently on his upper arm.

He felt an unexpected trickle of calmness running through his body, as if he'd gone on holiday and just stepped off a plane into the hazy heat. He stood still, enjoying the sensation and not wanting it to end.

If he didn't have a daughter, if he wasn't bereaved, if he hadn't shared a smile of connection with Yvette on the bridge—this might be a moment he'd invite Liza back up to his apartment for a coffee. His mouth felt dry and he had to swallow before he could say, "Good night."

"Night," she said in return, and got into the cab. "Thank you for the heart. I love it."

Mitchell felt his stomach flip as she drove away. And, as he raised his hand to give her a late wave, he felt the lightest specks of rain on his fingertips.

22

BISCUITS

A wind had started up and the gray sky seemed to press against the windows, making Mitchell's bedroom feel darker and smaller. The sun skulked behind a dark cloud and the air in the apartment felt claggy and still.

At the breakfast table, Poppy slumped with tiredness after staying up late. She ate her muesli in silence, grunting at Mitchell's questions about her school project.

He called Russ's PA, Clarice, and explained he needed to take some more time off work to collect his tools. He also admitted he'd finished work early on a couple of other occasions. Embarrassingly, Clarice knew all about his accident and gushed that a couple of the girls in the office had been talking about him admiringly. Russ knew about his extenuating circumstances, and they came to an arrangement where Mitchell would use part of his annual holiday allowance to cover his impromptu time off, including the collection of his toolbox.

After escorting Poppy to school, Mitchell made his way across the city toward the address sent to him in the mysterious text message. He wondered why the person had reported their own brother.

Trash rustled along the street and pressed against his ankles as he walked to the house on Whitby Street. On a brown patch of ground, two mongrel dogs tore around a broken pram.

This was an area in the city Mitchell never ventured to. There was a pressure building up behind his eyes that he attributed to the change in the weather. He rubbed the space between them and read the message on Barry's phone again to make sure he'd got the right address.

Pop music blared from inside the house. Mitchell rang the doorbell and waited until the door opened a little. A safety chain tugged tight across the opening and an eye appeared at the gap.

"Yeah?" a woman demanded.

"Um, I'm Mitchell Fisher," he said. "I'm here for my toolbox."

"You on your own?"

"Yes."

The chain rattled and the door opened fully. "Follow me. The culprit is on the sofa. He can get real nervy about strangers."

Mitchell followed the woman along a red carpet that was specked with grit. She wore hoop earrings with the circumference of small saucers and supermarket style Ugg boots. The white walls of the hallway were full of scuff marks and cheap framed pictures.

"I'm Margie, and Petey is very sorry." She raised her voice as she entered her front room. "He's *very* sorry. Aren't you, Petey?"

Mitchell didn't hear a response.

"Come in, love."

They entered the crowded sitting room, which was covered in piles of objects. He spotted a full-length mirror, a large shiny lamp and a stainless steel shovel. He wondered if they were ready to be taken to a charity shop or car boot sale. A teenager sat slouched in an armchair, scratching his arm and watching an Australian soap opera on the TV. Mitchell took a second look at him. He recognized him from Redford, carrying a shovel, just before Yvette fell.

Margie swiped his hand away. "Stop picking your skin. What have you got to say to the man, Petey?"

"I dunno."

"You're very sorry, aren't you? Very, *very* sorry."

"I'm very sorry, Margie."

"Say it to 'im, not me."

The young man gave Mitchell the briefest look. "Sorry."

"For *what*?" Margie shouted at him.

"For taking your toolbox, mister."

Mitchell followed Petey's sheepish gaze to where his toolbox sat in the middle of the floor. On top of it were a pizza cutter and a chunky necklace made out of plastic gems.

Margie picked up a silver sequined skirt and tossed it off the sofa so Mitchell could sit down. "He's got this thing, you see," she said. "He collects shiny stuff, can't help it. It was okay when he was a kid, funny even. But now he's an adult..." She shook her head. "Had a busy one, that day, he did. Came back with a right load of gear I'm trying to trace and return, a flippin' shovel included."

Petey looking longingly at Mitchell's toolbox.

"Eyes off," Margie snapped. She moved the necklace and pizza cutter off the top of it. "You've caused enough trouble, you 'ave."

Mitchell heard the strain in her voice. He had originally

thought she was in her forties, but now glancing at the dark circles under her eyes, he could see she was much younger. "It's okay," he said softly.

"No. It's not." She rubbed her face with both hands and held them there for a few moments, as if she was counting during a game of hide-and-seek. When she let them fall away, her eyes glistened with tears. "Look. Can I make you a brew or something?"

"A cup of tea would be good."

As soon as she left the room, Petey turned up the volume on the TV even higher. Australian voices boomed around the room.

"Turn that down *now*," Margie yelled.

Petey stuck his bottom teeth over his top lip and stared at the TV, before switching it off. Then his face appeared to morph into a child's and he flashed the sweetest smile at Mitchell. "Sorry, mister."

Margie set a cup of brick-orange tea on a glass coffee table, in front of Mitchell. "No biscuits, sorry."

"It's fine, I'm just relieved to have my tools back. I need them for work."

"Look through the box before you take it. Make sure nothing is missing. I didn't tell Petey you were coming or else he might 'ave vanished and took your box with 'im."

"How did you find me?"

"My boyfriend, Malcolm, saw a note on the bridge, and then he saw Petey's *new* toolbox. Put two and two together, I did. Petey told Malcolm he'd got a job, and the tools were for that." She tutted loudly. "I told 'im our Petey can't concentrate on work. Had a fall when he was a kid that damaged him." She tapped her temple. "Never been the same since. I was supposed to be looking after 'im that day. One minute

he was sat on the bed and next thing he's on the floor, crying 'is eyes out.

"As he got older, we could tell things weren't quite right
with 'im. Ma blamed me." Margie wiped at her nose. "She
couldn't deal with 'im being different so she scarpered and left
us to it. So, I got 'im. Had to be a flippin' ma and a sister to
'im after that. He's a nice kid really, but can't resist shiny stuff.
Walks around the city with sticky fingers." She leaned forward
and squinted at Mitchell. "You gonna tell on 'im or what?"

Mitchell shook his head. "No. Please don't worry. I'm
pleased to get this back."

"You've got to be honest, don't you? Luckily the police have
been good with 'im. 'Petey up to his old tricks again?' one
said when I took a necklace to the station. He just gets obsessed with stuff." She raised her voice again. "Did you steal
this man's toolbox from the bridge, Petey?"

"He left it there. Jumped off, he did," Petey replied.

"Don't tell me no fibs."

"It's true," Mitchell intervened. "I helped a lady who fell
from the bridge into the river. When I got back to the bridge
my toolbox was gone."

Margie closed an eye. "I heard about that. Was she all
right?"

"I'm still trying to find her."

She nodded once. "Oi, Petey. Did you see that woman on
the bridge? Did you see where she went to?"

"Stop it, Margie."

"You need to tell this fella. Tell 'im, or he might have you
down the station again. You 'ear me?"

Peter pulled on his T-shirt sleeve. "She wore yellow."

"Yes, she did." Mitchell sat forward. "The woman who fell
wore a yellow dress."

"She met her twin."

"A twin? Really?" Margie said. "Any other nuggets in your 'ead?"

"*She* was shiny. Not like you," Petey snapped back.

The two of them glared at each other, and Petey folded his arms. He peered at Mitchell through his fringe. "Her twin was shiny." He pressed a finger to his collarbone and drew a semicircle.

Margie puffed out her cheeks. "Might have known it. You spotted 'er necklace."

He nodded. "Big and gold and shiny."

"You should keep your eyes to yourself."

"Big, shiny pineapple."

A shiver ran down Mitchell's spine and Liza's photo flashed into his mind. The three sisters in a row, Liza, Yvette and Naomi. They looked so alike.

"So, you saw a woman and she wore a gold pineapple necklace?" he confirmed.

Peter nodded and his eyes glowed. "Shone like the sun, it did."

Margie tossed her head at Mitchell. "That mean something to you?"

Mitchell breathed deeply. He stood up and took hold of his toolbox handle without checking all the tools were inside. "Yes. It does. Can you tell me anything else about the twin?"

"You're wasting your time," Margie said. "He'd have been looking at her necklace more than her."

Petey shrugged a shoulder, agreeing.

Mitchell nodded. "Thank you, Margie. I should give you a reward."

"No need for that. Just doing what's right." Margie bristled. She stood up and wrapped her arm around Petey's neck in a headlock. She shook her fist in his face before pressing the lightest kiss against his forehead. "He's all right, really. Not such a bad 'un."

Peter grinned up at her. "Love ya, sis."

Margie accompanied Mitchell to the door. "It don't get no easier," she sniffed as she unfastened the latch.

He wasn't sure what he could say. "You're doing your best."

She shook her head and opened the door. "It never feels good enough."

As Mitchell walked away, the clouds had grown even darker and rain pricked his cheeks. He pictured Poppy making a crown with her fingers behind her head, and Liza doing the same.

But most of all he saw the large gold pineapple necklace that Naomi Bradfield wore in the photo of her laughing with her sisters. Had she really been on the bridge that day, at the same time as Yvette? What was she hiding from them?

When he turned the corner, the rain fell harder, drops hissing as they hit the still-hot pavement. After texting Liza to tell her he was going to call around on his way home, Mitchell dug his hands into his pockets. He walked quickly, curving his back against the weather, wondering just what was going on in the Bradfield family.

23

PINEAPPLE

When Mitchell approached Liza's house, he felt fidgety with nerves at what he had to tell her. The rain had yet to come down fully, but the clouds were growing even darker and wet specks were more frequent on the pavement. He placed his toolbox on Liza's doorstep and knocked on her door. As he waited for her to answer, his insides churned.

She greeted him with a friendly smile and it felt good to be so welcomed. "This is a nice surprise," she said. "Luckily for you, I'm not working this afternoon."

"Hi," he said, the lightness in his voice not reflecting the turmoil he felt.

When he followed Liza into the hallway, he noticed there was something different about her today. Her perfume had a tropical, fruity aroma and her lips were bright pink when they were usually bare. He wondered if he had caught her on her way out somewhere, but she didn't mention anything.

"You've got your toolbox back," she noted happily as they reached the kitchen. "That's so great. Cup of tea?"

"I thought it was gone forever." He could hear that he sounded too chipper. "And I'd love a drink."

She picked up her teapot and dropped in a couple of tea bags. "Where did you find your tools?"

"A young man called Petey took them from the bridge."

"He stole them from you?"

"I don't think he could help himself."

She stared at him quizzically.

"He collects shiny things," Mitchell explained. "I think his sister has a lot on her plate dealing with him and the stuff he brings home. He took my toolbox and a shovel that day."

"Hmm, that's most unusual..."

Mitchell pursed his lips, thinking of how to broach the subject of Naomi. He must have paused a bit too long, because Liza noticed.

"Anything wrong?" she asked, setting down two teacups and a jug of milk on the kitchen table. She sat down and poured him a cup of tea.

Mitchell pulled out a chair and joined her. He sipped the tea slowly. "Well, um, Petey said he saw Yvette, before and *after* her accident," he said. "I think he might have been watching her..."

She raised an eyebrow. "I don't like the sound of that. It seems suspicious."

"No, not in that way." He realized he had to just spit it out. "Petey said he saw Yvette meet with her twin on the bridge. Someone who looked like her, and she wore a gold pineapple pendant. I thought it sounded like Naomi."

Liza digested his words and began fiddling with her pink Perspex earring. "Well, it can't possibly have been," she said snippily. "This Petey person stole from you, so he can't be very trustworthy. Naomi would have said something to me, if she'd seen Yvette that day."

Mitchell held her gaze. "He gave a clear description of her."

Liza blew into her tea but didn't drink it, nursing the cup instead. "You're right," she said after a long while. "This is very strange, and I'm not sure what to think. Why would Naomi have been on the bridge with Yvette? She can't possibly have seen Yvette and not told us…"

"Perhaps you should ask her," Mitchell suggested gently.

"But then she might think it sounds crazy, too."

For a while, the only sound between them was the rattle of china cups against saucers as they sipped their tea.

Eventually, Liza gave a loud tut and Mitchell wasn't sure if it was aimed at him or not. "I'll have to speak to her, won't I? She's the only one who can tell us that Petey was mistaken. He might have seen Naomi on the bridge another day, or he could have totally concocted this story. That's possible, isn't it?"

Even though he thought it was unlikely, Mitchell nodded.

Liza took her mobile out of her pocket. Her eyes swept around the room as she waited for Naomi to answer the call.

Mitchell's heart pumped and he straightened up a place mat on the table.

"She's not picking up." Liza gnawed on her bottom lip. "Maybe she's gone shopping or something. I need her to tell me that she wasn't on the bridge that day, and that she doesn't know anything about Yvette's disappearance… She can't possibly have lied to me about this."

He heard urgency rising in her words. "We can go there now, if you like?" he offered. "I just need to be at home when Poppy gets back from the school club."

Liza hesitated at first, but then nodded. She grabbed her jacket from the back of her chair and pushed her arm clumsily down the sleeve. "Please. Let's go."

When she and Mitchell got outside, they both slid silently into her car and the sky above looked gloomier than ever.

Naomi's house was a half hour drive away. She lived on an estate of executive semidetached brick houses, which had at least two cars sitting on each of the driveways.

"I like this area," Mitchell said, looking around admiringly. He imagined insurance brokers and business owners might live here. It was somewhere he and Anita would have aspired to live.

After parking, Liza pulled on her handbrake. "I'm really proud of her. She's totally gorgeous and has a lovely home and family. And Yvette is so clever, too..."

She didn't elaborate further and Mitchell thought she sounded rueful. He was an only child himself, and wasn't used to the intricacies of growing up with siblings and the competition that might bring about. Sometimes Liza was so bright and full of life, and at other times her vulnerability felt raw to him. He side-glanced at her deep brown eyes, and couldn't remain silent. "You're all those things, too," he said awkwardly.

Liza's cheeks flushed. "Thanks, that's nice to hear, among all *this*... But, I wasn't fishing for compliments, you know?"

Mitchell opened his car door. "Come on," he said kindly. "Let's go and find out what's going on for ourselves."

When Naomi answered the door, she wore a string of spaghetti stuck to the front of her T-shirt. Her greeting was harassed rather than friendly. "Oh, it's you guys. Was I expecting you?"

Liza shook her head. "It wasn't a planned visit."

"We were, um, passing by," Mitchell said, and it sounded false, even to him.

"Well, that's okay. I mean, I was in the middle of tidying up, but..." She cast her hand around weakly at the piles of toys and shoes in her hallway. "Sometimes it's difficult to make even the slightest impact on this stuff."

Mitchell and Liza followed Naomi through to her kitchen.

"I've run out of tea bags, but I have black currant cordial," she said. "Or milk."

"I'm not thirsty, thanks," Mitchell said.

"Me neither," Liza agreed.

"Just me then." Naomi made herself a glass of cordial and smiled expectantly, waiting for Mitchell or Liza to speak.

Liza cleared her throat. "Well, we're here because after Mitchell helped Yvette from the river, someone stole his toolbox from the bridge... We didn't mention it over dinner."

Naomi looked at him. "Oh, sorry about that." She shrugged slightly, as if she didn't understand why she needed to know this.

"My friend made a poster to appeal for its return," Mitchell said. "A lady got in touch to say her brother had taken it. When I went to collect the tools, he told me that Yvette met with a woman, after her accident."

"Oh...right."

Mitchell saw the tendons tighten in Naomi's neck.

"Did you meet Yvette on the bridge that day, Naomi? After Mitchell rescued her?" Liza asked firmly.

Naomi placed a hand against her chest. Her eyes appeared hurt, questioning how her sister could possibly suggest such a thing. *"Me?"*

"Yes, you."

Naomi's nostrils flared. "No, of course not," she said sharply. She took a gulp from her drink then poured the rest into the sink.

Liza observed her. "The man said Yvette met her twin on the bridge, and she wore a gold pineapple necklace."

Naomi's face flushed bright pink.

Liza leaned forward as if she was about to leap over the table. "This is important, Naomi. Yvette could be in danger. Did you, or did you not, meet her on the bridge ten days ago?"

Naomi plucked at the piece of spaghetti on her T-shirt. "What danger?" Her voice shook.

Liza took the letter, signed with a V, from her pocket and tossed it onto the table. "I found this in her mailbox."

Naomi tentatively picked it up. As she read it, the pink in her cheeks became a mottled red. "At Yvette's apartment?"

"Yes." Liza took the letter back from her and read aloud. "'Don't worry, I'll find you. Won't be long. I have eyes and ears everywhere.'"

Naomi shrank back.

"If this is from Victor, he could be closing in on Yvette," Liza pleaded.

"I can't tell you *anything*."

"But you do know something?" Mitchell prompted.

Naomi pressed her back against the sink. Liza stood up and placed a hand on her sister's shoulder. "What is it? What do you know?"

Her sister shook her head frantically. "I just *can't…*"

Mitchell and Liza shared a look. They both silently agreed Naomi was keeping a secret.

"You said Victor had been in prison after Yvette discovered his stealing," Liza said. "We think he's written to Yvette and he sounds angry. What if he gets to her before we do? Our sister has been missing for almost a *year*, Naomi. Mum's health is getting worse, too."

"I care about Mum—" Naomi interjected.

"Yes, so if you know something, anything at all, you've got to tell us. *Please*. Do you know where Yvette is? You don't have to speak, just nod your head. That's all you've got to do. Then we can help her. We can help you."

Mitchell and Liza sat for what felt like the longest time before Naomi gave a slight nod.

Liza exhaled. "Good. We're getting somewhere."

"I made a promise." Naomi slumped against her worktop.

"Why haven't you said something before?"

"Because she's my sister."

"I'm your sister, too," Liza snapped.

"But I *can't* break Yvette's confidence."

Liza threw her arms up. "So where do we go from here? How long have you known where Yvette is? When were you going to tell me and Mum?"

"I've only known since she called me ten days ago from the bridge. She asked if I could help her. She's been—" Naomi cut off her own sentence. "Look, it's been hard, keeping this from you."

Liza's gaze was steely. "But you're refusing to say anything else? Like how she is, or where she is? Or why she went missing?"

Naomi squirmed. "I know less than you think."

"Only a few minutes ago, you said you knew nothing at all."

The two sisters refused to look at each other.

Mitchell picked up the letter from the table. "If Victor did write this letter, and it looks like he did, could Yvette be in trouble if he finds her? If you're not sure she'll be safe, then please—tell us what you know."

"I won't break Yvette's confidence, but I *will* speak to her," Naomi said eventually.

"Good. Thank you." Mitchell tried to catch Liza's eye to indicate they should leave and let things settle. But she wouldn't look at him, either.

"I'm so sorry," Naomi said. She placed her hand on Liza's arm, her eyes pleading for understanding.

But Liza shook it off. "You need to speak to our sister. *Pronto,*" she said with a point of her finger. "We'll let ourselves out."

She stormed into the hallway and yanked the front door open. Mitchell struggled to keep up with her.

As they strode away down the path together, Naomi shouted after them, "I made a promise to Yvette, what could I do? What would you have done?"

SWIMMING

Mitchell needed something to occupy his mind until he heard back from Liza. She was hanging on until Naomi got in touch with Yvette and he needed a distraction, a plan of action to concentrate on.

"You're quiet," Poppy said, joining him at the breakfast table. She pushed a hand into the muesli box and pulled out a raisin to nibble on.

"Am I?"

"Yep. You're usually happier when you've spent time with Liza."

"Really?" He realized he did feel cheerier when he was with her, during those moments they were talking about music or making chili together.

"She's sunny," Poppy said.

It was a good way to describe her, not a word he'd think to

use about someone. "I thought we could go swimming this morning," he said. "We've not been to the pool for a while."

"With Liza?" she said hopefully.

"Just me and you. Liza's busy with family stuff. She *thinks* she's found Yvette."

Poppy's eyes widened. "Where is she?"

"I'm not sure yet." He ran a hand through his hair. "But I'm sure everything's going to be all right."

Poppy sprinkled muesli into her bowl. "Ace."

As they ate their cereal together, Mitchell's throat felt tight, and he couldn't really be sure if he'd just told Poppy a lie or not.

The swimming pool was an obstacle course of people. There were the serious swimmers who wore black latex caps and goggles and front-crawled with the determination of Olympic athletes. Kids with orange inflatable armbands splashed around with their parents, and a large group of teenage boys pushed each other's heads under the water.

Mitchell and Poppy bobbed around in the middle of the pool, where Poppy could just about stand up.

"How many lengths should we do?" Mitchell asked. "Ten? Fifteen?"

Poppy tiptoed from one foot to the other. "Can't we just play?"

"It's good to have a target. Good exercise, too..."

"It's good for *you*," she muttered.

He watched as she sank down until the water slipped over her head. She swam around on the bottom of the pool, circling him like a shark.

When she burst upward, he felt bewildered, not sure how to join in the game. Anita had been the playful one in the pool, and he was the one who remembered the towels and

money for the lockers. "Shall we do a length and time ourselves?" he suggested.

She shook her head. "Remember when you used to swish
me in the water and pretend I was in a washing machine?"

He smiled as he recalled it. "You were only little then."

She stared at him, her eyes a bit puffy. "Sometimes I don't
want to be big." She turned and swam away from him until
she reached the far edge of the pool, hanging on to the side.

He breaststroked quickly after her. When he reached her,
he said, "I'm sorry, Pops—I kind of forget how to have fun
sometimes. I'm not much good at it."

She swiped her hand in the water so it splashed his face.
Her eyes instantly widened apologetically at what she'd done.

He was about to tell her off, but thought of her words,
about her wanting to be small sometimes. He felt the same
way, too. So, he slapped his hand against the water, splashing both of them.

Poppy gave a delighted giggle and he took hold of her
under her arms and pulled her away from the side. He spun
her around him, back and forth.

"Washing machine," she laughed. "Put me on a spin cycle,
Dad."

His arms ached and they both knew she was too old for
this, but for the next few minutes they didn't care.

After Mitchell had let her go, Poppy reached up onto the
side of the pool and pulled two yellow floats into the water.
"You've got to swim with your feet together, like a mermaid,"
she told him.

Mitchell was about to protest, but she had already kicked
off from the side and all he could do was follow her. "I'm a
dolphin instead," he called after her, and an elderly woman
nearby gave him a strange look. "Watch out."

After they'd got out of the pool and dried off, Mitchell met

Poppy beside the dispensing machine in the café. She hadn't dried her hair properly so water created a dark bib around the neck of her T-shirt.

He remembered how she used to love putting money into the slot and watching the crisps and chocolate bars jiggle along until they dropped down into the drawer below. They hadn't done it since Anita died.

"Do you want to share a bag of crisps?" he asked.

Poppy studied the contents of the machine. "Salt and vinegar crisps make me cough," she said.

"I like ready salted best."

"Boring," she sang.

"They're a classic, like me." He produced a pound coin. "How about we compromise, with a big bag of cheese and onion?"

She lifted her chin and quoted at him. "It's not a compromise. It's adapting to each other's needs." She took his money.

Mitchell wondered where these words had come from, because they sounded too grown-up. But then she flipped to being a child again, excitedly peering into the machine as the crisp packet juddered toward her.

They bought hot chocolate from another machine, in plastic cups too hot to hold. The murky brown liquid burned their tongues.

When the phone vibrated in Mitchell's pocket, he ignored it, wanting to focus on the time with his daughter.

It was only when they arrived back at the apartment that he picked up the message.

I've spoken to Yvette, Liza informed him.

Her words were too short, for her, and he replied immediately. Do you know where she is?

Yes x.

Mitchell felt a wave of relief hit him so hard he felt he might topple over. Liza hadn't offered up any further information and he didn't want to pry, so he simply asked, Do you need me?

Her reply took ten minutes to come through. Yes, she said. I think I do.

Just tell me where and when, he replied.

He met Liza in the Dala café an hour later.

Poppy had insisted she was okay to remain in the apartment on her own for half an hour. She was going to make toast and listen to music. "I'm nine years old, Dad." She rolled her eyes at him. "Not a kid."

He told her to call him if she needed anything at all and he left to meet Liza.

When Mitchell saw Liza nursing a coffee cup to her chest, she looked like a smaller version of herself. He bought a soda and sat down next to her.

"Are you okay?" he asked, unsure.

She nodded. "I just feel dazed. I can't believe I'm sitting here and my sister has been missing for all this time, and now I've just spoken to her on the phone, and it's like all this hasn't really happened at all. I feel as if I've got off a roller coaster and I'm all unsteady and can't even walk straight. It was so amazing to hear her voice," she said breathlessly. "But she didn't sound like herself."

"She's been gone a long time. It must be very strange."

"I know—I'm going to see her this evening. We can talk, and I can hug her and find out what the hell has gone on." Her lips trembled and then she was crying, her shoulders jerking and tears flooding her cheeks. "I'm sorry," she mumbled as she tried to wipe them away. "It's all the relief and worry and stress coming out of me."

He shot out his arm and pulled her close to him, feeling her wet face against his shoulder.

"This is *so* embarrassing."

"It's not. This is a huge thing that you've found her."

She let her emotions flow. Each time she tried to say she was fine, her chin shook and the tears came again. "Sorry," she kept saying.

"It's okay," he repeated. "It's okay."

He wished that he had been able to let himself go like this, allow his grief to flood out of him after Anita died, so it had somewhere to go rather than churning inside him. He sometimes imagined it as a sponge in his stomach, all squeezed up in a tight ball, trying to avoid the day it might expand.

She peered up at him and patted her nose with a paper napkin. "I'm *so* glad I met you, Mitchell. You've been amazing."

Her words made him swoon and he took a moment to enjoy the feeling. He'd tried so hard with Poppy for the last three years, never sure he was achieving the best for her. And now he'd felt like he'd got an A star in a school report from Liza. "I'm glad I met you, too," he said.

They smiled shyly at each other.

Liza took a few moments to compose herself. She sipped her cold coffee and smoothed a hand over her hair. "I'll need to put my makeup back on before I meet Yvette, or else she won't recognize me. I just wanted to see you first. It's like you're a defibrillator or something, giving me a shot of energy."

"You, too," he admitted.

They held hands under the table and it felt right.

After a few seconds, Liza glanced at the watch on her other wrist. "I should go."

"Do you want me to come with you?"

She shook her head and stood up. "This is something we

need to do as a family. Me, Naomi, Yvette and Mum. The Bradfields together."

He understood. "Okay, just let me know what I can do to help."

"Will do."

He walked with her to the door of the café. "I'm going that way," she said, pointing in the opposite direction to Angel House. "Wish me luck."

He watched her weave around people on the pavement, the purple highlights in her hair gleaming, and then she was gone. And Mitchell felt a slug of unease about what Yvette's story really was, and why she had hidden from her family for so long.

Later that evening, after he and Poppy had looked out of her bedroom window and she was settled in bed, he received a text from Liza.

Yvette wants to meet you in person, tomorrow if you're free? I can look after Poppy.

His heart leaped and he held the phone to his chest for a while, savoring this moment. Images flashed through his head of Yvette in her yellow dress, her smile on the bridge and lying in his arms on the riverbank.

Although he'd been on a few dates, it was the first time he'd felt the sweetness of a connection to another woman since Anita. He now knew it hadn't been desire, or a longing for her. It had been more of a recognition that she was someone in need of help in her life, too. Her smile, and helping her from the water, had helped to jump-start his life again.

"What is it, Dad?" Poppy asked him.

Mitchell showed her the message, and she nodded readily that she'd like to see Liza.

"Are you excited about meeting Yvette?" she asked.

"Yes." He nodded. "I'm intrigued, and relieved, and exhausted. I'm glad Liza has found her."

Poppy chewed her lip. "We will still see Liza, won't we? Now Yvette has been found."

Mitchell pondered upon this. Although he'd hadn't known Liza for very long, he already couldn't imagine his life without her in it. However, what the shape of their relationship might be was too complicated to think about right now. "Yes, of course," he said.

"Good." Poppy smiled.

Mitchell read Liza's message and tapped out his own in reply. Where and when should I meet Yvette?

It took half an hour before she got back to him with more detail.

In the park tomorrow, the conservatory at noon.

25

PARK

It felt ridiculous to him, but Mitchell had no idea what to wear to meet Yvette. He toyed with donning his work polo shirt, so she might recognize him more easily. Or should he dress smartly, or wear his usual weekend outfit of jeans and a T-shirt?

In the end, he decided on his newest dark blue jeans and a short-sleeved white button-up shirt.

The conservatory was somewhere he used to go with Anita when she was pregnant with Poppy. With her heightened senses and rounded belly, she couldn't get enough of the smell of the chrysanthemums. They used to trail their hands across soft ferns and talk baby names. The thought of going there again without her felt unbearably painful.

At 11:30 a.m., Liza parked her car briefly on the pavement outside Angel House and Poppy jumped in. They both waved at him and he was left alone, in this strange situation, where he was finally going to meet the stranger he had helped two weeks ago.

Before he set off to the park, Mitchell sat on the bed and took Anita's still-sealed lilac envelope out of his bedside drawer. He set the letter down on his lap.

"This is it," he confided to it. "I'm going to meet Yvette and I don't know how to feel, whether this is some kind of closure, or the beginning of something new."

He looked to his side, hoping Anita might be there with all the answers to his emotions and the thoughts rattling around inside him. He wanted to see her copper-brown curls and her smile, but there was only him.

When he placed her letter back in his drawer, he noticed the ones he'd left on top of his nightstand were gone. Poppy must have picked them up to pass on to Liza to look through for her school project, and he was glad he'd removed any unsuitable ones.

As Mitchell headed toward the park, he huddled under an umbrella against the rain. He felt his meeting with Yvette was going to be a momentous occasion, like starting college, or a first day in a new job. Her fall had shaken up his life like a snowdome, and he hoped meeting her would help things settle back down. But somehow, he knew things wouldn't ever be the same again.

As he neared the wrought-iron gates of the park, Mitchell rehearsed in his head what he might say to her. By the time he approached the conservatory, his heart was pounding. He wished the rain wasn't hammering down so hard, and that it was a sunny day, so the conservatory would be flooded with light. The anticipation of meeting Yvette again and discovering her story made reverberations thump through his body.

Each step he took thudded loudly, each of his breaths deafened him.

He saw a woman open one of the conservatory doors and shake out her red umbrella. She was blonde and wore a beige mac with a wide navy scarf around her neck—not Yvette, he thought with a bolt of disappointment.

He wondered why she hadn't chosen a café to meet instead. However, he supposed if Victor was at large, then a conservatory in the park in the pouring rain was less conspicuous.

When he entered the conservatory, he saw the red umbrella propped against the wall, water pooling on the ground. There were four rooms, he remembered, and the blonde woman stood in the next one, bending over the roses.

The air was hot and the hundreds of small panes of glass surrounding him were all steamed up. There was a small fountain made out of a wooden barrel and a terrapin let the water trickle down onto its shell.

He stood at the door, looking out for Yvette, but he didn't see anyone else. After a few moments, he headed into the other room. He cleared his throat to warn the woman in beige of his presence so he didn't take her by surprise.

When she turned her head to the side, he saw the slight hump on her nose.

His pulse soared.

A voice in his head told him, *"It's her,"* but his brain argued against it.

If this was Yvette, she didn't look how she did in his memory. He wondered if he had assembled a Photofit image of her in his head that wasn't holding together in real life.

She looked at him then gave a second glance.

"Are you Mitchell? Mitchell Fisher?"

And when he heard her voice, he knew it was her.

"Yvette?"

"Yes. *Yes.*"

They grinned at each other and this was the moment he had been hoping for, since their encounter on the bridge and on the riverbank. The few seconds that passed between them felt like an hour, as their eyes met and stayed with each other.

"Sorry. Gosh, you look so different," she said. "To how I remember..."

"I do?"

"It's funny, but in my head, you were really tall, like, six feet two."

He felt his jaw stiffen defensively. "You had dark hair, when I last saw you."

"I decided to go blonde for a change." She ran her hand through her soft waves.

"It's great to finally meet you again," he said. His hand gestured in the air, not knowing where to go.

"You, too."

They stood facing each other like children in a school play, waiting for a cue from a teacher.

"I don't know what to say. Everything is..." She shook her head. "It's so surreal. And I really want to hug you, to say thank you for helping me. Is that okay?"

He smiled and stepped toward her. Touching her would confirm she was really here.

Yvette moved forward, too, but she placed her arm diagonally across her body. "It's a little tricky," she said.

"Yes, it is. An unusual situation."

"Oh, I mean...this." Yvette looked down.

It was then Mitchell noticed that her scarf was some kind of sling. She reached out to him with one arm, but made a rocking motion with her other one.

Mitchell looked down and saw two small blue eyes peeping back up at him from inside the folds of the fabric.

"Connor is just waking up," Yvette said. "I think he wants to meet you, too."

The words *Yvette has a baby* streamed through Mitchell's mind. He told himself she could be looking after it for a friend, but there was something in the way she held Connor, as if she loved every inch of him. He could tell she was the baby's mum.

"Is he the reason you've been away?" he asked gently.

"Partly. It's a long story." Her hand shook as she pushed a strand of hair from her cheek.

"I'd like to hear it," he said.

They walked along the aisle into a room bursting with bright blooms. He remembered sheltering from a thunderstorm here once with Anita. She had laughed when he placed a stray flower behind her ear.

Yvette sat down. "Connor was the secret I couldn't share until the time was right. I'm so sorry for what I've put my friends and family through." She lowered her eyes guiltily. "I expect you have many questions for me, too. You risked your life to save me."

"I did what anyone else would do."

"No, not everyone…"

"Then I found out you were missing."

Yvette nodded, her face drawn. "I'll try to explain. It's difficult to know where to start."

"Maybe at the beginning?"

She smiled gratefully. "I was seeing a guy I knew through work for a few months, Victor. I knew Naomi, Liza and Mum wouldn't approve of him, so I didn't tell them. He was an alpha type and took charge of everything. And I liked that at first. But he was also obsessive. I saw him parked outside my house one morning, watching me. As time went on, I grew more unsettled by him. And then I found out he was skimming funds from mutual clients. I broke things off between us immediately and did some fishing around. When I found out the extent of his theft, I had to do something about it. I battled against my decision, but I spoke to my manager and she assured me it would all be handled discreetly.

"Then I found out I was pregnant. I felt sick when I saw those two blue lines on the test. I didn't want Victor or a baby. I was in line for promotion at work, had a holiday booked and I lived in a fancy apartment.

"I went to the hospital and hoped they'd tell me I'd got it wrong, that I wasn't pregnant at all." She gave a laugh of disbelief. "But I had a scan, and when the doctor told me I was sixteen weeks pregnant, I couldn't believe it. I'd felt dizzy at work a couple of times, and I'd put on a few pounds, but it didn't cross my mind that I might be pregnant. I'm forty-one and hadn't seen having a child as part of my future.

"However, when I saw this little one on the monitor, I knew I wanted to be his mum. I moved the buttons on my skirt along and kept everything to myself, needing to get my head around it all.

"I remember going out for dinner with Liza, Naomi and Mum one night, and I was trying to find the right moment to tell them the news, but I couldn't do it. I knew Mum would interrogate me about who the father was, and ask me a million other questions. She'd try to organize my life and I couldn't tell her the father was a criminal. So, I decided to wait until after my midpregnancy scan, when I knew everything was okay with the baby." She looked down at Connor and gave him a wistful smile. "Except it wasn't…"

"I'm sorry to hear that," Mitchell said.

"The scan showed the baby had a heart defect. It felt like I heard the words but couldn't take them in. It was like someone else's life unraveling, rather than mine.

"Again, I kept everything to myself. I went into work as if

nothing was wrong. I think I was in denial, wishing my time away until my next appointment."

Mitchell thought about how Anita had breezed through her pregnancy with Poppy. He imagined how horrendous it would be to discover your unborn child had a serious problem.

Yvette cradled Connor's head. "When Naomi was pregnant, Mum used to crowd her with advice, always quoting statistics and articles she'd read to her. I couldn't bear to go through all that. I was going to tell Liza and Naomi, but then the hospital gave me more bad news..." She took a long breath. "They confirmed that they couldn't operate on Connor until he was born. That's if the pregnancy progressed for that long. And I felt like I was falling from the top of a skyscraper.

"I can't even remember leaving the hospital after that visit. I just kept on walking, unaware of where I was heading until I found myself standing on a bridge in the city. I looked over the railing and stared down at the water for ages. And I knew in those moments that I had to fight for my baby's life. I'd do whatever it took for him to be okay, for me to be okay, because we had a chance.

"I stayed in bed until my next appointment. I couldn't sleep from worrying about the baby. I became a real mess.

"The heart specialist was based in a different hospital a couple of hours away, and she was willing to keep an eye on me throughout my pregnancy. I thought it would help to move closer to her, and I was finally going to tell Mum, Liza and Naomi about my situation. But then Victor found out that I'd told on him. He showed up at my apartment one night. He was yelling and banging on the door, and I was so scared to see him, especially if he noticed if I was pregnant. I hid for ages until he'd gone and, in the middle of the night, I got into my car. I was shaking like a leaf, and I didn't want to wake Naomi and the kids, or scare Mum, or disturb Liza. I just had to get away.

"I drove to the hospital where the specialist worked, the first place I thought of rather than the police, and I begged a nurse to help me. I just wanted to protect the baby.

"She helped check me into a hotel for the night. Her friend let out an apartment I could stay in, so I could be close to the hospital. I wrote to Liza, and to Jean, and Naomi, but I didn't want them to know where I was, because I was paranoid Victor would find out.

"The next weeks went by in a daze. I had assessments and scans and I plunged into depression, the darkest place. The nurse, now a friend, brought baby clothes for me and food for my fridge. And I managed to get by.

"Then one morning, when I was almost eight months pregnant, this little one decided to come early. I gave birth to him alone in the hospital, and I called him Connor after my dad. As I lay there recovering from my labor, the specialist carried out the first operation on him, and I had no idea if it would work or not. I didn't know if I'd have a baby to hold at the end of it.

"I sank even lower and was diagnosed with postnatal depression. I got it into my head it was truly best for Mum, Liza and Naomi that I wasn't part of their lives any longer. I had some moments of lucidity and was able to write a few letters here and there. But all I wanted to do was keep me and Connor safe in a protective bubble. It was such a relief when I found out Victor had been sent to prison, out of the way.

"All the hospital visits and Connor's operations meant that time evaporated. I got good support, took medication and the mist began to clear, but it took months before I could allow myself to believe things might turn out okay for us."

"Is Connor okay now?"

Yvette gave the smallest nod. "He'll need regular check-ups and possibly more surgery in the future. We have to take each day as it comes.

"One day, I felt a bit stronger and was drawn back to the bridge. I wanted to take a first small step out of the gloom and hang a padlock for Connor. My friend, the nurse, got it engraved for me and was the only person I trusted to look after the baby. I used to sing Auntie Jean's song to him when he was in my tummy, and the words felt perfect. 'My heart is always yours.'"

"That was the day we saw each other on the bridge..." Mitchell said. "Before you fell?"

Yvette nodded. "I was deep in thought, looking at my padlock when I noticed you."

"We shared a smile," Mitchell reminded her.

"It's all such a blur. After I hung the padlock, I felt my earring fall out. It bounced and then disappeared. Liza bought them for my birthday and I love them."

"Golden cacti?" Mitchell said.

"*Yes*. You know about them?"

"She told me."

"I leaned over the railing and I could see it there on the ledge. I reached farther and farther over, and felt the blood rushing to my head. I was still weak from looking after Connor and I lost my balance and fell. I remember the icy water, and then you in the water beside me."

When Mitchell looked back to that day on the bridge, he wasn't sure why Yvette had caught his attention. Perhaps it was the sticky heat of the day, or because her curls reminded him of Anita's, or maybe because a pretty woman had smiled at him after his years in the wilderness of grief. Perhaps he had recognized something within her, that she was a lost soul, too.

"The doctor who helped me on the bridge wanted me to

go to hospital," Yvette said. "But I didn't want to go. I was desperate to get back to Connor, but I was in a state. So, I used the doctor's phone to call Naomi rather than Liza, because she has children, too. She met me on the bridge and it was the first time I'd seen her in almost a year. I didn't want to put her in a difficult position, but I swore her to secrecy, until I was ready to come home properly. But then she told me that Victor had been released from prison... And I wanted to hide away all over again."

"Liza and I found a letter from Victor at your apartment," Mitchell said.

Yvette's face grew pale. "He found out my new mobile number and texted me. He wants to meet me tomorrow in the city."

"How did he find it?"

"I don't know..."

"You're not going to see him?" Mitchell stated, astonished she could be considering this.

Yvette bit her lip. "I'm scared about what I did, reporting him, but he's Connor's father, Mitchell. I didn't tell him I was pregnant but somehow, he found out. It's best if I meet him, in public, and get this over with. I'm so tired and I just want to face up to my past so I can move on."

"You'll need someone with you," Mitchell said. "You can't meet him on your own."

"Liza said she'd look after Connor for me. I don't want to worry Mum. I've put Naomi through enough, asking her to lie for me..."

"You should tell a police officer."

She shook her head. "He went to prison because of me, but Victor has never harmed me—I don't think he'd do anything violent."

"He was locked up because of something *he* did, not you." Mitchell thought for a while. "I'll come with you."

"I can't ask you to do that. You've done enough for me already."

"I want to do it," he insisted. He again thought of Anita and his sense of shame and loss. This time he could help. "I want to be there, for you and *all* of your family."

She took a while to consider this and gave him a small nod. "Thank you."

After leaving the conservatory, they headed back through the green wrought-iron entrance gates of the park. Yvette attempted to hold her umbrella over Mitchell's head, but the spikes jabbed where his stitches had been.

"Ouch."

"Sorry," she said. "I told you I was clumsy."

"You did. On the riverbank." He remembered. "You knock over wineglasses."

"And spike people in the head, it seems."

They shared an awkward small laugh that made them both feel stronger. And the smiles on their faces remained as they walked along the path.

The rain pelting against Yvette's umbrella sounded like a drumroll and Mitchell wondered what the hell they were both going to do when they encountered Victor.

26

BENCH

The following day, when Mitchell sat in Liza's sitting room with the Bradfields, the air was thick with tension. He was glad Poppy was out of the way in her school club.

Sheila sat on the sofa, clasping her hands anxiously. Naomi flitted around, plumping cushions, fetching glasses of water and squeezing Yvette's shoulder reassuringly. Liza pasted on a smile, though Mitchell could see the stiffness of her body and the strain in her eyes. Yvette sat rocking Connor on her lap, soothing and whispering to him.

They had all gathered here together before Mitchell would accompany Yvette to see Victor. She'd arranged to meet him in the middle of the Slab. Out of all the city bridges, Mitchell was glad it was this one. It was plain and wide, without any ornate railings or intricacies in its design. It meant Yvette would be in out in the open with lots of people around. Even so, his stomach was a tight knot, uncomfortable as he sat on the sofa beside Sheila.

"Are you sure about this, Yvette?" Sheila asked. She kept a hand pressed to her chest and her breathing was heavy. "I'm so worried about you. We've only just got you back, and now you're going to meet the man you tried to escape from. I blame him for all this."

"It wasn't all about Victor, Mum," Yvette said. "It's more about the decisions and actions *I* made over the last twelve months. He *is* Connor's father."

"We've read his letter," Naomi insisted. "I saw him in the café with you, and how he treated you. He's been in prison…"

Yvette nodded solemnly. "I'm scared of him, too. He's shaped my life for a long time. But this is more for me than him. I'm desperate to start afresh. I want to feel stronger with no more running or hiding. I want to be with my family and not have to look over my shoulder. I know I could do this officially, through mediation, but that could take weeks and months to set up. I thought about writing him a letter, but I'm just so tired and I want to take charge of things. I don't want anything hanging over my head any longer."

Mitchell could see both sides of the situation. He could feel the worry and stress humming around the room. However, he could also understand how Yvette wanted to take this big step forward and move on.

"I'll be with you," he told her. "You're not on your own."

"Thank you." She nodded nervously.

The others didn't say anything and Mitchell's spirits faded when he sensed they didn't think he was enough.

"Everything will be fine," he assured them. "Really."

Liza raised her eyes at him. "What if that's not enough?"

The air was warm and thick outside, so Mitchell's breathing felt labored as he walked with Yvette toward the Slab. She looked twitchily around her, and Mitchell's own legs felt jel-lylike from nerves.

"The last time I saw Victor, he was hammering on my apartment door," she said. "He's probably still furious with me."

"We'll be in a public place. You're not alone."

She walked without speaking for a while. "I know. Thanks for coming with me, Mitchell."

Everyone who passed them was in a happier place, buoyed on by the reappearance of the sunshine. Dogs scampered along the pavement, joggers wore smiles along with their Apple earbuds and office workers donned sunglasses and chatted on their mobiles.

Mitchell and Yvette reached the middle of the bridge five minutes before the agreed rendezvous time with Victor. The pavement was lined with low concrete benches. A couple lay draped across one of them, kissing languidly. On another, a man lay on his back with his socks and shoes off and a news-paper covering his face.

Mitchell and Yvette approached an empty bench. She perched on the edge, and her feet shuffled on the ground. Mitchell decided to stand a few meters away, surveying his surroundings until Victor arrived. He pressed his back against the railing and when he crooked his leg, he felt his mobile phone pushed down in his pocket.

Last night, he had used it to call Graham, and he thought back to their conversation.

"What can I do for you, Mitchy Boy?" Graham had asked when Mitchell said he'd like to call in a second favor, if pos-sible.

"I'm trying to find out what I can about a man called Vic-tor Sonetti. Yvette knew him through work and discovered he was embezzling funds. She reported him to her company and Victor was sent to prison. He got out recently and Yvette could be in danger. Do you think Mason and Tony can help us at all?" He recalled Graham's words, about how he was glad the men were his friends not his enemies.

"I told you, Mitchy Boy. They know everything about everything. Do you want them to do some digging around?"

"It's just some background information, if we need it." Mitchell explained the situation further and told Graham he was accompanying Yvette to meet Victor.

"Do you want the boys to come along, too, as backup? Brute force?" Graham asked.

"Hopefully I won't need that. And I'm sorry to ask you to do this."

"That's what friends are for," Graham said. "Now what do you want to know?"

On the bridge, Mitchell saw Yvette's eyes widen. He sensed her stiffening as he watched a small bald man walking a Pomeranian dog on a leash. He whistled nonchalantly as he approached them.

Mitchell frowned, thinking this couldn't possibly be Victor. In his head, he'd imagined him to be big and muscly with tattooed arms, or maybe a slick guy in a pin-striped suit. But this man was now smiling. He wore jogging pants and a faded lilac T-shirt. "Is that *him*?" he asked.

"Yes," she murmured. "Appearances can be deceptive."

"It'll be okay."

She nodded at him and stuck out her chin. "We'll see."

"Yvette." Victor picked up his small dog and held it to his chest. Though his tone was friendly, he didn't acknowledge Mitchell's presence. "It's wonderful to see you. You look fantastic—well, maybe a touch pale. This is my new friend, Penny. I brought her to say hi."

Mitchell studied the man. Although he smiled, his eyes were small and purplish like pomegranate seeds.

Yvette shrank like a caterpillar curling against touch.

Victor lowered his dog to the pavement. "Where's Connor?" he asked lightly, looking around.

"He's at home with my family."

"That's a shame, I so wanted to meet him. You kept it from me that I was a father, but that's not the only thing you didn't tell me, eh? I only borrowed that money for *us*, you know, so we could have a better future together."

"You stole thousands, Victor. What did you expect me to do?"

"Didn't expect my own girlfriend to turn against me, that's for sure. And you didn't tell me you were pregnant, either."

"I didn't know about it, until later."

"Would it have made any difference? Would you have kept your mouth shut? We could have been a family with nice cash to spend."

"No," she said firmly.

His eyes narrowed instantly. "I thought not, should have known you were a conniving cow."

"That's enough." Mitchell stepped forward. "Yvette agreed to meet you here as planned. Don't abuse that."

Victor's lips twitched into a smirk. "Ah, you're the new boyfriend I presume?"

"Leave him out of it," Yvette ordered.

Victor raised an inquisitive eyebrow at her before he suddenly lurched forward, squaring up to Mitchell.

Mitchell's heart thumped. However, he was used to people reacting aggressively when he stopped them from hanging padlocks on the bridges and he was not going to let Victor intimidate him. He'd played a big part in bringing Yvette and her family back together again, and this angry man wasn't going to taint that.

Mitchell got in Victor's face. "I'm a friend of the family."

"And I'm supposed to be impressed by that?"

"I don't actually care what you think," Mitchell said. "I'm here for Yvette and the Bradfields. You're a thief and Yvette was so worried about what you'd do to her, she ran away from you. She was protecting her unborn baby. A baby with a heart defect. Does that make you feel like a proper man?"

A flicker in Victor's eye told Mitchell he wasn't used to being questioned. He grabbed the front of Mitchell's shirt. "Don't you *ever* speak to me like that again," he hissed.

Mitchell jerked away and shoved the smaller man so he stumbled backward. Mitchell reared up to his full height. "Yvette wants to start afresh. She acknowledges you're part of Connor's life, but you are not going to see him if there is any risk to the baby, or to Yvette. You need to speak civilly to her and prove you're worthy of them both."

"I would *never* hurt my own child."

"Really? From my perspective, you look exactly like the kind of man who would do that."

Victor's eyes bored into him, but Mitchell stood his ground. "Yvette did what anyone with proper values would do when she found out you were stealing," he said.

Yvette inched forward. "I'll take steps for you to see Connor through the official, proper channels and you need to go along with that, if you want to see him," she said.

Victor smirked at them both in turn. "What if I'm not an official kind of guy?"

"Well then," Mitchell said. "A couple of friends of mine have told me a few more things about you... Very interesting things."

Victor's eyebrow twitched up. "Who?" he growled. "What?"

"Never you mind." Mitchell began to circle him, caging him in. He bent in close to Victor's ear. "This is what I know about you..."

He reeled off all that Mason and Tony had passed on through Graham, about Victor's other dodgy business dealings. They had uncovered several businesses he'd set up under a fake identity, where he had stolen funds from investors before disappearing. The information could easily land him with more months, even years in prison, if brought to light.

"If you *ever* do anything to jeopardize Yvette's and Connor's happiness, I will be onto you," Mitchell threatened. His words made him feel stronger as he spoke them. "My friends will not let this go."

Victor barked a laugh, but it sounded hoarse and unnerved. He picked up Penny again and gave her head a ruffle. "Hey, no need for that. I just care about my son. I'm a changed man since I got of prison."

Mitchell stared at him disbelievingly.

"It's true." Victor looked over at Yvette. "I've made bad choices. Had therapy for it, to understand myself better. I just want a second chance."

"I saw the letter you sent to her…"

"If it's any consolation, I'm sorry about that. It was a mistake. I'd found out I was a father through the grapevine, and I was angry at first. But now I can see why Yvette did what she did, and why she ran. She's a decent person, and I'm not." He smiled at her. "I don't blame you for any of this, okay? I brought it all on myself. Can we just talk for a while?"

Yvette eventually nodded. "Okay. But I want Mitchell close by."

"No problem. Anything you want. I apologize for how I spoke to you before."

Mitchell paced up and down for twenty minutes. He watched, making his presence known, as Victor and Yvette talked together.

Eventually, Victor walked over to him. "Thanks for that,"

he said gruffly and held out his hand. Mitchell reluctantly shook it. "I'll wait until Yvette gets in touch, okay? No trouble from me. I just want to get to know my son. You have stuff on me and I know it."

Mitchell jerked his head in acknowledgment. He watched as Victor and Penny walked away, and he returned to Yvette. "Are you okay?" he asked gently.

She nodded in reply before taking a deep breath. "I've done it. I've taken another step to returning to normal. I can look forward to everything being okay again. As much as it can be."

"I'm here whenever you need me," he said. "If you're ready to go home, I'll walk back with you."

"You don't need to. I can do it alone."

"I want to make sure you're back with your family safely."

She smiled at him gratefully, and they started to move away from the bench. "I heard from Liza that people call you the Hero on the Bridge. And you really are," she said.

Mitchell took a moment to let this sink in. He hadn't felt truly worthy of the label before, but reaching out to others had helped lift some of his guilty burden about not being there for Anita.

As he walked into the shadow cast by a tree, Mitchell's face felt briefly cool. But when he stepped out of the gray chilliness, he felt the heat of the day again, warming his cheeks. He smiled as he walked into the sunshine.

27

FAMILY

As Mitchell walked with Yvette through Upchester, he had a new bounce in his step, a pride in himself that he hadn't felt for a long time. When he'd helped Yvette from the river, it had been a gut reaction, an impromptu act that he didn't have time to consider. But this was different. It felt even bigger.

He and Poppy were a great team and they always would be, but it felt good to be a key part in helping the cogs of the Bradfields' family life to start turning again.

Mitchell could already see that Yvette looked brighter, too. Her body seemed lighter and her steps more determined as they headed along the main road and past each of the bridges. She asked Mitchell about the opening ceremony for the new white bridge and if he was going to take Poppy along. She said she might try to take Connor, making even more effort to bring herself back into the outside world.

Their conversation together felt warm and natural, and Mitchell realized that he didn't feel any attraction to her, other than the enjoyment of spending time with a friend.

When they reached Liza's house, she opened her front door and reached out to take Connor. Her face was etched with concern. "How was everything? Are you both okay?"

Yvette nodded tentatively. "I think so. I feel so tired after seeing Victor again. We talked, though I'm not sure if he's the changed man he says he is. When he first meets Connor, I'll make sure it's a supervised visit. I want to give him that chance, for Connor's sake."

"You look worn-out. Why don't you call Mum and then go for a lie down?" Liza suggested. "She's gotten herself all worked up, so I drove her home. Naomi had to get back for the kids."

"I'll do that, thank you."

"Poppy is upstairs, too," Liza told Mitchell, avoiding looking at him. "She was reading a book, but dozed off about half an hour ago."

As Yvette made her way upstairs, Mitchell could detect a coolness exuding from Liza, directed at him. He wondered if it was worry about Yvette. She walked into her sitting room and sat down heavily in a chair. He wasn't sure if it was an invitation for him to follow her, but he did so anyway.

Over the couple of hours he and Yvette had been away from the house, purple shadows had appeared under Liza's eyes. She sat with her body turned at an angle away from him. The air of worried tension in the house had gone, replaced by something more unspoken and unsettling.

Mitchell sat down in the armchair opposite her. "Has everything been okay?" he asked cautiously.

"With Poppy, yes." Liza folded her arms and directed a piercing glare at him for a split second.

"Um, is anything wrong?" he said.

There were footsteps on the stairs and the sitting room door swung open. It bumped against the arm of the sofa. Poppy bumbled inside, yawning.

"Whoops, sorry. I fell asleep," she said. "I've got a crease on my cheek, see."

"Oh, yes." Mitchell looked closer. "It's a crumple."

"Crumple?" She laughed, as if hearing the word for the first time.

"It is a funny word," Liza agreed.

He noticed that when she spoke to Poppy, she used her usual warm tone.

"Liza and I read some of your letters, Dad. She helped me set up my PowerPoint presentation, and she had a brilliant idea, too. She said if there was a centenary website then people could leave their messages on there, instead of hanging padlocks on the bridges. She designed her own music lesson site and it's cool. All shades of blue."

"It's just an idea," Liza said.

"I *love* it."

"It's great," Mitchell agreed. "When the padlocks are removed, people can still share their love, but in a different way."

"It would take quite a lot of work to set up," Liza muttered.

"Are we going home now, Dad?" Poppy asked as she played with the end of her plait. "Do I need to put my shoes back on?"

He nodded, and she sped back into the hallway.

Liza stood up. She focused her eyes on the painting of cherubs above her fireplace. "Shall I call a cab for you both?" she asked Mitchell flatly.

"It's okay. We'll take the bus."

Silence prickled between them, until Poppy carried her

shoes into the room and fiddled with her laces. She looked at him suspiciously, and then at Liza. "Is everything okay?"

"Sure," Liza said.

"I think so," Mitchell said.

Poppy continued to study them both. "Um, okay."

Liza reached up and toyed with her earring. "Perhaps you can check to see where Sasha has gone, Poppy. Can you see if she's in the garden, or if she's snuck upstairs? Perhaps you can feed her for me?"

"Okay." Poppy tied her laces and left the room.

"What's wrong, Liza?" Mitchell stood up. "Are you angry with me about something?"

Liza jutted her chin. "No, nothing."

"I think you are."

Liza fixed her eyes on her handbag on the sofa for a long time before snatching it up. She unzipped then fumbled inside it. "When Poppy gave me the letters to read, the other night, *this* was among them." She spun to face him and held out an unsealed cream envelope.

Mitchell stared at it and a chill ran down his spine. He could already see a couple of lines of his own handwriting on the letter inside it. Poppy wouldn't have taken one from inside his nightstand drawer. So, it must be one he'd written to Anita that he'd left next to his bed.

They both stared it as if it was a bug found in a restaurant salad.

Mitchell's head whirred as he tried to recall the contents of the letter. No individual words or sentences came back to him, but he remembered how he'd felt when he wrote it, after he thought he saw Anita at the ice rink. He had been weary, and confused and downhearted. He had written about Liza and Yvette. "I can't remember it properly," he admitted.

Liza pursed her lips and slipped the letter out of its envelope.

"Perhaps I can remind you," she said. She started to quote his own words back at him. "'*She talks too much, and wears garish clothes, and I feel like I've stumbled out of a nightclub, woozy in the early hours of the morning, after I spend any time with her. She's not calm and together, like you—*'"

"I write to Anita still," he cut in. "It's something I do to help me to cope."

She ignored him and continued to read. "'*I'm not sure I can ever move on. Being with anyone other than you would be a compromise too far.*'"

She stared at the paper and then at him. The look she gave him was loaded with so much disappointment, his insides shriveled. "I thought you *liked* me," she said. "I didn't know I was just some kind of rebound for you."

"I wrote it at a bad time…"

"It's here in black-and-white, Mitchell. Your true thoughts about me."

"Of course I like you."

She lowered her eyes. "I'm not calm or together enough for you. You want Anita or someone like her, and that's not me."

Mitchell struggled to think of what to say. He had felt something for Liza, feelings of real warmth, but confusion, too. Anita was still very much in his thoughts and in his heart, and he couldn't surrender her. "I said things clumsily. I apologize." He tried to take the letter from her, but she clutched it to her chest. Her lips were set in a fine line.

"I looked after Poppy and we formed a bond. You and I held hands and really talked. I allowed myself to think that—oh, it doesn't matter. I should be used to this by now."

He reached out to touch her arm, but she jerked away.

"You still love Anita. I was here as a distraction and I totally get that now. You enjoyed helping my family because it made *you* feel better about *yourself*. None of this was ever about *me* or *us*."

"That's not true, Liza," he pleaded. "I have felt things for you. It's just that—"

Poppy reentered the room. She carried Sasha under her arm. "She's eaten all her food, and I gave her water."

Mitchell and Liza's conversation halted sharply.

Poppy eyed them. "Are you two okay?"

You two. It was a phrase she used to use about him and Anita. Mitchell lowered his eyes, uncomfortable.

"Sure," Liza said lightly. She crumpled Mitchell's letter into a small ball. "Now before you go, have you had enough to eat and drink?"

Poppy nodded and picked up her bag.

Connor's cry rang out from the stairway and Yvette entered the sitting room, jogging him on her hip. "I've tried to get him to settle, but he refuses to go to sleep."

Liza pushed a hand through her hair. "Okay, I'll see Mitchell and Poppy out and give you a hand." She led them into the hallway. Poppy skipped toward the door and opened it. She jumped down the step onto the path.

"I don't know what I was thinking," Mitchell said quietly to Liza.

"Neither do I." She pushed the balled-up letter into his hand. "I appreciate everything you've helped us with, Mitchell."

Poppy fiddled with the strap on her bag. "Thanks for having me, Liza," she said.

"You're very welcome."

Mitchell stepped outside, too. He tried to take Poppy's bag from her, but she wouldn't let it go. A pencil dropped out, and as he stooped to pick it up, his eyes grew watery.

"Bye now," Liza said, and closed the door in his face.

Mitchell saw Poppy frown. She looked at him for an explanation, but he couldn't give her one. He tightened his hand
around the ball of paper. He had seen the letters he wrote to
Anita as something that helped and supported him. But now
his words had ruined something very special.

"Come on, then," he tried to say cheerfully to Poppy as
they walked down the path. "Let's go home."

PIGEONS

Before he even reached the Victorian bridge, Mitchell knew he didn't want to be at work today. The sky was as heavy and gray as the gurgling river rushing beneath the bridge. Through the wire fences, he could see droplets of rain hanging from all the padlocks like tears.

Ha, people won't try attaching them today in the drizzle, he thought, noticing that some of his grumpier old emotions toward the locks were resurfacing.

As he trudged across the city, he ran through yesterday's conversation with Liza in his head. She had been a good friend to Poppy, and to him, too. She had welcomed him into her family and, although the Bradfields were a dysfunctional bunch, he had liked the feeling he was helping them. And now he had upset her greatly.

He recognized there was a switch in the air when he was close to Liza, but he hadn't identified it as *chemistry*. That was something he'd shared with Anita when they sipped cider together for the first time and throughout their life with each other.

There hadn't been anything instant with Liza. His feelings for her had crept up on him gradually after spending time with her. At first, he thought it was friendship and now it felt like much more. But whatever there was between them, he had spoiled it.

He told himself that Liza had found Yvette, and the Bradfield family was reunited. Mission accomplished. Perhaps he should also try to move on and let them be. He had schedules and plans to make for Poppy's next school year—tennis shoes to buy, the new school bus timetable to learn, and they hadn't been to the city museum for a good few weeks.

All would be fine when things returned to normal.

He just had to stop thinking about Liza Bradfield.

Mitchell found Barry at the end of the Yacht bridge. His friend held on to a huge roll of blue tissue paper.

"I've got new duties," Barry groaned, as he tore off a wad. "Russ wants the bridge to be spotless when it opens. I'm cleaning it, checking it over, helping the contractors with whatever needs doing. I'm here to serve."

"Russ hasn't told me any of this," Mitchell said, feeling prickly at being overlooked.

Barry shrugged. "You've not been in work." He nodded over to the stage at the end of the bridge. There was a hive of activity, with people buzzing around and equipment being unloaded from the white vans.

"I can't get to the padlocks to cut them off."

"Enjoy it while you can," Barry said. "Russ is over there if you want to speak to him."

Mitchell turned to move away, then he remembered to ask. "How are you and Trisha doing?"

Barry's face flushed. "We're doing great. She's not weird at all. Progress, huh? Now we just need to get you fixed up. Liza is very—"

Mitchell held up a palm. "I know," he said more snappily than he meant to. "But it's complicated." He began to walk over toward Russ.

"That's life," Barry called after him.

Russ gripped a clipboard and his hair was sticking up from stressfully running his hand through it. "Mitchell?" he frowned. "You're back?"

"I'm reporting for duty."

"Right. I wasn't expecting you."

"Any reason?" Mitchell asked sharply, not liking the feeling that everyone and everything could function without him. "My holidays have ended."

"Well…" Russ hesitated. "I just heard you harassed one of the contractors, desperate to get to a padlock. Then, very strangely, a whole panel of them went missing overnight. I wondered if you're okay…you know, emotionally?"

Mitchell worked his jaw. He could feel his neck flooding with color.

"Did you have anything to do with that?"

"Um…" Mitchell said.

Russ raised an eyebrow. "I can watch the CCTV footage."

Mitchell felt like he was sinking into quicksand. He furiously grasped for things he could say, that might get him out of trouble. But he was enough of a disappointment to himself already without resorting to lying, too. Instead, he found a sheepish shrug.

"I see. Well, I think you should go home, Fisher." Russ glanced at his clipboard. "Take some time out."

Mitchell scowled. "I'm absolutely fine. I'll carry on."

"You're not hearing me. I know you've been through some

tough times in your personal life. You saved someone and ended up in hospital. You've been acting rather strangely. Your well-being is important."

"Yes, but—"

Russ held up a hand. "You know the council mantra—*a supportive working environment for all.* There are important celebrations coming up and our team is in line for a few awards. I need things to run smoothly, so I'll see you back at work in seven days. Take more time off, if you need it."

"No," Mitchell protested. His fingers gripped the handle of his toolbox. His job gave structure to his life, holding it up like scaffolding around an unstable building. Without it, the structure might collapse. If he could work and fill his time, he'd feel okay again. He'd lost the Bradfields and he couldn't lose his job, too. "I want to work. I *have* to be here."

"Go home."

"No." He heard his own desperation in that one word.

Russ fixed Mitchell with a concerned stare. He tucked his clipboard under his arm. "Then you leave me with no choice. Mitchell Fisher, you're officially suspended for a week."

Mitchell mouth slackened. "You can't do that."

"Yes, I can. We'll pay you while you're off. Now, take your toolbox, go home and sort your head out. It's for your own good."

Mitchell opened his mouth to protest, but Russ waved to a man in a yellow hard hat and strode away.

Mitchell sloped back across the bridge and found Barry had gone. There were no cars or couples, only him, alone.

When he reached the street, he trudged alongside the river past a florist booth where the heads of the blooms hung heavy with rain on their petals. A hole in the canopy of a fruit and vegetable stand allowed water to cascade down onto the melons. An earthy smell rose up from the river, and the grass verge was marred with mulchy black mud. He didn't know where he was heading and felt like he was wading through a swamp.

He longed to go home, not to his apartment, but to the house he shared with his family, to make daisy chains with Poppy and watch TV cuddled up with Anita. For a while, he shut his eyes as he walked, imagining reaching out with a key in his hand. He always felt she was still at home with glittery, crafty things on her lap. His fingers twitched in his pockets, wanting to run his hand through her curls one more time.

When a siren pierced the air, breaking his thoughts, Mitchell stumbled over a pile of soggy boxes. His eyes snapped back open.

A police car and an ambulance were parked on the pavement, their blue lights spinning. A car had smashed into a wall and crumpled like a cereal box. Steam rose from its bonnet.

Mitchell came to an abrupt halt, as if he'd smacked into the wall himself. As he surveyed the scene, his eyes filled with tears so everything blurred.

A picture of Anita's accident flashed into his head. He'd seen her crushed car in the pages of a newspaper.

And now, he swore he could hear her car tires squeal against wet pavement and the thud and hiss of metal hitting metal. He pictured her pretty face, pressed into an airbag. Granules of windscreen glass speckled on the road like salt crystals.

It felt so real to him that he shuddered, suddenly chilled to the bone.

His face puckered as he furiously blinked away the tears that spilled down his face. He wiped them with his wrist and straightened his back, trying to defy his emotions.

A policewoman eyed and then approached him. "Are you feeling okay, sir?" she asked. She was petite with dark skin and ebony eyes.

Mitchell stared ahead, not wanting to look at her. "Yes.

Um, just something in my eye." He moved away and could still feel her watching him.

"Sir?" she called out.

"I'm fine." He waved a dismissive hand.

I'm just tired of letting everyone down, he thought. *Including myself.*

Mitchell had never felt so glad to see the white bricks of Angel House. The rain had soaked his clothes and small puddles shimmered on the top of his toolbox. His socks were soggy and squelched at the end of his shoes. He walked past the Dala café and caught sight of his reflection in the window. His clothes hung off him, wet and too large, and his hair was plastered against his forehead.

Just look at the state of you. What would Anita think if she saw you now?

Only three years ago, he was a family man, with everything he could ever want in life. He had a loving, supportive partner, a career, an amazing daughter and a family home. He had done a great job of ruining it all.

And now he'd stamped on a burgeoning friendship with someone who was simply wonderful.

Liza.

His chest felt like it was filled with sharp tacks.

Mitchell saw Carl ahead of him with a broom in hand, brushing vigorously at white stuff smeared on the pavement. It looked like a dozen ice creams had been dropped at the same time.

"Pigeon poo," Carl said as he noticed Mitchell approaching. He gestured to the top of the building where the gutters were streaked with white vertical stripes, like stalactites. "I don't know where all those birds have come from, or why they're using our roof as a toilet. Any idea, Mr. Fisher?"

Mitchell pictured the piles of oats that he and Poppy sprinkled onto the slates. "Maybe they like the view," he murmured. Not in the mood for any further conversation, he tried to edge away.

"Do you know your eyes are all pink, Mr. Fisher?" Carl asked.

"Hmph."

As Mitchell neared the entrance doors to the building, his foot slipped on the white mess. His legs shot out from under him and he banged down onto the pavement, landing on his tailbone. Pain shot through his body and his toolbox crashed down onto his knees.

Carl dropped his broom and ran to his aid. "I'm *so* sorry, Mr. Fisher. I should have cleaned this mess up sooner. Are you okay?"

"It's not your fault," Mitchell said through clenched teeth. "It's mine."

"How can it possibly be *yours*?"

Mitchell managed to get to his feet. He picked up his toolbox and limped toward the front steps, not wanting Carl's sympathy.

"The lift has stopped working again," the concierge called after him. "It was fine earlier on, then, kaput."

Mitchell gritted his teeth.

"Oh, and something arrived for you this morning. I left it outside your door on the landing. That's okay, isn't it?"

Mitchell blinked against the rain. "It's all absolutely fine," he grimaced. He opened the door to Angel House and maneuvered his toolbox inside.

By the time he'd climbed all the stairs to the fifth floor, the weight of his tools had almost pulled his shoulder out of its socket. Mitchell dropped it to the ground with a thud and rotated his arm like a windmill to loosen it up. He kneaded his fingers into the muscles of his shoulder blade.

The delivery waiting for him was a voluminous black bin bag. It didn't have an address label and he wondered who'd sent it.

As he wearily dragged it into his apartment, he felt like Santa Claus on Christmas Eve, exhausted after delivering all the presents to find he'd left a bag behind at the North Pole.

The bag was tied too tightly, and instead of attempting to unfasten it, Mitchell ripped it wide-open.

An avalanche of letters spilled out, covering his feet.

Mitchell stared at them in disbelief, kicking them off. There must be hundreds of them here, maybe even a thousand.

After sitting down heavily on his sofa, he surveyed the giant pool of correspondence lying on his sitting room floor. He saw his name, repeated over and over, in a multitude of different writing styles—Mitchell Fisher, Mr. Fisher, the Hero on the Bridge.

Just looking at the envelopes made him feel like he was drowning in a sea of people's expectations. He wasn't a hero, or a celebrity, or a confidant. He was just a man, nothing more and often less.

Anger surged inside him, and he took off his wet shoes and threw them at the letters, one after the other. He stood and took a running kick at them in his socked feet, so they skittered across his floor. But all he did was make the place look untidy, a total mess.

He rubbed the back of his neck, wondering what Poppy would make of the scene when she returned home. Breathing deeply, he tried to let his distress subside, for her sake.

He began to push the letters together again, using the side of his foot. Then he bent down to use his hands. He gathered them roughly and stacked them into a series of piles so they surrounded him like molehills.

His eyes gravitated toward an envelope on top of one of the piles. It was lilac, the same color as Anita's last letter to him.

For the briefest moment, he wondered if her letter had somehow found its way out of his nightstand drawer, into his sitting room. Or if she'd written to him from beyond the grave. A shiver ran down his spine.

Even though he knew this was impossible, he reached down and picked up the lilac envelope anyway.

The writing sloped in a different direction to Anita's, definitely not hers. But he slid a finger under its flap and tore it open.

Dear Sir,

I'll turn eighty soon and have lived in the city all my life. So much has changed and I'm dismayed that many of my friends, those remaining, insist on living in the past. They shut themselves away, making their sitting rooms their comfortable prisons. "You only live once," I tell them, but it falls on deaf ears.

Throughout my many years, I've watched red phone boxes evolve into tiny devices that fit into a pocket. I've seen padlocks appearing on the bridges, and watched the new white bridge taking shape. High-rise buildings have sprouted up on land I played on as a child, and I walk past the school where I once wore short trousers. I sometimes wish the city could stay the same, the comfort of familiarity. I suppose these are the selfish longings of an old man.

Regardless, I shall be present on the bridge to celebrate its opening and will wave my flag with enthusiasm and pride. My friends will probably drink cocoa and watch it all taking place on TV, but that's their loss. My wife, Elsie, passed away twenty years ago now, but she always said, "One should always keep on moving, or else you might take root." I try to follow her advice.

Edmond Wright

Mitchell held the letter for a while, rereading it and think-ing how Poppy might like its combination of history and emo-tion. He thought that Edmond's advice to keep moving made perfect sense, even if he himself had been stationary for three years. He felt comforted after reading it, as if he'd sipped a warm cup of tea.

He picked up a chunk of letters and they felt solid in his hands. They were various shapes and sizes, some fat and some slim, their textures pleasing to touch. Some envelopes were handwritten and others were neatly typed.

He told himself that people must be attracted by the prize money, but many who wrote to him wanted to share a se-cret or a story. Could his act of leaping into the river to save a stranger have really triggered all *these*?

He opened another.

Dear Mr. Fisher,
We don't know you personally and I doubt you know us. How-ever, we read about your courageous act and wanted to pass on our kind regards and admiration. Our son Simon lost his life in the same river last summer. Although people tried to save him, it was too late.

He was our golden boy, our only child. The chasm he left behind is beyond measure. Each day without him feels like for-ever. Our only consolation is we knew he loved us and every-one loved him. He'd want us to continue our lives without him.

We are setting up a campaign to warn people about the dan-gers of open water, and would be most grateful to hear if you'd be interested in becoming involved.

With warm regards,
Ben and Melissa McDonald

He clung on to the letter. *Yes*, he wanted to call out to them. *Yes, of course I'll help you.*

A sense of urgency to read another one washed over him and Mitchell's eyes fell upon a postcard sticking out. It had an image of two black-and-white kittens on the front, peering out from under a blanket. He read the words on the back.

Pussycat

You make me feel like a puddle
You make my body giddy with glee
And my brain feels like an explosion
Will you marry me?

Third time lucky x

The corners of Mitchell's mouth twitched upward at this one. He wondered if the writer wanted to get married for a third time, or if they'd asked *Pussycat* three times? Was an exploding brain a good thing, or not?

As he pondered, a small polka-dot envelope caught his eye, and he opened it and read the note inside it. The paper was small and lined, torn from a spiral bound pad.

Mr. Mitchell Fisher,

I'm in love with Jessica and have tried to show her this—letters, flowers, a padlock on the bridge, without success.
  She told me what you did, saving a woman, and says you're a hero. Will you write me back so I can try to win her over, one last time? I'd appreciate that.

Cheers,
Damon

Mitchell noticed the writer had left a return address, and for a moment he considered picking up a pen to reply. Perhaps it might help Damon to win Jessica back. But he placed the letter to one side, thinking he might respond, sometime or other. And he should write to Ben and Melissa McDonald, too.

He decided to read some more.

He buttered toast while he read a postcard propped up against his kettle, and a poem on his bathroom sink while he cleaned his teeth. If letters were distasteful or didn't make sense they went onto his recycling pile.

He put a sizable stack of letters aside for Poppy's school project. And, as the stack grew taller, he imagined Poppy and Liza sitting side by side, reading them together.

The thought of that not happening again made his heart heavy with regret.

He tried to banish these thoughts for now because he had many more envelopes to open.

His task carried on for hours, into the midafternoon. Mitchell drank numerous cups of tea and placed more letters on top of Damon's letter. They were ones he wanted to reply to.

As he studied them, a strange feeling crept up on him, an awareness that he was willing to read and respond to letters from strangers. However, Anita's lilac envelope remained still unopened in his nightstand drawer.

He stood up and left the pool of correspondence behind. He walked to his bedroom and took her letter from its resting place. As he held it to his nose, his breath quickened. The hint of her violet scent was almost gone and he inhaled more deeply, desperate to smell it again.

He sat down heavily on his bed and tried to imagine her writing it.

Had she sat at their kitchen table, furious with him? Or had she written it from the Italian restaurant? Had tears streamed down her face, or was her back stiff and proud?

He'd always assumed her words would seal the end of their relationship, cementing his guilt and shame.

But do I know that for sure?

There was only one way to find out.

He traced his fingers around the perimeter of the envelope, the corners now worn from his constant handling.

For a moment, he sensed Anita's fingertips running down his back, assuring him it was okay to open it. The sensation was so real, he shivered and looked around him. His window blind rippled from a breeze that swept in and he heard bird wings flapping on the roof.

A sign?

Whatever it was, he knew it was finally time to open and read her letter.

29

AN UNLOCKED HEART

Mitchell's fingers felt huge as he tried to peel back the gummed flap of the envelope and he failed several times. He stood up and paced across his bedroom, trying to muster up his courage.

Finally, he stood with his back against the wall, wedged between his bed and nightstand. He pressed his outer thighs against them, needing the support.

After slipping his finger into a small gap at the top of the flap, he eased the paper apart. With shaking hands, he slid the letter slowly out of its envelope, its prison for three years.

Then he held his breath and read the last words Anita ever wrote to him.

Dearest Mitchell,
I want to hate you, but I can't. I'm going to go for lunch, our lunch, with my friend Jane instead. We are going to drink cham-

pagne and eat strawberries and laugh with the waiters, because I
suppose I want you to be jealous even if you're not here to wit-
ness it. I'm going to try to be positive in this letter. However,
I'm not sure how much longer I can manage it.

The last few months have been hard for us both, you es-
pecially, because you're the one who's spending so much time
away from Poppy. I know you're working hard to help us have
a better life, and I am, too. I just wish you didn't have to do so
much. I was really looking forward to dining together, but there
will be other times, I hope.

We're supposed to be a family, Mitchell, but a lot of the time
it feels like we aren't. When I look at you, I want to see the man
I fell in love with. I want us to drink cider in a beer garden to-
gether. I want to see Poppy's seashell eyelids when we both hold
her for the first time. I want to share tiramisu with you. Above
anything else, I want Poppy to be happy. I want you to be happy.

Love always,
Anita xxx

Mitchell slid down against the wall in a heap. He grinned
and cried at the same time.

After Anita died, he'd convinced himself that she despised
him, that he'd failed her. But her words told him differently.
Among them, there was hope. She'd still been willing to fight
for their relationship. It could have been good again.

When he held her letter to his chest, he felt her words
against his skin and tendons loosened inside him. He bowed
his head and thought about her curls and her laughter.

If she was here, they would still be together. And now, although she was gone, he knew she'd want him to be happy
and hopeful.

And he could strive for that.

It could provide part of the framework he needed to move on. Perhaps he could try harder and feel better.

When he was ready, he stood up and placed the letter and envelope under his pillow.

He knew what she'd want him to do.

Poppy's mouth dropped as she surveyed the strange scene in the sitting room—Mitchell sitting on the floor surrounded by piles of letters everywhere.

"Um, like, wow," she said.

"A fresh delivery from Susan." Mitchell shrugged.

She wandered over and stared at them. "There's hundreds here."

"Yep, and I'm going to read them all."

Her eyes widened. "What?"

He smiled and held out his arm, inviting her to sit down beside him. "I think your mum wants me to do this."

She sank down cross-legged onto the floor. "Why?"

"I think she'd want me to read people's stories and help, if I can."

She nodded in agreement. "Have you been off work today?"

Mitchell explained how Russ had told him to take seven days away from his job. With embarrassment, he wiped away a rogue tear that escaped from his eye.

"Are you crying, Dad?"

He blinked up at the ceiling. "No."

She eyed him then ran a hand across the letters, shifting them under her touch. "I've got something to make you feel better."

"A miniature chocolate?" He found a smile.

"No. Stay here."

When Poppy returned with her hollowed-out dictionary, Mitchell looked at it warily. He didn't want to revisit his sparse writing-home efforts.

But she took out a letter and handed it to him.

Mitchell reluctantly unfolded the piece of paper.

Dearest Anita and Poppy,

The sun is out in the city this weekend and everyone is having fun, all except me. I miss you both so much when I'm away. At first the apartment felt like an adventure, but the longer I'm here, the farther away the both of you feel. Poppy, I miss your hugs in the morning and even seeing your unicorn T-shirt looking through the washing machine door at me. Anita—I miss your smile, and eating breakfast with you and, well, everything.

The bridge project is going well, but it's hard work and I've been naive about how much of my time and commitment it would take. I want to talk about the future and where we go from here.

I wish I was at home with the two of you.

Love always,
Mitchell/Dad xxx

As he read it, Mitchell remembered sitting at the kitchen table in the apartment on his own with his pen poised. He had heard the sounds of the city below him, while he was cut off from his family. He imagined Anita and Poppy carrying on their lives without him, going to play netball, making sandwiches together and eating popcorn at the cinema.

When his letters to them filtered out, it wasn't because he was a bad person, but a stressed one instead.

"I liked getting them." Poppy rested her head on his shoulder. "Everyone likes receiving letters."

"Yes, they do."

She went quiet for a long time. "It could have been you in the car, too." Her voice trembled. "With Mum."

He looked at her with a frown. *"What?"*

"If you'd met Mum for lunch that day... I might have lost you both."

"Oh, Poppy," he gasped, devastated. He'd not thought of things that way before. "I'm *so* sorry," he said. A tear cascaded down his cheek and this time he didn't try to hide it.

Poppy took his hand in hers and squeezed tightly. "It's not your fault," she said quietly. "It was an accident."

His throat felt so tight he could only whisper. "Thank you."

They wrapped their arms around each other and held on tightly. The pigeons cooed on the roof and lilac shadows shifted across the walls.

After a while, Poppy let go and unfolded her legs. "I think Liza really likes you, Dad," she said.

He felt a flutter inside when he thought about *her*. He let out a sigh. "I like her, too, but I don't think we're suited. If I were a letter, I'd be one that had been dropped in a puddle and the ink had all run. Liza would be a cheerful postcard with a sunflower on the front." He looked up at the naked light bulb hanging above his kitchen table and thought how much nicer it would look if it had a shade.

"Dramatic much?" Poppy nudged him in the ribs, making him grin. "I've been thinking about my school project."

"Again? You're getting obsessed," he teased.

"I know. I'm going to work on my PowerPoint presentation, but I like Liza's idea for a website, too."

"It could be really good." He looked at all the stories spread around him. He thought about the initials and messages on the padlocks. People would have a place to share their feelings and thoughts with others that wouldn't affect the environment or clog up the city bridges.

"I think Liza would like to do it, too," Poppy said.

An image dropped in Mitchell's head of him, Poppy and

Liza reading through letters together, and his fluttering feeling intensified, as if there was a colony of bats trapped inside him.

He realized he wanted Liza in his life.

After reading Anita's words, he felt it was what she would want for him, too.

This awareness made him feel like laughing out loud.

"What are you grinning at?" Poppy eyed him.

"Am I?"

"Yes. You look crazy."

He didn't want to keep these feelings to himself. "It's Liza," he said. "I think I really like her, too."

She fixed him with a stare. "Well, *that* took forever."

"You don't mind?"

She considered this for a while. "She makes a great banana milkshake, and Sasha loves you. Liza's good at shopping, and she uses music to make people happy. She likes Taylor Swift. That's lots of good things. And I think she likes me for me."

Mitchell smiled, warmth radiating through him, but then it faded. "I may have messed things up between us…"

Poppy shook her head. "Doesn't surprise me."

Mitchell knew she was right.

"The question is," Poppy said, "what are you going to do about it, Dad?"

Mitchell didn't know. He suddenly felt exhausted from his day. All he wanted to do at this moment in time was to flop on the sofa with his daughter.

When he felt stronger, he decided he would take the time to respond to all the correspondence. When he did, he would ask an important question.

Would you be happy to share your letter online?

But as for how to tell Liza what he felt for her, and how sorry he was, he really didn't know where to start.

30

PROJECT PADLOCK

Mitchell agreed that Poppy could skip her school club for a few days, so he could help her further on her presentation.

She read through all the letters that suited her project while Mitchell wrote back to people who had requested a response, left a return address or asked him a question. Also, to ones that tugged at his heartstrings.

He and Poppy sat at the dining table together, or lay on their bellies on the sitting room floor, chatting and sharing the letters, their emotions soaring and swooping at the stories of strangers.

Mitchell found there were lines and passages he wanted to share with Liza, topics he wanted to discuss, letters he and Poppy found to be hilarious, knowing that she'd laugh, too.

On his third evening of letter writing, Mitchell took a walk with Poppy to the park. When they returned to Angel House, they bumped into Carl in the lobby. To thank him for his care and concern after he slipped on the pavement, Mitchell invited him up to the apartment for supper.

The concierge grinned and asked if he might bring Susan along, too. "We've been seeing a lot of each other," he admitted shyly. "Would that be all right, Mr. Fisher?"

Mitchell readily agreed.

Later on, Mitchell and Poppy made homemade pizza and garlic bread together, and they sat with Carl and Susan around his dining table to eat.

Susan announced she was working on an article for Upchester News about the growing revival of letter writing in the city. "I'm convinced it's the big story I've been looking for," she said. "And it will show my boss I'm back on track."

"Poppy thinks if we encourage people to write letters, it could take their attention away from hanging padlocks," Mitchell said. "They could write them on paper or online."

"Great idea," Susan said. "I like it."

Mitchell asked her a question that had been playing on his mind. "Where did this last huge number of letters suddenly come from?"

Susan nibbled awkwardly on a pizza crust. "My boss took a day off work and I found out he'd been throwing any letters that arrived into a big box underneath his desk. I stuffed the black bin bag full of them."

"Then you left them with Carl to drop off for me?"

Susan nodded and she and Carl shared a look so full of love, it was impossible for Mitchell to feel angry with them.

"I still think you should pick the winner of the prize money," Susan said. "They're your letters, after all. Did any stand out for you?"

Mitchell surveyed his apartment. There were letters on

every surface, piled neatly on the coffee table, on the end of the sofa, laid out on the floor, and even some under Poppy's bed.

He recalled Edmond, the eighty-year-old man who loved the city, and the enigma of Third Time Lucky whose love was like a puddle. There was the delightful Annie, who shared her first kiss with Douglas on the bridge at the end of the war, and foreign exchange student Henri who was worried about the effect that the locks and keys would have on the wildlife.

As he scrolled through all the letter writers in his mind, there was one that sprang forward. Mitchell was sure that Ben and Melissa McDonald would welcome the prize money toward their safety awareness campaign about the dangers of open water. "There's a married couple I think should win the competition," he said.

Susan looked around her. "If you can find their letter, I'll get in touch with them."

Mitchell remembered the emotion and dignity in their words, as they wrote about their son, Simon. "Actually, do you mind if I write to them instead?" he said. "I think they'd appreciate the personal touch, and I want to offer to help them, too."

Throughout their conversation, Carl sat quietly, not asking any questions. He folded a weird shape out of paper and, when he'd finished it, Mitchell couldn't tell what it was supposed to be.

Susan and Poppy sat back in their seats and Mitchell collected their plates. "Did you finish writing the letter to your friend, Carl?" he asked.

Carl shook his head. He side-glanced at Susan. "I didn't need to. But I got lots of practice."

"Now you're an expert. Perhaps you can help me write back to all these people," Mitchell said.

Cheeks reddening, Carl's shoulders crept up toward his

ears. "You've been very kind to me, Mr. Fisher, but I need to tell you something. It's about all these letters. My letters…"

Susan rubbed his wrist with encouragement.

Carl's eyes dipped, embarrassed. "I can't actually read and write properly, Mr. Fisher. Never have been able to. Susan has been helping me learn."

"It's nothing to be ashamed of," she assured him.

He nodded gratefully though he still looked down. "I grew up with my dad and he never read with me, or showed me how to write. When I started primary school, all the other kids could at least write their first name, but I couldn't do it. I tried to hide it by asking lots of questions, and I was good at art, too. But writing was the one thing I couldn't ever get right, I just got left behind so easily. One of my teachers said I was hopeless, and it stuck with me."

"That's sad," Poppy said. "I think you're brilliant."

Carl peeped up at her with a smile. "I'm doing my best to learn now. But I'm not up to helping with these letters. I'm not letting you down, am I, Mr. Fisher?"

Mitchell shook his head furiously. "No, of course not. You're good at so many other things—everything else."

Carl's grin returned. "Thanks."

"It's a crazy idea, but we could ask Brad Beatty if Word Up might be interested in getting on board," Susan said. "The band could ask people to stop hanging padlocks and to write letters instead."

"That would protect the bridges," Mitchell agreed. "You'd be able to see their beauty again. Did you know the 1970s concrete one is called a beam bridge? It's like a log that—"

"*Dad.*" Poppy shook her head at him.

"The trouble is," Susan continued, "I spilled coffee on a politician, and I got stuck in traffic on my way to interview

Brad. We need someone who is cheerful, resourceful and great with people to ask him."

"That rules me out." Mitchell shrugged.

"We need someone inquisitive, who asks good questions and who is caring," Susan added.

Mitchell, Susan and Poppy slid their eyes over to Carl.

"Me?" He sat up in surprise.

Susan nodded. "We need a kind of glue that binds everything together."

Carl's face flushed more, right up to the roots of his yellow hair. "Well, I can try," he said eventually. "Do you think I can do it?"

"You'll be great," Susan said.

He took hold of her hand. "Thank you."

Mitchell looked around the room. He eyed all the notes Susan had jotted down so far. A project was underway, and he loved these planning stages.

Poppy looked at him inquisitively. "What are you thinking, Dad?"

"Hmm, I'm wondering if we need a spreadsheet to map all this out. Perhaps we need a schedule, a firm plan of action. Set some targets."

Under the table, Poppy kicked his shin.

"Ouch." He bent down and rubbed his leg. "It was only a thought."

That night as he lay in bed, Mitchell didn't feel like a bag of bricks was weighing down on him. He felt hopeful, even excited about the future.

When he reached under his bed, he found there was only one sheet of paper left in his Basildon Bond pad, and he wanted to use it wisely.

He opened his drawer and looked at all the letters he'd written to Anita. It was time to empty them out and add them to his recycling pile. She wouldn't ever be able to read them, and he wasn't the same person who wrote them any longer.

His ritual of writing to Anita was finally at an end.

The sense of loss he felt was tangible, and it was with both a heavy heart and a lightness in his fingers that he took up his fountain pen.

It felt both scary and exciting to start a letter to someone new. He wrote down his first words.

Dear Liza,

31

WEDDING DAY

Mitchell took his blue wool suit, which he last wore to Anita's funeral, to be dry-cleaned. When he got it back, he peeled off the cover and hung it on the back of his bedroom door. He felt odd about wearing it to Graham's wedding, a celebration after loss. However, it was a good suit. He felt Anita would encourage him to get use out of it. He was glad the fabric was more vivid than he remembered, a bright cobalt rather than a somber navy.

Mitchell placed Anita's last letter to him in the inside pocket so he could feel her close to him during the ceremony. He put the one he'd written to Liza in there, too, for safekeeping.

Poppy sidled into his bedroom and inspected the jacket on its hanger. She lifted up one of its sleeves. "Do you think it will still fit you?" she asked.

He raised an eyebrow at her. "What are you inferring?"

"Nothing. You'll just look silly if it's shrunk."

He smoothed down his shirt over the torso that was much slimmer than it had been three years ago. "I think it's more likely that I've shrunk."

Mitchell carried the suit into the bathroom and changed into it. In the mirror above the sink, he stroked its lapels. From what he could see, the jacket looked surprisingly okay on him. It was a bit baggy around the chest, and the trousers were an inch too loose on the waist, but not totally disastrous.

"Is it a bit too big?" Poppy asked as she plucked at the back of his jacket.

"It's the fashion," Mitchell said. "Or so I'll tell people."

They smiled at each other in the mirror. "I think Mum would say you look handsome," she said.

On the day of the wedding, Graham sported a gray three-piece suit, a red cravat and top hat. Apart from his broken front tooth, he looked every inch the dapper groom. He stood in the doorway of Brock's baronial ballroom and nervously greeted people as they filed in.

Mitchell stood proudly beside him. "It'll be okay," he assured him.

"I know, Mitchy Boy. It'll be marvelous, but I still feel jittery inside. I've even brought along one of Mum's hankies for my top pocket, so she's kind of here with me."

Mitchell smiled. "I've brought a letter from Anita, too."

"Well, aren't we big softies?" Graham said.

As the wedding party guests filed past, Mitchell saw they fitted into two distinct groups. Graham's friends and family could be identified by the men's tailored suits and mirror-shiny black shoes. The women wore feathered fascinators, floral-print dresses and court shoes. Rosie's guests donned lots of velvet and embroidery. Mitchell had never seen so many tattooed shoulders and primary-colored hairstyles at a wedding before.

The ballroom was a fitting venue. It had long stained-glass windows that cast prisms of light across the red carpet. The seating consisted of vintage turquoise velvet cinema seats, set out in rows. At the end of the wedding aisle stood a metal arch, the kind of garden trellis that flowers and leaves wove around. But this one featured something sturdier as its decoration.

Covering every inch of it, padlocks hung, bunched together so tightly that, from a distance, they resembled barnacles on a ship's anchor.

"What do you think of our centerpiece, Mitchy Boy?" Graham nodded toward it. "I said I wanted to do something special for Rosie."

"It looks amazing, totally unique, like the two of you," Mitchell said. He stroked his chin. "Hmm, I wonder where you managed to find so many locks."

"I have my connections." Graham winked. "I looked through all the locks and saved the ones with loving messages. Then I fastened them to the arch. We're going to get married under something that truly represents love. Do you think Rosie will like it?"

"I think she'll absolutely love it."

"Good, I hope so. And Brock will keep it to use for future weddings."

At the mention of his name, Brock appeared. He was dressed in smart jeans and a black T-shirt. He gave Graham a slap on the back and clasped Mitchell's hand in a bone-crushing shake. "PlayStation or Xbox?" he said.

"Excuse me?"

"Mitchell isn't a gamer," Graham said. "He's my best man."

"I'm going to try to be," Mitchell said.

The three men walked down the aisle together and stood in front of the arch. Poppy sat on one of the front seats and stood up to greet them. She looked pretty in her new clothes and shoes. Mitchell fished out her necklace from under her dress so her pug dog pendant was on display.

Brock turned and faced the room, and Mitchell and Graham shared nervy smiles as music started up. It sounded more like an Irish jig than a wedding march, all panpipes and flutes.

"Not my choice," Graham whispered to Mitchell.

When Rosie appeared, she wore a purple satin dress with a lace-up bodice, down to her bump, and a flowing skirt beyond that. Fluted sleeves hung down to her knees and she carried a small bunch of white roses and freesias. She smiled hello to guests on each side of the aisle as she slowly walked along it toward Graham. As she got closer, Mitchell saw some of the blooms in her bouquet were made out of Lego bricks.

Graham laughed when he spotted them. "I thought some of my pieces were missing," he said.

Poppy beamed. "She looks like a pregnant fairy princess."

Brock waited until people's chatter died down.

Graham and Rosie had written their own marriage vows, and they faced each other to read them out.

"I know you're like a unicorn and I'm only a donkey," Graham started. "You're a rainbow and you bring all the color into my life. You've made me a better person."

As he continued, Mitchell felt a lump rising in his throat, so large it might choke him. He swallowed a few times and stared down at his shoelaces to try to will it away.

His discomfort was broken by the sound of Poppy giggling at Rosie's speech, in which she promised to cherish Graham's Lego Death Star, forever and ever.

After Brock pronounced them man and wife, Rosie flipped Graham back in her arms and they conducted a minute-long, full throttle kiss in front of everyone.

Mitchell reached out and covered Poppy's eyes with his hand, and she laughingly batted it away. She spread her fin-

gers out behind her head in a crown. "They'll be sweet together forever, just like pineapples," she said.

The wedding dinner was a meat-free affair, and when
Mitchell read the menu card he groaned inside. The words
vegetarian buffet ranked only one lower on his wince list after
campfire jamboree.

However, when he and Poppy got closer to the long buffet table, there was a riot of delicious food. Roasted butternut
squash, beetroot couscous, grilled vegetable skewers and a nut
roast. Poppy attempted to coax two vegan enchiladas onto her
plate and Mitchell made her put one back.

They sat at the top table with Graham, Rosie and a few
close family members, drinking fizzy elderflower cordial from
purple plastic goblets with bendy straws. The knives and forks
were crafted from copper and had the initials *G* and *R* printed
on them.

Rosie stood up and revealed her wedding gift to Graham,
an elaborate tapestry featuring an embroidered unicorn and
a donkey. "It's our new family crest," she said and Graham
beamed with joy.

When most of the guests had finished eating, Graham
leaned in toward Mitchell and nudged him. "It's the time
you've been waiting for."

"Um, the wedding cake?" Mitchell said hopefully.

"Nice try. I think we're ready for your speech. On your
feet, Mitchy. Try not to embarrass either of us too much. Feel
free to keep it short and snappy."

As he stood up, Mitchell couldn't feel his knees. The chattering in the room died down and someone started to clap.
Others followed suit until applause rippled around the room.

"Go on, Dad," Poppy said eagerly. "You did okay around
the campfire."

He paused to tug gently on her plait and brushed the tip of her nose with it. "Love you," he said.

"Love you, treble that."

Mitchell's hands shook as he took his speech from his jacket pocket. "Thanks for coming, everyone," he said with a quivery voice. "I'm delighted we're all here to celebrate the wedding of Graham and Rosie." He lifted his purple goblet in a toast and stared at the sleeve of his blue jacket.

As he felt lots of expectant eyes upon him, a frost seemed to creep over him, stiffening his bones and cooling his skin, until he felt like his body might shatter if he moved. "I, um—" His words halted and wouldn't come through.

He set his goblet back down on the table and hung his head for a moment, trying to gather his thoughts.

When he raised his head, he imagined Anita walking down the aisle toward him. She wore her red coat and her smile radiated through him, as she walked to his side and then stood behind him.

He could swear he felt her hand circling around his chest and her fingertips pressing lightly against his ribs. Her breath was hot and sweet on his neck, and he was so sure she must be here with him, helping him find a rhythm to his breathing again. He reached his hand to his chest to feel hers, but his fingertips found only the buttons on his jacket.

"Are you okay, Dad?" Poppy asked.

Mitchell opened his eyes and, instead of Anita, his daughter stood by his side, instead. He felt such a tug of love for her, it overwhelmed him with its ferocity. "I'm not sure," he said.

Graham and Rosie watched him, their eyes full of concern. Mitchell nodded apologetically at them.

"It's fine," Graham whispered.

"Do you want to sit down?" Rosie asked.

Mitchell shook his head. He wanted to do this.

Anita would always live on through Poppy. She had both lots of their blood running through her veins. And Mitchell had to find the strength to start celebrating that, not to keep memorializing it. No matter how painful it was, he had to try to move on.

After taking a deep breath, he held it in his chest. He folded up the paper with his speech on it and left it on the table. He didn't think of any strategies or plan what to say. All the letters he'd read from strangers helped him find his own words and he spoke straight from his heart.

"Even though Graham's sweaters were too big as a kid, his heart was even bigger," Mitchell said. "We've known each other for many years, and have dipped in and out of each other's lives, but he's always been there in the background, like a bad guy in a slasher movie."

A collective laugh rang around the room, with Rosie's the loudest. Graham rolled his eyes and guffawed.

Mitchell waited for quietness to descend. He licked his lips before he spoke again.

"Some of you will know that I lost someone close to me—my partner, Anita. We didn't have the perfect relationship, and I've always felt guilty about that. However, I've read many love letters recently, and I now believe there's no such thing as perfection, just two people trying to make the most of their time together." He gestured toward the padlocks on the arch. "Love can be showy, or it can be quiet. It can be long lasting, or it can burn brightly and fizzle out. It can bring families together and tear them apart. It can be welcomed or unrequited. I've tried to think of its definition and I think that true love is simply *your* way of being together, in a way that makes you both happy. And Graham and Rosie are just made for each other in their own unique way, and that's what makes them special." He raised his glass. "To Graham and Rosie."

"To Graham and Rosie," everyone repeated.

Poppy raised a glass of lemonade and stared at the tapestry of the family crest. "I *love* that unicorn," she murmured.

Graham patted Mitchell's shoulder, in thanks and some relief. Rosie stood up and cradled her bouquet to her bump. She walked toward the buffet table at the other end of the room. Once there, she turned her back to her guests and raised the flowers to her chest. "Hup," she shouted and flung them with force over her head.

The bouquet soared through the air on a flight pattern directly back toward the top table. Mitchell saw it was about to collide with the goblets and tableware and, without thinking, he lunged forward.

Poppy's eyes opened wide with excitement that he was about to catch it.

Mitchell held his arms open and the bouquet crashed into his hands, then bounced out of them and tumbled to the floor. Petals scattered and Lego bricks exploded.

His jaw slackened as he stared down at the broken flowers, and a moment of silence in the room deafened him. But then a cheer rang around at his valiant effort. He picked up the smashed blooms and held them aloft like a trophy, with petals dropping down around him. "I tried," he said.

Poppy shook her head at him very slowly. "You are *so* embarrassing," she said.

"That's what dads are for," he said as he plucked out a white rose and handed it to her.

She took it from him and smelled it, and when she glanced back up at him, he could see Anita shining through in her smile.

32

LAST DANCE

For their wedding reception, Graham and Rosie had hired a Word Up tribute band, whose members were at least ten years older than the actual group. They played a few of the group's hits, then due to popular demand, launched into tracks by the Rolling Stones and Kings of Leon instead.

A group of children had transformed a long table into a den. They sat in a line underneath it with a tablecloth hung over chairs as an entrance canopy.

"Why don't you go and play with them?" Mitchell said.

Poppy tutted. "They're just kids. Can we go outside instead?"

The evening was filled with the promise of the hot weather returning and Rosie threw open all the windows and doors. Outside, Graham had laid picnic blankets and rugs on the grass. Candles were dotted around and shone like fireflies.

Mitchell and Poppy sat down next to each other on a tartan blanket.

"This is the best wedding ever," Poppy said.

"I think it's only the second one you've been to."

"It's still the best."

Mitchell thought for a while. "It's my best one, too," he said. "I've enjoyed it, despite having to do a speech."

"You did okay." Poppy picked up a daisy and twirled it between her thumb and finger as she thought for a while. "Why didn't you and Mum ever get married?" she asked.

Mitchell considered her question. "We'd only been together for three months when your mum found out she was pregnant."

"What?" Poppy's mouth fell open, aghast. "You never told me *that* before."

"You never really asked."

"I wish I hadn't." She pushed the daisy behind her ear.

"Your mum and I knew we loved each other, and we loved you. And we felt we didn't need to stand in front of a room full of friends and family to express that. The two of us knowing it was enough."

"The three of us," Poppy corrected.

Mitchell wrapped his arm around her. "Yes, the three of us."

They sat like this for a while, huddled together, and with Poppy staring up at the stars. "Do you think Mum is up there?"

Mitchell knew it wasn't true. How could it be? But for the briefest moment, he allowed himself to believe it was. "Yes," he said firmly.

"Which one? Which star is she?" She shuffled closer to him.

"The brightest one, of course."

"I think so, too." Poppy slipped her hand inside his jacket and roughly rubbed his chest. Then she wriggled her fingers. "You have something in your pocket."

"I know."

"Is it your speech?"

Mitchell reached into his jacket and undid the tiny button on his inside pocket. "I brought a letter from your mum, and I started one to Liza last night. I wanted to say sorry."

"*Just* sorry?"

He thought about this. "I should say more, but it's not that easy." He let out a sigh. "I'm not really sure why I'm carrying it around with me, and it's probably all too late anyway. I messed up."

He tried to think of Yvette now on the bridge in her yellow dress, the person who had sparked his outlook, but he could only see Liza. She wore aviator sunglasses, toadstool earrings and had a gingery dog at her feet. He saw a friendly smile and banana milkshakes and they came with a Madonna soundtrack. "Open Your Heart" started up in his head.

He thought about the feel of Liza's hand in his own in the forest, and the strange tension in the kitchen between them as they made the chili together, and the brush of their foreheads as they collected broken glass.

"You wrote to all those strangers, but Liza's our friend," Poppy said.

He liked how the words *our friend* sounded. It was a solid and warm word full of potential.

"You could write it now." She shrugged.

Mitchell gave a small laugh, but her face was serious. He looked up at Anita's shining star and it appeared to wink down at him. His laugh faded and everything suddenly felt so clear.

Liza wasn't a figment of his imagination, or a wish or a twinkling star.

He didn't want to wait until tomorrow, or the day after that, and then stick a stamp to an envelope and walk to a postbox. He wanted to tell her tonight how he felt about her, and to ask if she'd give him a chance.

He knew he'd been broken, but she had helped to make him feel more whole again.

He wanted her to be part of his future, and Poppy's, too. Not just as a friend.

Maybe they needed each other, and each other's families. It might all be too late for this, or she might not be interested, but he was determined to try.

"If I write the letter now, I could go to her house tonight to deliver it. Will you come with me?" he asked.

Poppy broke into a grin. "Yep," she said. "I'd love that. But what about Graham?"

Mitchell took a pen from his pocket and thought about his friend's new romantic nature. "I'm sure he'll understand."

He unfolded the letter he'd started to Liza and stared at his first few words at the top. Then he nodded to assure himself and allowed his feelings for her to flow onto the page.

Once he finished writing, he and Poppy found Graham and Rosie feeding each other wedding cake with their fingers. "I'm so sorry, but we have to dash away for a while," Mitchell said. "We'll be back as quick as we can."

Graham raised an eyebrow. "Liza?"

Mitchell touched his pocket where he'd placed his letter to her in an envelope. "How do you know? You've never even met her."

"I saw it written all over your face when you were twirling on the tire in my garden. Any man who uses up a lifelong favor to retrieve a padlock for a woman *must* be smitten. Knew you were a goner before you knew it yourself." He looked at his watch. "I'd love you to be back for our last dance, though. Don't want my best man to miss that."

"What time will that be?"

"Midnight. Rosie wants to do it to the twelve chimes of Upchester cathedral. You've got just over an hour."

Mitchell shot out his hand and Poppy placed hers in his. "Let's go," he said. "Are your new shoes good for running in?"

She looked down at her feet. "Yep."

Graham shook Mitchell's hand. "Good luck, Mitchy Boy."

"Thanks, I'll need it."

Mitchell and Poppy walked quickly through the ballroom, traversing around people dancing. They burst out onto the street and then started to sprint across the city together.

33

LIZA'S LETTER

As Mitchell jogged across the city with Poppy, he looked out for a cab to hail on the way. However, at almost 11:00 p.m. on a Saturday evening, all the taxis were occupied. If he phoned for one, it might take half an hour to arrive.

When he and Poppy ran over Redford, Mitchell didn't think about Yvette's yellow dress or where she hung her heart-shaped padlock. He didn't picture anything in his mind other than Liza.

At the end of the bridge, they stopped for a short while, panting together as they caught their breath. Then their feet were busy again, beating rhythmically against the pavement.

They passed late-night café bars where friends lounged around small plastic tables, drinking coffees and beers. They traversed around the street cleaners who were already tackling the day's rubbish on the pavements. A queue of people snaked from a crepe van, and the sharp smell of lemon contrasted with the warm smell of melting sugar. On another night, Mitchell would have stopped and bought Poppy a sweet treat. But for now, they had to concentrate on their mission.

When they eventually reached Liza's house, Mitchell marveled at how Poppy managed to look so calm and collected while he wheezed like an old man.

The lights were on both downstairs and up, and he saw a TV flickering in the sitting room that told him someone was home. There were no cars parked on the street to indicate that Sheila or Naomi might be visiting.

Mitchell took a moment to compose himself. He smoothed down his lapels and fastened a button on his suit jacket that had come undone. He made sure the white rose in his buttonhole was neat and tidy. Only then did he reach inside his breast pocket and take out the letter to Liza.

Mitchell's heart thumped as he rang her doorbell. He listened for her footsteps in the hallway, or a jingle of her keys in the lock, but no one came to the door. There was a small thud from inside the house and Sasha jumped up onto the windowsill to stare at him, her breath fogging up the pane of glass as she made a wet smear with her nose.

Mitchell could see the expectation and hope etched upon Poppy's face, and he felt it, too. He yearned for Liza to answer the door with a "Hey," and a smile.

He pressed the doorbell again. A curtain twitched at the upstairs window, but after a few more minutes, Liza still hadn't answered.

"I don't think she's home," Poppy said, trying to sound chirpy, though he could tell she didn't believe her own words.

Mitchell wanted to ring the doorbell again, but he didn't want to harass her if she wasn't ready, or interested in seeing him again.

"Are you going to post her letter instead?"

He nodded glumly. "It's the only option."

Mitchell took a pen out of his jacket pocket and rested the letter flat against the wall. He wrote an additional note to Liza on the envelope.

Dearest Liza,
Poppy and I called for you at 11:30 p.m. tonight. We'd hang around but I promised Graham we'd be back to the Jupiter Hotel by midnight, for his last wedding dance.

I hope to see you soon, and Poppy says hello, too.
Mitchell

He read over his note then inserted a small arrow on the line above his name. In very small letters, he added the word *Love*.

Then he posted the letter through her door.

When he looked back at Poppy, she looked smaller, standing in the shadows. "Come on," he said. "Liza can read what I've written and take time to think about things."

"I know. It's just… Well, I miss her."

He pursed his lips, understanding. "I know. And I do, too."

He placed his arm around her shoulder and they walked back along the street together and onto a main road. Their footsteps were slower, more forlorn, and Mitchell glanced back intermittently at Liza's house.

Poppy tugged his sleeve. "Come on, Dad. There's nothing you can do. We need to get back for Graham's dance."

He glanced at his watch and his eyes widened. "We only have twenty minutes. We can't make it on foot. I'll have to try to hail a cab."

Poppy looked around her doubtfully.

The traffic was busy and Mitchell felt as if he'd been dropped inside a computer game as cars shifted past him at speed. He lifted his head, up and down, to try to locate a taxi with its light on. He'd always meant to download Uber, but he and Poppy usually got around the city on the bus just fine.

"What are we going to do, Dad?"

Mitchell performed some calculations in his head. If they caught a bus in the next couple of minutes, they might just about make it. He held Poppy's hand tightly. "Let's hurry along to the bus stop."

As they sped toward it, three beeps pierced the air above the noise of the other traffic. A car pulled up alongside them and the window wound down. Liza leaned over toward them. "Hop in," she said.

Mitchell stared at her as if he'd seen an angel. "You're *here*."

"Yes. You're not hallucinating."

Poppy opened the rear door and slid into the car without question. Mitchell was slower at joining Liza in the passenger seat, still surprised she was here.

"We called at your house," he said.

"I know. And I wasn't sure if I wanted to see you at first. I hid upstairs, but then I heard my letter box rattle—and I read you have to get somewhere very quickly. I can take you there."

He swallowed nervously. "Have you read my full letter?"

"Yes. And we have lots to talk about. But for now, fasten your seat belt." She beeped and deftly pulled out, leaning forward in her seat so her nose wasn't far from the windscreen. Rousing classical music played on the car radio. "This is a fantastic tune to drive along to."

"Just so you know—I meant every word in my letter," Mitchell said.

She didn't reply, but gave him a quick smile that he couldn't decipher. "Sorry I took a while to get to you. I mean, a girl needs time to choose her shoes, even in a rush. I went for the fuchsia pink ones."

"Good choice," Poppy said from the back.

"Thank you, kind miss."

They drove past the five bridges, which looked so different at night, each lit up and seeming like they were floating above the river that flowed black, unseen, beneath them.

Liza glanced over at Redford. "I can see the appeal of that redbrick bridge more now," she said. "Never noticed it before. It looks rather solid and handsome."

"I'm getting to appreciate the new white Yacht one," Mitchell said. "It's different but stunning."

In the back of the car, Poppy sighed. "Please don't tell us about the concrete one again, Dad."

Mitchell grinned. "I'll try not to."

He found himself gripping his seat as Liza took a sharp bend in the road. She finally pulled onto the Jupiter Hotel's car park with a screech.

Mitchell and Poppy unbuckled their seat belts and opened the doors. They both clambered out quickly.

However, Liza stayed put.

Mitchell placed his hand on the car roof and bent down to speak to her. "Are you going to join us?"

She bit her bottom lip. "I'm not sure, Mitchell. It's late and I'm giving a lesson tomorrow. I dashed out of the house and Sasha will wonder where I've gone to…"

He gave her time to think.

The music on the radio ended and the presenter started to drone on in a sleep-inducing voice.

Poppy ducked her head around Mitchell's arm to speak to Liza. "Rosie made Graham a tapestry, a family crest," she said. "It's got a unicorn and a donkey on it. Because they're so different. You should come see *that*, at least."

Mitchell and Liza shared a smile, before she paused a few beats. The anticipation of her reply made his chest feel tight.

"Well, that sounds most interesting," she said. "Perhaps I should take a closer look."

Mitchell beamed. "It's 11:58," he said.

Liza flung her car door open and jumped out. The three of them ran across the car park into the hotel and shoved open the doors to the ballroom.

Graham and Rosie stood together on the dance floor. No music played as Mitchell, Liza and Poppy approached them.

"Bloody hell, Mitchy Boy. Talk about cutting it fine," Graham said. "We've been waiting for you."

"I'm so sorry."

"My fault." Liza pointed down at her feet. "I had to find shoes to wear. One was under my bed and it took a while to locate it."

Rosie broke into a smile. "I *love* those. Pregnancy has made my feet swell so I had to wear these." She hitched up her wedding dress to display a pair of purple Nike trainers.

"They're so cool," Liza said. "That look really suits you."

"I didn't know about *that*," Graham laughed.

"We can tell each other all our secrets, now we're married," Rosie said, and she wrapped her arms around his waist.

The first stroke of midnight sounded faintly from the Upchester cathedral clock.

"This is it," Graham said. He raised a hand and waved at Brock, who had also taken on DJ duties.

The opening bars of "Crazy For You" by Madonna started to play. Graham and Rosie held each other close and swayed side by side. Other couples filtered onto the dance floor to join them.

Poppy stood there stiffly. "I don't know this one," she said. "I might join the kids under the table."

"Go and play," Mitchell said. "Have fun."

She sidled away self-consciously, then broke into a skip.

"Shall we…um, get a drink? I'm in the mood for a glass of chardonnay, or do you fancy a nice red?" Liza gestured toward the bar. "Or you can show me the tapestry."

Mitchell followed her gaze. After running across the city, he could really do with a glass of cider. But there was something he wanted more. He positioned his arms as if ballroom dancing with an invisible partner. "I know I'm not perfect—far from it. But I'd really like to ask you to dance, Miss Bradfield."

She paused for a while, so he wasn't sure what her answer would be. Her eyes flicked away from his before she gave him a short nod. She took hold of her skirt and curtsied. "That's a nice proposition. Not something I've been asked before. I don't mind if I do, Mr. Fisher."

They stepped closer together and he wrapped one arm around her waist and took her hand. When she placed her hand lightly on the back of his jacket, he felt light-headed, in a good way. Her perfume had a hint of coconut and it reminded him of holidays and sunshine. And he knew he liked it. Very much indeed.

From beneath a table at the edge of the dance floor, among a line of other children, Poppy stuck her thumbs up at him.

34

THE NEW BRIDGE

Two days later

Mitchell and Poppy walked along the main road in Upchester, past the Slab, Vicky, Archie and Redford, toward the new Yacht bridge. The river ran beside them, a shimmer of smooth gray satin. Mitchell enjoyed being in the city with the sun warming his cheeks. It brought out a happiness in people, a bonhomie that didn't exist in duller weather.

There was an energy in the air, an infectious buzz about today's centenary celebrations and the opening of the new bridge. Families and friends waved flags and held on to bobbing balloons as they teemed toward it. Mitchell felt genuinely happy for the lovers who held hands and looked into each other's eyes as they walked along.

It was something he'd once had for himself, and perhaps he could again.

When he saw a swish of a red jacket among the crowds, Mitchell let it slip away, knowing it could never be Anita. He focused on what was ahead of him instead. He'd arranged to meet Liza and her family in the middle of the bridge, next to one of its huge masts.

Mitchell wondered if any of the people surrounding him might have written a letter to him, and received his own in reply. It made him feel a stronger connection to the city and everyone who lived in it, as if there were invisible threads binding them all together.

When he and Poppy approached the mouth of the bridge, Mitchell saw the barriers had been removed and food stalls and vans now lined its pavements. The smell of hot dogs made him feel hungry. Other vendors sold hats, T-shirts and commemorative posters with Jasmine Trencher's bridge design on them, and he could see how his own original plan had been steeped in the past. The new white structure that towered in front of him was majestic and beautiful.

At the far end of the bridge, a big Word Up logo spun around on a large screen above the stage.

Mitchell spied Liza with her back to him several meters away. She wore her white shirt with rows of dogs on it, and the purple highlights in her hair had a dragonfly-like iridescence. When she turned and they caught each other's eye, something bubbled gently and hopefully inside him.

A group of excited toddlers milled around Mitchell and Poppy, their parents trying to gather them all together in one place. When Mitchell halted to let them pass by, he felt a hand stroke down his arm, as if he was a cat.

Spinning around in surprise, he saw a flash of platinum blond hair and slash of scarlet.

"Mitchell. Salutations," Jasmine Trencher said with a smile that showed a smudge of lipstick on her front tooth. "*So* fantastic to see you. I wondered if you'd be here for the celebrations."

His mouth gaped and the color seeped from his face. He instantly started to sift through all the words he had screamed at her in his own head over the last couple of years to find ones that were suitable in front of Poppy.

His daughter squeezed his hand. "Dad?"

Mitchell swallowed the words down thickly. He ordered himself to think properly before he spoke to Jasmine. "It's okay, Pops," he said gently. "You go and see Liza, if you like?"

She nodded and skipped off, and he watched as the Bradfields embraced her, as if she was one of their own family.

Yvette wore a black sundress and cradled Connor in a white sling, lowering him so Poppy could take a peek. Naomi crouched down to wipe ice cream from her kids' mouths and Sheila enjoyed the attention of a street performer who played the guitar and sang to her. When they noticed Mitchell looking over, they each gave him a wave.

He raised his hand back, and a feeling of belonging rose within him. When he returned his focus to Jasmine, he found a calmness in his breathing. His smile didn't feel too forced. "The bridge looks beautiful. It's amazing to see everyone using it. You must feel very proud."

Jasmine pressed her lips together, looking bewildered at his generous words. "Yes, totally. A couple of years' hard work, but worth it. I mean, it's really magnificent, huh? I admired your original design, but it just wasn't..."

He held up his hand to stop her. "You were right, Jas. Okay? Your design is more fitting of the city. You just went about introducing it in the wrong way. But it's all water under the bridge," he said, not intending to make a pun. "I've made peace with it, and a lot of other things, too."

"Right," she said, taking this in. "Good. I mean, no hard feelings, right?"

He couldn't grant her that much, and he looked around him. "Are you here with anyone to celebrate your achievement?"

Her shoulders dropped and he noticed. "I, um, well—no, actually. Things are totally awkward at Foster and Hardman at the moment. Someone complained I pilfered a design from them. I mean, as if I'd ever need to do that. Why would I? It's ridiculous. I keep trying to grab Don for a coffee to explain, but…" She flicked her eyes away. "Um, are you still in touch with him, Mitchell? Perhaps you could…"

Mitchell cleared his throat. "I'm no longer part of that world. I've moved on."

"Yes, but he might listen to you…"

"Perhaps you could write him a letter to explain."

"Yes, but—"

He felt a hand slip into his, fingers weaving. Liza stood at his side. "Hi," she said with an apologetic smile. "I'm sorry to interrupt you, but Poppy is virtually begging me for ice cream. I didn't know if she'd already had one…"

"No, not yet. And it's fine. We were just finishing up our conversation, anyway."

"Great. We're all waiting for you, and Barry is here, too."

Mitchell looked over to where Poppy, Yvette, Sheila and Barry stood. "Friends and family," he explained to Jasmine. "Got to go. Sorry."

"But about Don…?" she said after him as he walked away. "What about me?"

He gave a shrug of his shoulders and concentrated on Liza's hand in his.

When they joined the others at the mast, Poppy stared intently at Connor. She hooked her fingers around his sling so she could see him better. "Look at his tiny fingers," she said. "His eyelashes are so cute."

Yvette rocked him proudly. "I'm going to take him home in a few minutes. I don't want the loud music to scare him when it starts."

"Auntie Jean called Mum this morning," Liza told Mitchell. "She had a day off from her tour. When she's completed it, she's going to come and stay with me for a few days. It will be such fun. I can't see her and Mum ever agreeing on anything musical, but they might find a common bond over Connor. I hope they can work out their differences."

"Let me know if I can help with any chili making," Mitchell said.

"I'll bear it in mind, though getting takeaway will be less stressful."

When Mitchell glanced over toward Barry, he saw his friend was slouched against a railing.

Liza followed his eyes. "Barry doesn't look happy at all. Do you know what's wrong with him?"

Mitchell shook his head.

"Chat to him, if you like? I'll take Poppy for that ice cream. Is she allowed two scoops?"

"Yes, and sprinkles."

When Mitchell joined Barry, his friend's shoulders slumped. "Things haven't worked out with Trisha," he said. "Her ex is still on the scene and making moves for her attention."

"I'm sorry to hear that."

"Why are things so complicated?" Barry huffed. "It looks like I'll have to go back into the wild again."

Mitchell patted his arm, and he thought about the last few weeks. "Why don't you leave things alone for a while?" he said. "Stop searching so hard and things might come to you."

Barry pondered on this. He nodded toward Liza. "That worked for you, yeah?"

"I think it did. Maybe the bad times help you to appreciate the good, when they happen."

Barry managed a small smile. "Whoa, that was deep."

"I *know*, right?"

"Maybe Liza might have a nice single friend or two…"

Mitchell shook his head slowly. "Come on, mate. Let's get an ice cream to cool us down."

Barry chose chocolate flavor and Mitchell got adventurous with mint choc chip. Poppy wanted vanilla with cherry chunks, and Liza went for strawberry.

Barry licked his cone. "I'll look after Poppy for a while, if you guys want to go for a walk together?" he suggested.

Poppy squinted against the sun. "I could interview Barry for my project, Dad. He's not a stranger and will have stories about the padlocks on the bridges."

"Good idea. If he doesn't mind?"

"Nah, go for it," Barry said, but then jokingly pressed a hand against his heart. "Nothing too painful, though. Go easy on the questions."

Mitchell and Liza ate their ice creams and walked back along the bridge to the main street together.

"I was almost late getting here today," she said. "My oldest client is taking his music exam tomorrow and I gave him a last-minute lesson this morning. He's very nervous."

"Still? At the age of eighty-one?"

"He's had a birthday and is eighty-two now. And if something's important to you, then a touch of anxiety can be good. It makes your body feel more alive and receptive."

Mitchell felt a drumming in his chest, his own adrenaline pulsing at being with Liza, and he knew this was true. "It's great he's doing this later in life."

"It's never too late to teach an old dog new tricks," she said. "Well, except maybe Sasha. I've been trying to get her not to pull on her leash for ages, and nothing works."

He smiled to himself and reached into his pocket. "I have something to show you." When he uncurled his palm, a small silver heart-shaped padlock glinted in the sunshine.

Liza pursed her lips. For once, she used few words. "For Anita?" she asked hesitantly.

"It's for us," he said. "The start of something. If that's okay?"

When her laugh rang out, it was full of joy and relief. She linked her arm through his. "It's more than okay. But I thought your job was to remove the locks. Won't you get in trouble for this if anyone sees you?"

"I'm officially still off work. Maybe just one more won't hurt."

"Well, I won't tell if you don't." She winked.

"Good. I know just the place."

He led her off the bridge, along the road and down a few steps that led to a grass verge. Crisscrosses of white struts supported the Yacht bridge underneath it. "If we hang the padlock under the bridge, no one will see it. But we'll know it's there."

They both ducked down, where the shadows were cool and soothed their hot skin. The sound of anyone else nearby was eclipsed by the shush of the river flowing past them.

"Is there a message on the lock?" she asked him.

He shook his head. "I thought about it, but some things are best said in person."

She looked into his eyes and opened her mouth to reply. He leaned forward and stopped her with a kiss to her lips.

She let out a small gasp before wrapping her arms around him. He cupped the padlock gently in his hand against her back.

They both melted into the moment, and Mitchell felt happy, like he was somehow coming home.

"Sometimes actions are better than words," Liza whispered.

Afterward, they glanced giddily at each other and attached the lock together. Mitchell put the key in his pocket rather than tossing it into the water, and they made their way back up onto the bridge.

When they reached Barry and Poppy again, they were chatting to Carl and Susan.

"Carl managed to get a meeting with Brad," Susan announced proudly as Mitchell and Liza joined them. "The two of them got on like a house on fire."

"I made origami figures of the band, Mr. Fisher," Carl said. "He really liked them, said they were quirky."

Susan nodded. "And Brad really liked the story of Upchester people being inspired to write letters. He says he writes songs very quickly and even jotted down a few lyrics while I was there, and—"

Her words were interrupted by a roar of applause that soared around them. Electronic feedback screeched through a speaker onstage and Mitchell frowned in the direction of the noise. A woman beside him whooped, and her boyfriend gave a loud whistle.

Onstage, lights swept to and fro. Lasers shot up toward the sky. A young man with spiky purple hair appeared and sat down behind a set of drums. A brief expectant hush fell across the crowd before the cheering started again, even louder.

Another man approached the microphone stand and thrust one arm in the air. This time, Mitchell felt bodies surging past him, trying to suck him along with them.

He wrapped protective arms around Poppy and Liza, holding them close.

"Ladies and gentlemen, boys and girls," the man shouted into his microphone. "I'm Brad Beatty and we are Word Up."

A fanfare of music blasted out. Poppy jumped up and down, squealing.

"We're going to kick off tonight's centenary celebrations with a new song," Brad said. "It's called 'Love Letters' and I hope you guys like it."

Mitchell, Liza and Poppy looked at each other and laughed.

He wondered what effect the song might have on the city folk of Upchester, and it was joyous to contemplate.

Then the first few bars of music kicked in. The crowd moved forward again, and Mitchell allowed himself to be swept along with them all.

★ ★ ★ ★ ★

ACKNOWLEDGMENTS

It takes a lot of people to bring a book to readers and I have a fantastic team around me. Everyone at my agency, Darley Anderson, does a fantastic job with special thanks going to agent Tanera Simons for her support and advice at the start of this book, and to my super-agent, Clare Wallace, for being there for me throughout it all. Also, to Mary Darby, Rosanna Bellingham, Darley himself and Sheila David.

A special mention goes to Janine McKown for her friendship and medical expertise in connection to Mitchell's, Yvette's and Connor's stories—thank you! Any possible inaccuracies are my own.

To all at Park Row in the US, especially my editors Natalie Hallak and Erika Imranyi, for their support, encouragement and understanding. In the UK, my appreciation and thanks go to my editor Emily Kitchin, Lisa Milton and the entire HQ team.

I'm lucky to have the support of many author friends, too numerous to mention here, but specific mentions go to B. A. Paris, Roz Watkins and Pam Jenoff.

To everyone who reads my books, enjoys and shares them—thank you! I love reading your reviews, so do keep leaving them. Each one really counts. Also, to booksellers and book bloggers everywhere for their continued support.

I couldn't write without my wonderful family around me, and love and appreciation go to my mum and dad, and to my son, Oliver. To Mark, thank you for your support and believing in me. And thanks to my dog, Rosie, for our many walks together. Also love to my friends for sharing the good times and bad, especially Joan, Mary and Belinda.

For reading group questions, writing tips and more information, please visit www.phaedra-patrick.com. I'm happiest on Instagram, and you can also find me on Twitter and Facebook.

THE SECRETS
OF LOVE STORY
BRIDGE

PHAEDRA PATRICK

Reader's Guide

PARK
ROW
BOOKS

1. *The Secrets of Love Story Bridge* centers on Mitchell's second chance at happiness after living in the shadow of shame and guilt about Anita's death. How did Mitchell change throughout the book? Did your opinions of him change too? Do you think men are more likely to lock their feelings away than women?

2. Mitchell's first instinct is to think about and look after his daughter, Poppy. Discuss their relationship. What were your favorite moments between them? Were there other times when you felt Mitchell could have been a better parent? Should parents always put their children first, or should everyone in a family be seen to have equal needs?

3. For much of the novel, Mitchell teams up with Liza to track down Yvette, the woman who fell from the bridge. What did you think of the ultimate reveal of what had happened to Yvette? Were you surprised?

4. What do you think the main themes of the book were? What feelings did the book evoke for you?

5. Liza has her own problems, especially with her sister Yvette being missing and keeping secrets. Do all families have issues, and how are these best resolved? Should they be kept within the family, or should outside help be sought out?

6. The people of Upchester begin to write to Mitchell and the letters ultimately help him to move on with his life. Which of these letters were your favorite? If you could write a letter to anyone in your life, past or present, who would you send it to, and what would you say to them?

7. Mitchell reluctantly performs a song around the campfire, unaware of how the words will resonate with him. What is your favourite song? What do the words mean to you?

8. Mitchell deals with his loss of Anita by making rigid lists, schedules and plans. Have you ever turned to coping strategies to deal with difficult times? What helped you?

9. The book is populated with a colorful array of characters. Who was your favourite character in the book and why? If the book was adapted into a film, who would you cast as the main characters?

10. What do you think the meaning is behind the title, *The Secrets of Love Story Bridge*?

Read on for a sneak peek at The Library of Lost and Found, *another perfectly charming read from bestselling author Phaedra Patrick.*

1

Valentine's Day

As always, Martha Storm was primed for action. Chin jutted, teeth gritted, and a firm grip on the handle of her trusty shopping trolley. Her shoulders burned as she struggled to push it up the steep slope toward the library. The cobblestones underfoot were slippery, coated by the sea mist that wafted into Sandshift each evening.

She was well prepared for the evening's event. It was going to be perfect, even though she usually avoided Valentine's Day. Wasn't it a silly celebration? A gimmick, to persuade you to buy stuffed furry animals and chocolates at rip-off prices. Why, if someone ever sent her a card, she'd hand it back and explain to the giver they'd been brainwashed. However, a job worth doing was worth doing well.

Bottles chinked in her trolley, a stuffed black bin bag rustled in the breeze and a book fell off a pile, its pages fluttering like a moth caught in a spider's web.

She'd bought the supermarket's finest rosé wine, flute glasses and napkins printed with tiny red roses. Her alarm clock sounded at 5:30 a.m. that morning to allow her time to bake heart-shaped cookies, including gluten-free ones for any book lovers who had a wheat allergy. She'd brought along extra copies of the novel for the author to sign.

One of the best feelings in the world came when she received a smile of appreciation, or a few grateful words. When someone said, "Great job, Martha," and she felt like she was basking in sunshine. She'd go to most lengths to achieve that praise.

If anyone asked about her job, she had an explanation ready. "I'm a guardian of books," she said. "A volunteer at the library." She was an event organizer, tour guide, buyer, filer, job adviser, talking clock, housekeeper, walking encyclopedia, stationery provider, recommender of somewhere nice to eat lunch and a shoulder to cry on—all rolled into one.

And she loved each part, except for waking people up at closing time, and the strange things she found used as bookmarks (a nail file, a sexual health clinic appointment card and an old rasher of bacon).

As she rattled past a group of men, all wearing navy-and-yellow Sandshift United football scarves, Martha called out to them, "Don't forget about the library event tonight." But they laughed among themselves and walked on.

As she eventually directed the trolley toward the small, squat library building, Martha spied the bulky silhouette of a man huddled by the front door. "Hello there," she called out, twisting her wrist to glance at her watch. "You're fifty-four minutes early…"

The dark shape turned its head and seemed to look at her, before hurrying away and disappearing around the corner.

Martha trundled along the path. A poster flapped on the door and author Lucinda Lovell beamed out from a heavily filtered photo. The word *Canceled* was written across her face in thick black letters.

Martha's eyes widened in disbelief. Her stomach lurched, as if someone had shoved her on an escalator. Using her hand as a visor, she peered into the building.

All was still, all was dark. No one was inside.

With trembling fingers, she reached out to touch the word that ruined all her planning and organizing efforts of the last couple of weeks. *Canceled*. The word that no one had bothered to tell her.

She swallowed hard and her organized brain ticked as she wondered who to call. The area library manager, Clive Folds, was taking his wife to the Lobster Pot bistro for a Valentine's dinner. He was the one who'd set up Lucinda's appearance, with her publisher. Pregnant library assistant, Suki McDonald, was cooking a cheese and onion pie for her boyfriend, Ben, to persuade him to give things another try between them.

Everything had been left for Martha to sort out.

Again.

"You live on your own, so you have more time," Clive had told her, when he'd asked her to take charge of the event preparations. "You don't have personal commitments."

Martha's chest tightened as she remembered his words, and she let her arms fall heavy to her sides. Turning back around, she took a deep breath and forced herself to straighten her back. *Never mind*, she thought. There must be a good reason for the cancelation, a serious illness, or perhaps a fatal road accident. Anyone who turned up would see the poster. "Better just set off home, and get on with my other stuff," she muttered.

Leaning over her trolley, Martha grabbed hold of its sides and heaved it around to face in the opposite direction. As she did, a clear plastic box slid out, crashing to the path. When she stooped to pick it up, the biscuits lay broken inside.

It was only then she noticed the brown paper parcel propped against the bottom of the door. It was rectangular and tied with a bow and a crisscross of string, probably left there by the shadowy figure. Her name was scrawled on the front. She stooped down to pick it up, then pressed her fingers along its edges. It felt like a book.

Martha placed it next to the box of broken biscuits in her trolley. *Really*, she tutted, the things readers tried to avoid paying their late return fees.

She wrenched back on the trolley as it threatened to pull her down the hill. The brown paper parcel juddered inside as she negotiated the cobbles. She passed sugared almond–hued houses, and the air smelled of salt and seaweed. Laughter and the strum of a Spanish guitar sounded from the Lobster Pot and she paused for a moment. Martha had never eaten there before. It was the type of place frequented by couples.

Through the window, she glimpsed Clive and his wife with their foreheads almost touching across the table. Candles lit up their faces with a flickering glow. His mind was obviously not on the library.

If she's not careful, Mrs. Fold's hair is going to set on fire, Martha thought, averting her eyes. *I hope there are fire extinguishers in the dining area.* She fumbled in her pocket for her Wonder Woman notepad and made a note to ask the bistro owner, Branda Taylor.

When Martha arrived home, to her old gray stone cottage, she parked the trolley outside. She had found it there, abandoned a couple of years ago, and she adopted it for her ongoing mission to be indispensable, a Number One neighbor.

Bundling her stuff out of the trolley and into the hallway, she stooped and arranged it in neat piles on the floor, then wound her way around the wine bottles. She found a small free space on the edge of her overcrowded dining table for the brown paper parcel.

A fortnight ago, on a rare visit, her sister, Lilian, had stuck her hands on her hips as she surveyed the dining room. "You really need to do something about this place, Martha," she'd said, her eyes narrowing. "Getting to your kitchen is like an obstacle course. Mum and Dad wouldn't recognize their own home."

Her sister was right. Betty and Thomas Storm liked the house to be spic and span, with everything in its place. But they had both died five years ago, and Martha had remained in the property. She found it therapeutic, after their passing, to try to be useful and fill the house with stuff that needed doing.

The brown velour sofa, where the three of them had watched quiz shows, one after another, night after night, was now covered in piles of things. Thomas liked the color control on the TV turned up, so presenters' and actors' faces glowed orange. Now it was covered by a tapestry that Martha had offered to repair for the local church.

"This is all essential work," she told Lilian, casting her hand through the air. She patiently explained that the shopping bags, plastic crates, mountains of stuff on the floor, stacked high on the table and against the wall, were jobs. "I'm helping people out. The boxes are full of Mum and Dad's stuff—"

"They look like the Berlin Wall."

"Let's sort through them together. We can decide what to keep, and what to let go."

Lilian ran her fingers through her expensively highlighted hair. "Honestly, I'm happy for you to do it, Martha. I've got two kids to sort out, and the builders are still working on the conservatory…"

Martha saw two deep creases between her sister's eyebrows that appeared when she was stressed. Their shape reminded her of antelope horns. A *mum brow*, her sister called it.

Lilian looked at her watch and shook her head. "Look, sorry, but I have to dash. I'll call you, okay?"

But the two sisters hadn't chatted since.

Now Martha wove her way around a crate full of crystal chandeliers she'd offered to clean for Branda, and the school trousers she'd promised to re-hem for her nephew, Will. The black bin bags were full of Nora's laundry, because her washing machine had broken down. She stepped over a papier-mâché dragon's head that needed a repair to his ear and cheek after last year's school Chinese New Year celebrations. Horatio Jones's fish and potted plants had lived with her for two weeks while he was on holiday.

Her oven door might sparkle and she could almost see her reflection in the bathroom sink, but most of her floor space was dedicated to these favors.

Laying everything out this way meant that Martha could survey, assess and select what to do next. She could mark the task status in her notepad with green ticks (completed), amber stars (in progress) and red dots (late). Busyness was next to cleanliness. Or was that godliness?

She also found that, increasingly, she couldn't leave her tasks alone. Her limbs were always tense, poised for action, like an athlete waiting for the pop of a starting pistol. And if she didn't do this stuff for others, what did she have in her life, otherwise?

Even though her arms and back ached from handling the trolley, she picked up a pair of Will's trousers. With no space left on the sofa, she sat in a wooden chair by the window, overlooking the bay.

Outside, the sea twinkled black and silver, and the moon shone almost full. Lowering her head towards the fabric, Martha tried to make sure the stitches were neat and uniform, approximately three millimeters each, because she wanted them to be perfect for her sister.

Stretching out an arm, she reached for a pair of scissors. Her wrist nudged the brown paper parcel and it hung precariously over the edge of the dining table. When she pushed it back with one finger, she spotted a small ink stamp on the back.

"Chamberlain's Pre-Loved and Antiquarian Books, Maltsborough."

"Hmm," she said aloud, not aware of this bookshop. And if the package contained a used book, why had it been left at the library?

Wondering what was inside, Martha set the parcel down on her lap. She untied the string bow and slowly peeled back the brown paper.

Inside, as expected, she found a book, but the cover and title page were both missing. Definitely not a library book, it reminded her of one of those hairless cats, recognizable but strange at the same time.

Its outer pages were battered and speckled, as if someone had flicked strong coffee at it. A torn page offered a glimpse of one underneath where black-and-white fish swam in swirls of sea. On top were a business card and a handwritten note.

Dear Ms. Storm,

Enclosed is a book that came into my possession recently. I cannot sell it due to its condition, but I thought it might be of interest to you, because of the message inside.

Best wishes,
Owen Chamberlain
Proprietor

With anticipation making her fingertips tingle, Martha turned the first few pages of the book slowly, smoothing them down with the flat of her hand, until she found the handwritten words, above an illustration of a mermaid.

June 1985
To my darling, Martha Storm
Be glorious, always.
Zelda

x

Martha heard a gasp and realized it had escaped from her own lips. "Zelda?" she whispered aloud, then clamped a hand to her mouth.

She hadn't spoken her nana's name for many years. And, as she said it now, she nervously half expected to see her father's eyes grow steely at its mention.

Zelda had been endlessly fun, the one who made things bearable at home. She wore turquoise clothes and tortoiseshell cat's-eye–shaped glasses. She was the one who protected Martha against the tensions that whirled within the Storm family.

Martha read the words again and her throat grew tight.

They're just not possible.

Feeling her fingers slacken, she could only watch as the book slipped out of her grip and fell to the floor with a thud, its yellowing pages splayed wide open.